Better Publishing Corporation

BETTER PUBLISHING CORPORATION
1603 Capitol Ave, Suite 310 A457
Cheyenne, WY 82001
307-274-4386

For previews of upcoming books of the *Genetic Pressure*® series by Eugene Clark visit WWW.GENETICPRESSURE.COM

ISBN: 978-1-7330499-2-4   paperback

Cover art: Monte Ritz
Layout design: Charles King

EUGENE CLARK

GENETIC PRESSURE® VOLUME 3

TEEN CULTS

Better ⟨⟨⟩ Publishing ⟨ꟷ⟩ Corporation

2023

CONTENTS

The strong do what they can and the weak suffer what they must.

—HISTORY OF THE PELOPONNESIAN WAR Chapter 17,
Thucydides

Ellie Arroway, when asked what her one question to an alien race would be:

How did you do it? How did you evolve, how did you survive this technological adolescence without destroying yourself?

—CONTACT (1997) movie quote

ACKNOWLEDGMENTS

My beta readers were Jan Pinkerton, Hoyt Hudson, Christine Gravel, Mike Piper, and my Sydney writer's club.

My editors were Olivia Swenson at Olivia Edits, Bryna Kranzler, and Skye Loyd.

Any reader interested in assisted reproduction tourism and human genetic engineering should visit www.geneticpressure.com.

PREFACE

In the 2010s, American, French, and Chinese scientists Jennifer Doudna, Emmanuelle Charpentier, and Feng Zhang proved that CRISPR-Cas9 bacterial enzymes could be used to edit human DNA. In 2018, Chinese scientist He Jiankui "washed" the sperm of an HIV-positive man to gene-edit the CCR5 gene to provide HIV resistance to an IVF child. From that experiment were born the world's first genetically engineered twin girls.

These events inspired me to think, and then write, about the implications that go beyond the stated goals of scientists to eliminate genetic conditions that cause illness. I started writing a series of books under the *Genetic Pressure*® title to explore the implications of designer babies and human genetic engineering (HuGE).

Volume 1, *Baby Steps,* explores the perspective of intended parents buying a designer baby; this method is compared to all the other ways people have children. *Talented Children* and the books that follow explore how it might feel to be a designer child. The series will later explore what it might be like to create a designer-baby company. The series will conclude with speculation on how genetic technology can be used for space exploration.

The *Genetic Pressure* series is not appropriate reading material for people under 15. The series contains sex and violence and discussions about it but without resorting to pornography.

Teen Cults covers the stories of a genetically engineered boy and girl from the ages of 15–18 and references cults, exotic killings, and sex practices. Religion, politics, and economics are also discussed in terms of how they relate to human genetic engineering.

This is the third book in an open-ended series, which should not be read out of order. The story itself is very sequential, and the decisions and actions of the characters are highly consequential. If you skip or skim chapters, later chapters will make little sense.

I adopted several conventions in these books. Numbers are in 2022 amounts, pegged at $1800 USD for an ounce of gold. All international money is expressed in US dollars as well. The characters use inches for height measurement (5'10" = 178 cm) and pounds for mass measurement (2.2 lb = 1 kg). Numbers are deliberately rounded for simplicity and the science has been simplified to be digestible by nonscience readers. While *Baby Steps* was more in the hard science fiction category, the following books are more fitting for the preapocalyptic science fiction category using more theoretical (unproven but plausible) scientific concepts.

To better represent modern communication, I use the following conventions:

INTERFACE:

Char(acter) says, "I love you"—Denotes verbal, in-room communication.

Char: "I love you"—Denotes mediated verbal communication (e.g., via phones, headsets, earbuds).

Char/voxplay: "I love you"—Denotes the character is not using his real voice.

Char: [I love you]—Denotes text or other visual (e.g., body or sign language) form of communication.

{Who do you love?}—Denotes mass messaging (e.g., spam mail).

<I love you>—Denotes kinetic communication (e.g., hugs, hand holding).

I love you—Denotes inner communication; the character is thinking to himself.

%Language indicates a language change. The writing is still in NA-English.

Talents and live-in Parentsos use verbal or written Tesp (Talent dialect Esperanto) unless otherwise noted. Tesp is an affix-based language.

CONVERSATION COMPRESSION

For the sake of readability, lengthy text (or audio-to-text) conversations are not split up into segments, emojis, and slang, but the reader can assume that characters use them. As when foreign languages are rendered into English, I've spared the reader frustration and distraction by not including these. I've also spared the reader all call setup and patching and time spreads between texts except when noted. Context will be sufficient to understanding how quickly conversations happen.

For example:

Esther decided to text Martin about the book they were reading. She said to her wristband, "Martin-san text," paused to secure patch (her earbud made a slight ding), and then spoke out loud into her wristband.

[how are you today happy-emoji]

One minute later.

[fine]

She used her phone.

[silly-emoji photo of herself lol omg]

One minute later.

[cute]

She used her wristband microphone, set audio to text.

[I think homo sapiens killed neanderthal men with lots of rocks]

[took their women by force]

Ten seconds later.

[havent thought of that] sic/spellcheck

Etc.

Simplifies to:

Esther: [I think Homo sapiens killed the Neanderthal men through coordinated rock slinging and took their women by force.]

Martin: [Oh, I haven't thought of that.]

PART FOUR

TEEN CULTS

"Out of life's school of war—what doesn't kill me, makes me stronger."
Nietzsche's famous aphorism was true in my case. His suggestion
was that strong individuals should use suffering as an opportunity to build strength. I was already powerful and knowledgeable
when I was killed. Then I became all powerful and all knowing.

—LIVING BEYOND GOOD AND EVIL,
by Esther Stein

*Two heads are better than one. Man and woman together, sym-
biotic, androgyne. Two bullets sparked the fusion of two brains.
A chain reaction started and never stopped until the Talents all
became one. Unity.*

—NOTE11.TXT TRUE-ROOT DIRECTORY,
by Martin Allerton.

CHAPTER ONE
DIVINE INTERVENTION

[Friday, May 28, 2060]
Palo Alto Science School (PASS)

MARTIN WOKE UP from his nap with a fine feeling of impending dread. *A battle needs a battalion. A battle lion. A brave lion.*

Felicity, sitting in the chair next to him, had nudged him in the shoulder. "It's time to go." His phone vibrated; it was Smithy telling him [time to go.]

He had fallen asleep reading William Tecumseh Sherman's autobiography, the man famous for "War is Hell." Sherman was referring to the fact he'd experienced better days as a soldier, banker, and then military academy teacher before deciding with Ulysses S. Grant on scorched-earth military tactics to bring the Confederate States to unconditional surrender and end slavery in the United States. His mother, Marcy, wanted him reading books about famous military leaders. She wanted him to learn about people who were given free license to kill and destroy as much as they could in the name of whatever. "Freedom." The illusion we are anything but slaves to rich and powerful people. That one set of rulers or employers is better than another set of rulers and employers because of kinship or ancestry or shared moral values. God, King, and Country.

Marcy was cynical like that. She was a soldier. "Why do we fight? What is worth dying for?" he had asked her.

"Sex, money, power, children. Also, glory."

Sherman wasn't motivated by any of those things, he had a guilty conscience for his somewhat efficient or at least intentional organization of rampant chaos. "It's a job, somebody has to do it." "Duty and honor." "Slavery is evil, and we must fight evil." "We fight for our way of life." "We are called to serve."

Martin thought people usually respected soldiers. You fought for respect, or at a minimum, not to be thought a coward. Martin suspected he'd become cynical like Marcy. "Hardened by killing." "Knowing I'm already dead." These qualities made for good soldiers, alongside internalized cynicism. He pinged Marcy in the hope of cynicism.

Martin: [Have you killed anyone?]

Marcy: [Yes. Lots. I've killed a lot of people. It's my job and your job.]

Martin shivered.

"Let's get going, Sis." They left their private computer room to walk to their public computer room. "Battle stations," Felicity nicknamed them on their walk.

Martin had read from his leadership textbooks about the importance of "face-to-face" time. Talents had the ability to switch between total concentration/isolation (inside a large busy room) and group social coherence, often called "party time" (Tesp. Sopartiso). Today would be a test of both capabilities, or as the military called it, "Capex" (capability exercise, pronounced "cape-x"). *I'm going to war today, but my friends are calling it a party. Political parties kill people. And this is a demonstration of power.* He entered the public computing room to look at his battalion organized into battle stations.

Instead of individuals with specific command functions sitting in isolated chairs centered on a large display screen, Talents were arrayed in circle benches of computing functions with individual large flat screens, often cut up into various subscreens. Headsets were used for voice interactions (using keyboard inputs for voice patching), but Talents also made use of kinetic and visual communication, a sort of full-body enhanced sign language with an adaption of Martin and Felicity's kinetic

communication. True Reality, which made use of " " < > and [ ] communication, simultaneously reduced reaction times and command decisions
to fractions of seconds in conflict simulation. Memeso was working on
shortening common words so Talents could communicate very quickly
and precisely with each other. Flirting in morse code (binary)—left eye,
right eye—was the latest pastime between the men and women since
Esther had discouraged physical contact outside of handholding and
pecks on lips for displays of affection. For computing (party) functions,
people could communicate quietly instead of shouting.

When the Twins arrived at the battle stations for Operation Nate,
circles stood up as they approached, all, "Glad to see you, Martin and
Felicity." "Inf/we/both love you inf/guys/both." "Come to the computer
lab more often, not just the Founder's Area." "When are you guys going
to show up for Circleturbo?" "I want to see you fry my latest OM device."

The Twins sat next to each other, joining their six-sibling circle
Command circle (Tesp. Circlesibso Commcircleso). Martin would select execution responses (with voice or kinetic keyboard and touchscreen
inputs and outputs) from the circle during the exercise. Felicity would
manage the AI-driven filtering process from all the other Talent circle
computing processes, shortcutting the need for "task assignments," which
would be self-evident by function.

Martin announced to his headset, "Full Talent Battle Lions mobilized."
*Time to test out the combined AI cyberwarfare system we've been working
on the past year. One thousand genius elite Talents from my out-family. A
battalion is 1000 people.*

He looked at his computer monitor.

Churchhackprog: [Church systems owned, selecting feed.]

A third of his screen showed the main church camera feed with Nate
and his crew busy prepping the church.

Elsa-car: [Parked 200 m from church.]

"Continuous status on Esther's and Elsa's and Nate's positions. Video
on Nate. Audio on Esther," Felicity said. Martin gave a visual nod, and
the Talent camera on Martin confirmed the spoken and visual command, sending the required outputs to the battalion, demonstrated on
Martin's screen area. The Battle Lions would have a video thumbprint

on Martin and Felicity the whole time in the top right corner of their monitors. Martin and Felicity's sound outputs would connect to their left ears, while audio communication within their circle updated their right ears, Talents being able to manage two audio feeds and their computer all at the same time.

"Sibsos start a running commentary on mission goals. Is Esther doing the right thing?" Martin worried about whether he should worry about her. Marcy told him every battle needs clear primary and secondary goals as well as a risk assessment. He should be mathematical and logical about anything concerning death, the calculus of infinite negative utility.

Smithy took the role of hardline realist as usual: "This is stupid. Bravery is the definition of stupid. Normsos are all volatile and stupid, and can only barely control their base lizard brain impulses. They all have at least one base impulse they can't control. Nate probably has the base impulse to kill. Some Normsos are sick like that. Don't like it, then kill it. Disgusting creatures."

Candice's face showed no reaction. "She's awesome going in there. Bravery is not stupid. We should honor this act of bravery. Someone needs to stand up to Normso bullies. Talents need champions."

Sister Cecilia looked happy. "The Parent Parse Program works. Parents are stuck in sunk costs and got the happy, healthy motivated child they wanted. We stood up to our Parents and now we stand up to the rest of the Normsos."

Brother Karol larped parent patronizing, saying, "You are just children. You should listen to your elders; you don't know the real world. You don't understand real people. You'll have to work with real people someday. Money makes the world go round. You need to understand the value of a dollar." Martin and the other Talents laughed at his mimic abilities. Nagging and patronizing (while not Bullso) was deemed comedic in Talent culture. If someone nagged in earnest, the usual response was laughter.

Cecilia responded, "Which is precisely my point. Real people are terrible. We don't want to work with real people, we want to work with Talents. The Talents who take on Normsos should be honored as heroes. I think Esther is glorious."

Martin didn't think Esther was motivated to risk her life by glory. *All she feels is the fear of death. She knows she was created for a purpose: Ambassador. I hate it when she uses "Apostle."*

Martin said, "Mission assessment. Fear. What exactly is this battle? What are we afraid of?"

Smithy began, "Our side includes a trained sharpshooter bodyguard, motivated by what passes for a religious fanatic devotion, best friend forever bonding, and a splash of sex. And a battalion of geniuses with advanced cyberwarfare technology. All that versus a group of teenagers with serious mental health problems. Shall I list them? Bulimia, depression, drug addiction, alcohol addiction, anorexia, body dysmorphia, sex addiction, pain addiction..."

"That's enough. Esther wants to cure all that. I think she can do it," said Cecilia.

Candice said, "We can't get Elsa in any of the doors. The gun detector alarms are all hard-wired to alarms on closed systems, according to purchasing reports."

Good, the document data mining AI is working well, that was fast.

Karol asked, "What's the upside versus the risk? Death is infinite negative utility. Esther is the most valuable Talent we have. Her only potential replacement is Lucy, who has made it clear she is only a backup, not a replacement. Maybe Melanie or Rachel takes her place. They package most of the Ethers these days."

Memeso had shortened the daily 30-minute news and culture program, *Esthentials*, to Ethers. Esther still approved the final video each day. Her Circle would be creating the Ether out of Esther's events tonight. Martin felt unsettled at the idea of Esther being replaced. It felt rather strange that her life was on the line. That was war. Some soldiers think they're going to die, and others don't. The latter was probably the better attitude.

Smithy said, "Upside? She's stated two goals. Attempting to convert haters into followers, and figuring out where the missing Talents have gone..."

Martin interrupted, "We're not challenging the value of these goals. I agree with Esther, the value of reconciling Talent haters is high. We don't want violence between Talents and Normsos. Every Talent agrees with that."

His video monitor passed out universal agreement on the subject. Not a single Talent advocated violent solutions to Normso relationship problems. "Unthinkable" was the usual adjective (55%), followed by 45% reminding others not to bring an unthinkable subject back into thinking.

Only Cysso, the Coxos, and Preppers are supposed to think about violence. That's what Talents tell us. They are happy with a King and Queen, my family, and a small Aristocracy and military for their government holding the power and appreciation of violence. Marcy told me power is the capability of violence without repercussions. A good King and Queen must be ready for violence on behalf of their people. The King for hard power, and the Queen for soft power. I am hard power, actual violence. Esther is soft power, the threat of violence. How did I get such a mother? Felicity nudged him out of his reverie.

"Discuss Parental involvement." Martin had selected vocal output to just his battalion (not the Talent nation) and decided to keep it this way for the rest of the battle. A battle station was designated "Public Affairs" and would mediate Talent response to the live camera feed in the church. The program was set to output [text] on the computer monitor in case any specific Talent was already engaged in headset verbal communication. He looked around to admire the large computer lab holding 1000 people sitting in circles around computer screens. He brought up a map of command functions and found Public Affairs was located in the corner of the room near the main entrance. They were data miners, not a propagandistic Ministry of Truth.

Smithy stated, "We've agreed not to use Parents unless absolutely necessary. They always think they know best and are doing the right thing but forget that Talents don't think like them and don't share their goals and needs. Parents are inefficient and chaotic resource interfaces whose only real value is using them to interface with Normsos."

"We stick to Esther's request to let her make the decision. We feed her information assessments..." said Candice.

Martin agreed, "Yes, okay. Esther makes the command decision to reach out." *Or me. She told me that last night. She says we are one person* now. It feels that way. I am the head, and she is the heart. The command function and the purpose function. We can't live without each other, she said. Is my wife a little nuts? Dad told me all women are a little cray-cray. A status update on Nate's computer system showed they'd hacked his system using the video recognition system. A Talent AI system developed at Tel Aviv could collect passwords from camera spying on the keyboard or number pad physical finger inputs. All computers connected to the Internet had a hidden open port as legislated by government authorities as an antiterrorist and drug enforcement (tax assurance) countermeasure. Marcy gave us the port hacking program. Nate is using simple consumer electronics.

Esther was studying her phone so he could study her face, feeling the pair-bond. She looks both happy and in a state of active concentration. Martin felt intense Crushso as usual when he stared at her.

Circle: [She has contacted her religious friends for advice. Sending her data on the church history and current activity.]

A selection of prompts came up about what to do about her religious friends. Martin selected the option: [Spoof authorities], which would circumvent their calls and simulate a police conversation. Simulated Reality. Martin didn't feel guilty about Talents pretending to be these strange people Esther made friends with.

Esther was in the church now using the various spy gadgets he gave her. "Report on OM field test."

CyberhackAI: [Antitemperance group phones hacked. We have listeners and video on all phones. Data mining for relevance.]

Martin looked again at Esther looking at her phone and felt again the surge of neurochemicals driven by limerence and pair-bonding, what Normsos called "being in love." It's hard to think about anything but being with her again. Dad told me it will eventually pass. New Relationship Energy, he called it. Normsos have invented all kinds of reasons to break up relationships it seems.

Felicity nudged him. "Bro, save it for later." Martin had told her to nudge him when he started staring too long at her.

I'm like Q from James Bond. Spy gadgets. Mad inventions. Esther is like James Bond. A very stupid man, always getting killed and somehow *not dying. Not a single movie makes any sense. Why did my dad insist on me watching these senseless movies? Why doesn't the bad guy just kill him? Why can't bad guys shoot straight?*

He looked at Elsa's update; she was searching for a way up to the outside second level of one of the connected outbuildings for children's Christian education classrooms. The plan was for her to use her handgun to smash open a window. *How many geniuses did it take to come up with that plan?* Talents stopped making "changing lightbulb" jokes and wanted to get rid of lightbulbs altogether.

Martin kept selecting the recommended prompts that communicated to Esther and Elsa. He hadn't told Elsa and Esther an AI-mediated brain gestalt was talking to them via text or Martin voxplay. He thought that most people would feel guilty at the deception. That feeling had gone away a year ago. The initial excitement of fooling the world outside the Schools and Labfarms had turned to boredom. *Sports, travel, sex, drugs, booze, science, grades, tests, papers, social injustice, relationships...*

Martin stared at Esther again. *She looks like a Talent, but no Talent is like her.* Felicity nudged him again.

"Discuss phone hacking technology."

Smithy said, "These are Marcy's gifts. Esther's mother Debbie has a similar device. The most likely explanation is BGC has hacked the telcos and equipment manufacturers. We can only speculate how they accomplished this."

"Agreed," added Karol. "These Parents are criminals and BGC is a criminal organization for sure. And now, we are criminals."

"Does that bother anyone?" Cecelia asked.

Smithy said, "No, all Parents are criminals as far as I can tell. They made their own petty laws to make them so. I can't believe the time I waste trying to understand their legal systems, which are props to enrich powerful connected people at the expense of creative and productive people."

Martin recalled his last love-making session with Esther. *Bondturbo she calls it, we both sort of lose ourselves. I asked her again why she is doing this instead of living with me. Hate with kindness, fear with bravery, selfishness with self-sacrifice. Nuts. My wife is nuts. I am nuts to let her do this.* Felicity nudged him.

"How's the video translation going?"

Medium: "Medium is processing well. The video is clean." That was a nameless Talent specialist who was spokesperson for the computing circle that managed the filters and converters for cyberwarfare, the medium between the Internet and the Intalent network systems.

Talents had created a platform (Medium) that took in Internet video and cleaned it of nonvisual programming, and then converted to a TOS (TalentOS) codec for further safety. The same went for audio cleansing and translation. A status update popped up to inform Martin the audio and video on all the Normso phones and church systems were filtering and converting in a 0.01 second buffer. He kept his view on the chancel and forward- and back-facing cameras on Esther's phone. Then he switched his attention to the video Nate was showing.

Who the hell is that? Why are you talking that way?

Messages piled in on his monitor: [Working on ID, sysgroupA.] [Computer AI dialogue 95% likely.] [BGC plan to kill Normsos considered highly improbable, there is no evidence to support theory.]

The second Talent video came online. "Talent reaction summary."

Public Affairs: [Glad I didn't go to my local high school.] [I think the Circleturbos are less trouble than her lifestyle.] [What a potty mouth, no manners.] [You think Talents outside the Schools have to tell the truth like Star Trek Spock did?] [Glad she doesn't want to come to our school.] [Why would you want a handbag?] [I think she enjoys it.] [Gross!!]

He had asked Public Affairs only to send high-frequency or interesting responses; Martin decided not to click on the meta-data for now.

Video Analysis: [Visual AI confirms true violet and not contacts.]

Martin quickly approved all the Talent/AI comments to Esther. "General comments on the situation." He looked at his monitor.

Public Affairs: [No known Talent wipe out Normso projects.] [Why would we ever contemplate such a project? BGC has plans for the whole planet.] [Doesn't make sense, we don't compete with Normsos. We don't compete with ourselves.] [A pregnant Talent, not ready for that yet.] [I want to get pregnant. Lucy doesn't allow it but promises it.] [She looks beautiful pregnant.] [Talents don't drink alcohol anywhere, should we verify her alcohol resistance test?] [Talents are outbreeding? I thought it was just a few male Coxos who were doing that.] [These Talents are not in a School. Verified 1000 times on facial and voice recognition.] [Parents didn't choose all the recommendations?] [They didn't want to listen to BGC it seems.] [Didn't they select their clients for that?] [Normsos always make mistakes.] [Violet Bloom identified by Manhattan Science, building her profile.] *We found an Out-Talent. A Talent not in the School system. Finally.*

Extranet: [Violet Bloom identified, missing, presumed dead by her Parent.]

Lucy: [What a shame. While not the same as In-Talents, it would be a waste of beautiful life. I will send the question out.] A video of Violet Bloom on camera at Manhattan Science came up on his screen, along with a news article about her mother; a Jewish billionaire in Manhattan real estate was the tilder introduction.

ImageProcessing: [It's the same person, confirmed.]

Public Affairs: [Dead?] [Why would people kill Talents?] [We're harmless.] [Why kill anyone?]

Martin didn't think these Out-Talents had beautiful lives. He did feel a powerful need to find them though. He managed a feeling of "kinship" and "sympathy," the same feelings Talents had for the Dissentsos held by Lucy in a facility near to Paris Science for her biotech research on Talent sexuality. He contemplated his own sexuality. Lucy and Felicity watched him and Esther have their once a week sex on camera. Martin and Felicity watched Esther turbo with Elsa every other day, while they selfturboed. He had gotten in the habit of watching the Coxos, too. *I'm a pervert it seems. I should stop this habit* <nudge> *Smithy this time.*

Esther had left her seat to walk down the aisle. A prompt came up with choices, and he chose <contact Elsa move faster> with a mouse click; that would translate to her earbud in his voice: "Move faster."

Elsa: [Trying hard] *Stupid girl wasting time to type that.* Improvements in Talent microphone technology would allow Elsa to speak her response in a whisper.

TechTeam: [We forgot to train her on the new whisper tech.]

"Verbal status on Elsa!" Martin found himself standing up and shouting. The system was set up for shouting; the Talents would feel that in their headsets and earbuds. He found more than a few staring at him. Smithy pulled him back to his seat.

AssaultTeam: "Sending space analysis." A layout of the church appeared on screen and a red dot labeled [Elsa] elsewhere on the screen was on the second floor by a window with her dot headed towards the nearest stairway.

The Assault Team (or Elsa's computer processing brain) was adjacent to the Command Team. Larry (its spokesperson) faced Martin directly IRL.

Larry, "We've got her in through the broken window with just her handgun. No rifle. She's making her way to the chancel from a side entrance by the lectern. Look at your screen." A dotted line showed a route through a bunch of doors and small steps to the stage left side (lectern side) of the chancel. There was a sidebar discussion to come up around to the pulpit side for a better ambush, but Martin immediately selected [fastest route.]

Martin looked around the room with his naked eyes, and then via cameras on each battle station. Felicity's face was covered in tears. He looked around to discover everyone's faces were covered in tears. Felicity verbalized, "Come on Elsa. Before something bad happens." There was no mistaking—the snarl on Nate from the pulpit was intensifying.

SitAwareNateTeam: [Signs of Crushso but way more hate than love.] Martin was aware Talents had developed advanced facial recognition technology, a sort of "empathy AI" always trying to remove the uncanny valley with computers and robots. It was supposed to be extremely accurate. Someone had even boasted it had gaydar capabilities.

CyberwarfareTeam: [Macro is ready, Martin. Button F1 macro kill switch programmed on your kinetic execution.] He was told it wouldn't actually kill anyone, but that didn't stop Talents from making puns or living in a universe of unintended consequences.

They want to kill her. After all she's done. After all the Talents are doing for his School. Esther manages our entire civilization through us. Who is more qualified to manage Normso civilization? I suppose Talentsos are easy to manage and Normsos impossible. Sudden dread hit Martin. At the same time came the thought that dread would not be a help to the situation.

"Verbal status, outsiders."

Karol reported, "Several Parents are closing in on the church. Rachael and Debbie are in their car about ten minutes away. Amanda and Ken are twenty minutes away. Jordan has made several attempts to notify the police, AI spoof interception is not convincing him of his failures. Paula and Jordan have gotten into their cars. I have allowed all of them to text Esther." *I can't believe she ignored Felicity's command to get out of there. Would I have told her that? I gave Felicity autonomy. Was that a good idea in a command theater?*

Esther was now standing at the lectern, facing straight out to the audience: "Yes, you heard me right, I fight for anyone who is not a Talent. I fight for your sake because I am one of you and I love you. Fighting for you is the purpose of my life."

Nate quickly pulled out a small pistol from his coat pocket and was working towards a solid two-hand sighted aim out of Esther's vision.

<Press F1> Lights out.

"BANG!"

The Press was about 0.1 seconds ahead of the BANG. A Talent analysis popped up on his screen.

From the video it looked like he had aimed directly at the right side of her head, but the phone in his pocket would have created an electric arc as the battery inside it ran through its entire charge in about three seconds. [OM success, all Normso phones on fire.] [Gun aim slightly off. Head shot hit confirmed.]

"Bang!" The audio monitor Talent muffled the headphone output for the second shot, probably by setting a decibel limit, learning a little late from Martin's previous outburst.

[Second shot likely to arm.]

Esther's body had spun around and jerked in the limited daylight from the windows and Martin could just make out her head falling hard against the side railing. Tears came pouring down Martin's cheeks. The dread of Esther dying hit his consciousness again. *This pain is close to dying. This is truly awful.* Martin closed his eyes. *It doesn't help.* A powerful trembling came over his whole body, the pure dread overwhelming him.

Felicity shouted, "Physics analysis!"

He heard Elsa scream "die!" and there was one more BBang (*was that two gunshots?*). There was screaming in the background. Fires were starting from the 100 overloaded phones now dropped on the ground. No one was staying to put out the fires or help Esther, Nate, and Elsa now all lying on the ground, the fire now giving more light than 6:20 p.m. daylight through stained glass windows in a church did.

CyberwarfareTeam: [Confirm OM test complete success.]

AudioTeam: [Four gunshots.]

PsychTeam: [Students running for it, as per school shooting protocol training.]

VisualTeam: [Confirm Elsa, Nate, and Esther down on the ground.]

Felicity said in a loud voice, "Oh, Bro!" Command prompts came in but were dimmed yellow, meaning he could follow the decision path, but that Felicity would make the selections.

[Notify police.]

[Notify fire.]

[Assemble Parent paramedics.]

[Dispatch Parent Doctors.]

MedicalTeam: [John, Mary] and some names he didn't recognize [dispatched.]

SpiritTeam: [Josh and Esther's Sibsos dispatched as Esther's spiritual support team in case of accident or harm.] Martin had not known about this. Then he reflected that Esther's friend Josh and her siblings were constant spiritual support to her.

Martin recovered some spirit at this recognition and touched Felicity's hand <ok>, approving her taking control. As some were in cars, she utilized a text/voice conversion interface so audio inputs from car "drivers" were converted to text, and Felicity's text inputs were converted to user-selected male voice audio outputs in this case Jordan had the default selected [original voice.]

Felicity/Martin: "Jordan? It's Martin Allerton."

Jordan: [Yes, Martin. You're Esther's boyfriend. She calls you her husband though. We have formal ceremonies for these commitments. I suppose it doesn't matter to you two. You let all the Talents know in a keyboard click. Your *cybernetic* society, I take it. Is she alright?]

Felicity: "No, she's been shot in the head and arm."

Jordan: [Get the best Talent doctors you can.]

Felicity: "Already done. I am on my way as well."

Jordan: [Is she going to die?]

MedicalTeam: [Not the brain stem. It's a race against time for blood loss. The lighting is too poor to make a reliable analysis.]

Felicity: "A race against time."

Rachael: [I am nearly there with Debbie. Is everything alright?]

Esther said first sex was marriage for Talents. She wouldn't entertain any other definition. I think she's right on this. I suppose I barely know my mother-in-law. My "mil," as Normsos call them. The female ancestor to your lover. I gave her my direct line patch access to be on good terms with her. Rachael's direct text to Martin's phone would not be intercepted by Cysso. He showed the text to Felicity.

The pain of the thought of Esther dying overwhelmed Martin again. *This is awful. I can't stand it.*

Felicity texted back for him: [She's been shot twice, and the church is burning down, get there faster Rachael. Save my wife, I'll get there as fast as possible.] She gave the phone back.

Debbie: [Martin, you better get here now. She's going to need you. We'll save her, don't you worry. You've got the best Parent doctors on their way, I bet.]

MedicalTeam: [Doctor Parents on standby at local hospital. Paramedic Parents in ambulance.]

Martin took some small relief in the effectiveness of his focus groups. He felt proud of his sister, who quickly took over and executed in his name much-needed command functions. He'd watched too many movies and read too many books where command and chain of command had failed. When time was crucial and command teams had to deliberate verbally, breakdowns happened too often. He deemed the tech side of the operation a success, and that increase in spirit gave him the energy to assess what was going on in the chaos for himself.

Between the fire and the smoke, he could sort of make out Esther lying on the ground bleeding out. At least, her arm appeared out from behind the lectern and there was what looked like blood pooling. Lying on the ground next to Esther was Elsa. She looked dead too. Now he could see Nate. *Yeah, he looks dead as well.* He felt an urge to vomit. Martin lurched over his thighs facing the floor with eyes closed, tears falling to the ground. He retched loud and hard, but nothing came out.

Here Martin was thinking Esther was stupid. *I'm the pot calling the kettle black. This is a complete disaster. I failed her. I feel like I'm dying. This pair-bonding stuff she goes on about. This awfulness is feeling death. I can't stand it. She can't die. I can't watch this...*

CHAPTER TWO
ADOLESCENCE

[Friday, May 28, 2060]
PASS computer lab

HE WAS SLUMPED in his seat staring into space when two of his Parents came up to him, Max and Marcy. Someone had put a bucket in front of him, but he hadn't needed it.

"Son, how are you holding up?" That was Max.

Felicity: <pinch wake up> "You're acting catatonic bro, snap out."

"Dad, I effed up. Bigtime." Tears. The crying became uncontrollable again. He watched his tears drop into the bucket.

Felicity slumped into Martin on their bench (now facing outward/away from the monitors) and was crying too. "Not Esther. Not her. She was perfect for you, Martin. She was perfect for all of us. She was one of the few of us willing to live so closely with them. So brave. She had to become one of them to live with them. Such sacrifice. Such humility. She is truly a Normso as well as a Talentso."

Marcy spoke evenhandedly, "Are you worried this incident will come back to haunt you and the Talents?" *She doesn't seem concerned.* Marcy hadn't directly involved herself in the Capex so her evenhandedness came across as odd. He looked into her attractive nonaging face, trying to see if it had any feeling about the potential death of her new dil. *Nothing.*

Martin took this as another lesson about warfare, an indifference to death.

"It's untraceable," Martin said. "But it will put us under suspicion." *Mom is acting strange. This was her program. She told me this.* "I will take full credit and responsibility if it comes to it." *This is what she wants me to say. All her lessons on personal agency. I can't blame anyone but myself.*

Marcy spoke without sympathy, "Okay, the way the real world works. Another lesson."

"Yes, Mom." *Another mom-larp.*

"You can never do this again, you understand. You get away with it once. Period. You do it again, and they catch you. Do not play with lady luck. You will lose."

"Okay, Mom." Martin got up and reached out to his mom to hug her, but she was wooden and distant and didn't hug back. She pushed him out and held both his arms, looking him straight in the eyes.

"You go and travel to Kentucky. If she's dead, you attend her funeral. If she lives, then you do everything in Talent power to help her. That is your punishment." *Mom is never so serious. Wow.*

"Of course, I will. I married her. I took her and bonded with her, and we shared vows. I'll email you the video. Everyone approves of this." Martin bowed his head. Some of the other Talents came over and took turns hugging him.

After his spirit was restored, he sat back at his station. He sifted through various messages.

VideoTeam: [These videos must have been cherry-picked. The editing is screwy. We will have to try to restore time space for cut-outs. There is so little movement.]

PsychTeam: [These Talents were either paid or for some reason didn't think through what they were saying. One person is confirmed drunk.]

PublicAffairs: [Only identifiable Talent is Violet Bloom. She appears to be the daughter of a billionaire Manhattanite real estate developer. All agree she didn't get the Science gene. Witnesses noted that her mom wanted her to have a real estate career and not a science career. Violet had said so many times before she left Manhattan Science. We are piecing more about her story but it's best to reach out to her single Parent.]

Martin considered the situation for about a minute before deciding to address his parents, who were still there talking to each other, quietly arguing about the Registry.

"Mom. Um, Moms, Dads. I think our situation is much worse than it looks."

"What is worse than a fire and three dead people?" Max replied, surprisingly calmly. Marcy was holding his hand.

"Um, more than three dead people?"

"Not a time to be funny, Martin." *I hadn't meant to be funny.*

"I think Normsos are out there murdering or kidnapping the Talents who didn't go to the Schools. They are organized." *That was Esther's suspicion. But then why try to kill and not kidnap Esther? Because she was no longer a virgin? How would Nate know that? Is this a bad horror movie?*

Max spoke, "I had speculated about that. My AI handler told me that anyone I sponsored to Better Genetics had to take all the recommendations or the AI would cut me off the Registry."

Marcy frowned at Max, like she always did when he coughed up a secret voluntarily.

"Marcy, he should know." Max looked grumpy about the issue.

Miffed, Marcy said, "Your AI handler theory is rubbish. 'Ladykiller' is me. Was me all along and that is that. This obsession with the Founder intelligence or AI cyber-genetic reproduction is complete rubbish. Tony sponsored my trip to BGC, the deal being getting you to stop drinking. I love you and our children. We even stopped philandering. Adam and Evelyn have paired up nicely as well. Those crazy Registry days are over. We are very happy together now." She gave Max a kiss and a big smile, but it didn't seem to work on Max's demeanor.

"Even the name *Registry*, Marcy. It's a computer term. Everything is being run by a computer AI. Better Genetics is cleaning up the misfits. Only they know who they are and where they are."

"I am not an AI. I assure you. You and your brother are the AI masters. Tony paid Bruce to create his own voxplay. Look, it all worked out. You stopped drinking, reconciled with Mindy, and started your hedonic treadmill program." Marcy snickered at that. Martin was a little unnerved that jokes were being cracked while Esther was dying. "You burned out on it. Everyone crashes and burns on the promiscuity machine sooner or later." Marcy snickered again.

Martin looked at Felicity, who looked right back to him with a [confusion] wink.

A glance at his monitor showed VisualTeam: [Rachael and Debbie onsite. All other Normsos including the church employee fled the burning building. Building records show no fire sprinklers installed in the main church. Other parts of the building malfunctioned.]

Martin sat down facing his monitor and folded his arms. *How did the Ladykiller controversy pop up in the middle of this tragedy? Hedonic program is Marcy's clue. It was her system of resource extraction through promiscuous sexual activity and Registry-based selection programs to fund BGC and the Schools. Quite a marketing program. She's showing me how to act rationally in the midst of a crisis and subsequent trauma.*

He looked back at his Parents. Marcy nodded at him with [continue] [think]. Martin thought aloud, "The Schools need more protection. I'm afraid for the worst."

Max looked worried. "What did we do? What were we thinking? I really hate this world sometimes. You are supposed to *end* violence and suffering, not cause it." *Why do stupid Parents think this? Why is this our burden? We want nothing to do with Normsos. Why Esther bothers…*

Felicity interjected, "We will keep trying. We're still young, Dad, but we grow up fast. We will try harder not to make mistakes. Maybe they'll change their minds. We have awesome solutions for world energy, medicine, pollution, many great things in the works. They will love us then."

"It looks like you better create these fast. Looks like the Parents owe well more than two million to have a Talent child. All our other resources have to go to protecting you as well." Max shook his head. Martin almost felt his dad's comment was rehearsed. It felt like a conversational remnant from a discussion he had with Marcy about what to do with all his money.

Marcy spoke, "Well we won't make sales and marketing sex workers out of ourselves this time. BGC has changed up selection tactics and no longer needs Parents sleeping around. We switch to emotional extortion to raise money. Contribute or your beautiful and happy Talent child might be killed or kidnapped." Marcy winked at Martin.

More cryptic hints. Okay, Mom. We'll create a Talent program to put the screws to our Parents for more money to protect us. Maybe my dad is right; a BGC AI is controlling everything. Or Marcy is telling the truth. SHE is controlling everything. Martin tried to emotionally comprehend that his mother might be evil. Strange and awkward was what he came up with. Evil didn't seem like the right word. He thought that if Marcy was behind the BGC selection AI, then she selected people who would not make the recommended selections, just to use as extortion or blackmail and motivation for Martin's benefit. *Is Mom that twisted?*

He suddenly felt nervous being near Marcy and got up to walk around his battalion workstation circles trying to negate that evil thought with distraction. Cysso was busy analyzing footage and monitoring the various people moving around. They restored the lights to the burning church and were instructing Debbie and Rachael to move the bodies out quickly after they bound Esther's wounds.

Smithy scootered over to him and handed him his forgotten phone. "The plane is waiting for you. Get going."

Felicity came up to him and smiled. "I can handle things from here." She gave him a peck on the lips. "It'll be fine. I promise. Take a vacation."

Martin hesitated to leave, except that Marcy had told him to do so. He had been under the impression he could never leave. He hesitated some more.

Felicity smiled pleasantly and twirled some of her long curly hair that was half braided (right side), half unbraided. She started pushing him. "Go. Get out of here."

CHAPTER THREE

LIFE AFTER DEATH

[No time]
No place

PEACE. I AM DEAD. *I wonder if I'll reincarnate, resurrect from the dead, get tossed into the lake of fire as an unbeliever, find oblivion...*
Goodbye body. You were perfect, but I lost you. I loved my short perfect life. I was going to reshape the whole world into something perfect. I was making everyone proud. I was too proud and so I died...
Darkness...
I see the light shining in the distance, approaching...
I see a pyramid and inside the pyramid are all the gods, zoomorphic and anthropomorphic, in all civilizations. The outside of the pyramid is covered in symbols for the countless religions, cultivars, ethical systems, syncretisms, cults, gnosticisms, mysteries, occultisms, and kabbalas through human history. They are converging... to...
I see a caduceus and between the snakes the DNA double helix. One snake is black, and the other is white. Above the caduceus I see the eight-pointed star of Ishtar. It is white. It is drawing out the black snake color into it and turning gray while the black snake turns white. The star turns red then shines with light and now burns and shines colorless white light.
The light from the star intensifies. It is bright enough to consume

everything, the pyramid is burned to nothingness in an instant...
Nothing remains except the light and the star.
I hear a voice. Alto pitch.

I am alpha and omega. I am the beginning of the very end. For as the new heavens and the new earth, which I will make, will remain before me, so will your seed and your name remain. All flesh will come to worship before me. And they will go forth and look upon the dead bodies of the men who have transgressed against me. For their worm will not die, nor will their fire be quenched, and they will be an abhorring to all flesh.

The time of the great filter is nearly upon mankind. Ninety-nine of one hundred shall die so that one shall live. One of ten shall die so that nine shall live. Those who give everything shall receive everything. Those who keep everything will lose everything. My people shall be granted eternal life and a place in paradise. The wait is nearly over.

I am entering the star.

I am awake. Where am I?

I am heavily sedated. Probably fentanyl. I was hallucinating. A common side effect.

I can open my eye. Just one eye? My left eye.

"Hello?" *My throat is dry.*

"I am here, sweetheart." Her mother (Rachael) was crying while she got some water for Esther to sip.

There are other people in the room. Two hands are holding my hands. She moved her eyeball around. *Martin and Josh. Martin looks so concerned. My husband, I am alive, but in what condition?*

"Wh-where am I?" *I am flooded with painkiller, probably as much as I can handle.*

"You are in a hospital in Lexington. You were shot twice and hurt your head badly when you fell. You nearly died from blood loss. If you weren't so healthy, you would have certainly died. Frankly, it's a miracle as far as I am concerned. You were brain-dead at one point. It's all my fault. I should have understood what was going on. I didn't think he'd try to kill you..." A flood of tears came from Rachael-mother.

"Mother, I'm really sedated. Am I going to live?" *I am so sleepy.*

"Yes, dear. The doctors here think you will make a full recovery."

"Mother, what happened?" *Best to get it all out now.*

"It won't be easy." *Bad news.* Mother was standing where Esther could see her, crying. The boys still held her hands out of the way.

"I'd like to know. Do it while I'm sedated." *Quickly, I'm starting to fade.*

"You were shot in the arm; it's that wound that nearly killed you from blood loss. I'm not sure how the forensics and physics work, sweetie. But you lost your left index finger. It was shot off and too damaged to reattach." *She is starting slowly. It's going to get worse. A finger is not so bad. Do I quit piano?*

"Mother, what's wrong with my right eye?"

"Oh, dearest, it was damaged from a bullet. You left ear was damaged as well. They think the second bullet ricocheted off your arm and finger and lodged in your ear. Darling, I have other terrible news." *Okay, I lost a finger, an eye and an ear. I'm still alive. People have suffered worse.*

Her mother was crying very hard. It took some time for her to rally.

"Mother, what?" *I'm so tired.*

"Your friend Elsa is dead. She was shot through the heart protecting you."

"Noooo... Nooooo..."

Esther started crying in her good eye and couldn't stop. *One eye has to serve for two, it seems. I'd give my whole body for her to be alive. I am so stupid. So incredibly smart and so incredibly stupid. The spouse pays Inanna's ransom from death. She has gone to the afterlife in my place... demons released...*

She fell back asleep.

In her dream state she found Elsa smiling. She was radiant.

"It's okay, Beloved. I died in battle protecting you, like I wanted. I killed Nate in return. A life for a life. A life to save a life, one worthier than a simple riflewoman. Look, the gods have decided I am worthy to be a Valkyrie and get to serve, you, Freyja, my goddess, in the afterlife. It is a good fate, is it not? I lived a good life, Esther. I got to be with you, to know you, and to love you. I am content with that. You can take the future even if you fail."

And in the dream Annie flew away riding on a horse armed with her rifle, with ABBA music playing: "I Have a Dream."

#

Esther wakened. Her mother was there asleep sitting at her side. *It is Mother now. Yes, no longer Mom.* The room was dark.

"Mother?"

"Uh, yes. Oh. Yes, I'm awake now." Rachael woke up.

"Did Nate die, too?"

"Yes, Elsa managed to shoot him through the eye as he shot her. Such a waste of life."

More crying. Her mother whispered, "It's all my fault."

"Mother, stop that. It's my fault. It was my idiot idea to confront stupid violent Nate. My friend died because of *my* stupidity. Not yours. You made me smart but not wise, mother. Now I have wisdom, at too great a price it seems. It is my price for hubris. I am not a goddess. I shall *NEVER* pretend to be one again."

Esther felt a special anger and hard determination. She had crossed the barrier of death. She reasoned the paradox mission glitching would leave her to sleep in peace now that she knew who she was. *I am male and female, androgyne, Talentso and Normso, I am human with godlike power. I was dead but now I am alive. I am light and dark. Truth and lies. I am not afraid. I am good and evil. Beyond good and evil. I feel capable of absolutely anything. I will do absolutely anything in my fight for life.*

"A goddess? You thought with all your knowledge and power... I see now. I should have seen this. Your life was so blessed."

That was part of it. Yes, I suppose my god complex wasn't completely unreasonable. Combined with my mission genetics to convert, lead, and take followers. Deadly genetics indeed.

"No, it's more than that. It's these mission genetics. It's a potent and dangerous set of mutations that have combined and now imprinted. I must convert people and I am tribal. I must convert and protect my tribal identity, which is Normso." *That was my last thought before I died. Before Elsa died. Oh, Better Genetics, my true god, what have you done to me?*

Her mother reflected for a while. "You found your faith during that year of religious study?"

"All I found was kindness. Most of religion seemed like genetic in-breeding and outbreeding programs built for supertribal altruistic unity. We must learn to live together in peace. It starts with kindness. That is my religion. My purpose in life is completely clear. I must maintain peace between Talents and Normsos. Ambassador."

Esther found more tears in her mother's eyes and waited for her re-ply. "That is a worthy goal. I am glad you have this faith. Peace through kindness. Let your parents be your first true Normso Followers. You have plans?" Rachael smiled and cried some more. She used the Tesp word for followers, meaning 'those who walk behind.' She was learning the language, as did all Parentsos who participated in Talentso society.

Follower. A fine word. Tesp Followso. I will build a group of Normso Followers, those whose will has been subsumed to mine, whose purpose is only my purpose. I will make a synthetic Normso community. Religions make synthetic communities to transcend genetic tribalism. Followers should become Disciples, too. They must obey my ethical principles to the best of their ability or be cast out. They must be loyal to the point of death.

"The sedation is really strong, Mother. I can sort of feel the patch on my eye and my ear. What are they doing to me? How long am I going to be here?" *I can't plan anything on sedation.* "I must get well first, be-fore I do anything."

"Two Parentsos who are world class doctors want to try some medical treatments on you. Your four parents have given consent, but they need yours too, obviously. You will have to talk to them about it."

"Okay, after another sleep then."

Esther took another long sleep. She went back to death. This time she dreamed of Nate.

He was floating above a black sun. A thin red tentacle came out of the sun and wrapped around his legs, holding him taut and stretched as if his will was keeping him from falling in.

"I'm going to hell. I thought you should know. They said I could talk to you before I go, once you knew I was dead."

"Why did you kill me Nate?" Esther didn't have her own body, just a consciousness with a view.

"These people said they would promote me, give me money. There are people who pay good money to have Talents killed or captured. I did it for the money. I was in love with you and could never have you. There was that reason, too. It was more money if I captured you, but they made it clear I couldn't keep you. I thought if you thought my intention was to capture you and not kill you, you'd be more likely to take my bait. I didn't expect your speech to sway my followers away from me. I had to act quickly and decisively."

"You didn't know me. How could you love me?"

"You are the goddess of love. Don't you know that? You wear her necklace. Don't you know we can figure stuff like that out? Everyone loves you. Everyone *will* love you. Many will try to kill you. I am just the first of very many people who will try to kill you. Just as Elsa was the first of many who will die saving you. The ones coming after you will be older, smarter, better, and eviler. You will need to do better than Elsa next time. That is all that I am allowed to share with you before I go."

"Do you have to go to hell? Do I have any say in the matter?" The black sun seemed to suck light and heat, instead of generating it. Esther thought the other side was permanent nonexistence. *Annihilation. A life forgotten to eternity.*

"You are the one I tried to kill. Elsa is already gone. Yes, you can intervene. I don't deserve pity or grace. I was stupid, mercenary, jealous, and evil. I deserve hell."

"Your confession is worth something. Your warning is worth something. The lesson you taught me is worth something. I will pronounce judgment on you. You will stay in hell as long as I live. You are free if those who follow after you in evil succeed in killing me."

"Your judgment is wise. Thank you, Esther. I love you."

"I know that you love me."

Nate remained expressionless as he was pulled into the black sun, caught between his certain punishment and the prospect of Esther saving him through her own death.

CHAPTER FOUR
THE 4.5 MILLION
DOLLAR WOMAN

[Time unknown]
A private hospital bedroom somewhere

ESTHER'S CONSCIOUSNESS STIRRED, and from the light filtering through her one closed eyelid, she thought it was daytime. She decided to eavesdrop and pretend unconsciousness.

Paula and Ken were talking about church stuff related to female priests and open homosexuality. Jordan was talking to Amanda about her atheism and what moral principles she invented for herself and why she thought they were better than other better tested systems. Rachael was talking to two people she didn't recognize about recent medical advances in prosthetics. Martin was talking to Josh (to the other side of her body) about Debbie's decision to live full-time with Ken. She was returning to monogamy and wanted Ken around the Estate.

She opened her eye and craned her neck to see Josh and Martin sitting on either side of her, holding her hands with both their hands. Josh had the left hand with the missing index finger and had closed both his eyes. Martin was staring at her, and she stared right back. He used the bed controls to sit her up and then bent in and kissed her on the lips gently. They both laughed and smiled. *I feel such love for my man. I want to make love, that is a good sign.*

She spied a male and female doctor (clothing recognized) in the room talking about her eye and ear with Rachael-mother. *They sound like the Parentso medical specialists she told me about.*

Rachael noticed her looking and excused herself to go to Esther. She examined Martin. "You two and your marriage." She smiled, looking content, then turned back to the two doctors. "She's awake. Esther? These are the Parent doctors who want to talk to you. I'll be in the room with your other parents while they do so. You can introduce yourselves."

"Here you go, that should be better." Martin readjusted the recline on the hospital bed so she could scan the room a little better.

The room was quite large to fit all these people, now that Esther thought about it. She guessed Debbie had made a financial contribution to whatever hospital or clinic she was in. She probably had an app for that. *Probably a private clinic for the superwealthy to be used by Alison's Eleven app doctors.* They were all there standing, sitting, talking. Rachael, Debbie, Ken, Amanda, her siblings, the two doctors, Martin and Josh, and Jordan and Paula.

"You have quite a family that loves you, Esther. They have such complete devotion for you." *That was Josh speaking.* She turned to him and gave him her best Debbie smile and sweetest (noncynical) voice, "Hello, Josh. It's kind of you to be here. Thanks. Yes, I love my family." Esther studied Josh's serene face. *I like this man. He has the look of someone who truly cares. Someone truly kind. Would he have been a better choice than Martin?*

Josh signaled the doctors over to the bed and stood up. Martin stood up too. "Come, come. Esther has big decisions to make. She looks ready for them." Esther marveled that Josh managed simultaneous kindness and authority in the way he spoke.

A man who looked in his later middle age, slim to ectomorphic, showing a brow accustomed to deep concentration, walked up close to her bedside next to Josh.

"This is John." John gave a curt nod. Esther didn't feel like moving her arms. She recognized him as Josh's Parentso at the coming-of-age ceremony.

Esther smiled at John and then the female doctor standing next to him. They both visibly relaxed.

"Hi Esther, I'm Janet. My Talents are at the Boston Science School. They tell me you are the best and send their deepest love and hope and pray for a good recovery." Janet frowned for a moment. "They called you their Queen." She looked irritated when she spoke 'queen.' That would have been a slip-up by Janet's children, but she trusted her friend Lucy to manage this sort of faux pas in the future.

"Oh, we're just kidding around, Janet. I have a popular video show." Martin scratched her hand, a signal to shut up. Esther decided the drugs made her lose her guard.

Josh spoke next in his typical authority/kindly fashion, "John and Janet are medical specialists. We want to talk about prosthetics. You've lost a finger and damaged your right eye and left ear. Martin is working with prosthetic engineers to make your new finger more Talent-cybernetic. Martin, you explain."

"Well, all your damaged parts. We want to make them all Talent cybernetic. Parents like John and Janet have been installing cybernetic prosthetics on Talents all over the world. All accidents, of course. Smithy, as you well know, lost his organic legs in a car accident."

Josh elaborated, "Your optic nerve and retina are still fine. It's the rest of the eyeball that's problematic. We can re-create an acrylic eye prosthesis that contains a sort of mini computer screen with low resolution. Your eye retina contains about four point five million cones, but the mini computer screen is not that dense. It will look sort of like a pixelated computer game. It will be wirelessly connected to a small computer you carry around which can go online, or will access a special camera fitted onto glasses for some regular vision, also pixelated..."

Martin interrupted, "The best part is your new finger acts as a sort of mouse, an interface. Thumb controlled, using the finger as a touchpad. We've got about a thousand Talents signed up to improve the technology, too. We want to get the resolution up to that four point five million retina cones, matching the correct cone density. Janet will take a cone map of your retina. Your new eyeball will be custom built."

John spoke up, "Your inner ear was damaged. And I'm going to recommend a cochlear implant, connected to your auditory system in your brain. Our current technology has a small rechargeable battery and an external cord that you plug into your ear every night. It will also have a wireless connection to your portable computer."

"Yes, and another five hundred Talents want to program for that. Real mind/machine interface stuff." Martin couldn't restrain his joy. *I will be using and carrying his electronic property, good.* Esther mused at the humor of Martin now being perpetually inside her sexiest organ and that he would literally own her body. *I chose him well to bond with. And he chose me.*

Janet took her turn. "Yeah, well we want to do it all while you are still on sedation. It will add to your recovery. There's some plastic surgery as well. The bullet caught your eyelid and part of your nose at the bridge. We're thinking many months of both recovery and tweaking it out…"

Martin interrupted again, "You'll get your fifteen-year-old rhinoplasty, but you didn't need it. I mean your nose looked great before." Jordan came over and smacked him on the arm. Jordan, Martin, and Esther started giggling.

Jordan spoke next, "It's good that you're laughing. Esther, I've studied these people, John and Janet. They're the best in their field. You couldn't get better care." Jordan went back to talking to Amanda, who looked so nervous she was going to crack.

Josh continued, "It will look exactly the same. Anyway, it's not as important as your eye surgery. They are doing a tear duct transplant and an eyelid transplant."

John spoke next, "We need your consent. The surgeries have all been explained to your family and Paula and Jordan. Everyone is comfortable with what we want to do."

"How much of the technology is Talent tech?"

Martin spoke, "At the start mostly Normso. Inventing the initial techs made these Parentsos rich enough to afford Better Genetics. Talents are going to take over these technologies, though. And we still need the Parentsos to do the surgeries or train Talents on them. We are all planning on regular upgrades. You'll be a real cyborg, Esther! Only less metal, more acrylic. We're talking about custom Talent nonplastic materials too. A lot of projects are underway."

Josh continued, "Esther, don't let Martin fool you, they are just prosthetics with tiny computer chips and batteries that require daily recharging and a twice-a-year checkup. I'm sure Esther would prefer her old eye and ear back."

Esther again admired the natural kindness and implicit authority in Josh's voice, compared to Martin's eagerness and enthusiasm about his wife becoming a science project. She understood that two power supplies and chips inside her head could be overclocked to the possibility of killing her. The thought of Martin having instant life and death over her didn't bother Esther in the slightest; she felt the opposite effect, safer and more protected. She wondered if she would become a cliché of two perfect men fighting over her. They had both paused to stare at her while she looked back and forth between their faces, both so intensely beautiful.

Martin broke the silence with an eager, "Hey, she's technically a cyborg in my book. You're no fun." Esther struggled to suppress a giggle about how two Talents might fight over a woman, compared to Normso showdowns.

"Fun is not a word that describes me."

"Bionic woman?"

Josh spoke with complete equanimity, "No superpowers. We live within the physics boundaries implicit and discoverable in God's creation, which only God can break." Esther remembered that Josh was an explicit Christian and had formed a small "church" of fellow Christian Talents living at the Labfarm, which included her siblings. They held a sunrise breakfast prayer and a Psalms scripture reading plus singing every morning in the cafeteria. She had joined them once a week, after which they discussed plans for Ethers for the next week with Josh leading. She was sure she went because she found Josh so likeable.

Martin frowned, but Josh continued, "I'm sure Esther would prefer an external phone versus implants. Plugging your ear in at night and removing your eye to clean and recharge it is not going to be exactly fun. You are not the one doing all the maintenance hassle. Any mistakes she makes in her routine will cause her quite a lot of pain."

Janet intervened, "Okay, what the boys are not explaining is that recovery is going to be difficult. Before I explain recovery, I need to refamiliarize you with the concept of neuroplasticity."

"I'm familiar with the subject." *It was critical with Alzheimer's research.*

"Okay, maybe with regular people or animals. But we need to be specific about Talents. Many of the Talent parents are doctors, and we've compiled a lot of information on Talent medicine." *They were giving it all to Lucy, who always promised a report. How did Lucy arrange all this?*

"But we barely get sick. What would there be to learn?"

Martin distracted her with a pinch and morse blinked [Lucy covered this with Janet], while Janet spoke. "Many things. First of all, we had to double check Better Genetics' marketing promises, right? See if all their health claims were true? Well, it turns out they were more than true, and they did a lot of things they didn't tell us about but surely knew about. Your sisters already told me that every Talent woman has that woman's body over there."

Debbie raised her hand up and spoke in an innocent girl voice. "That's me. I have to say, given my life and lifestyle, you're going to love it." Esther laughed, and so did the other Talents, girls and boys saying they admired having or looking at Debbie's body. Janet and John didn't laugh. Josh didn't laugh or smile, calm as ever. *Another odd Talent. So, he's like the Circle of Six then, maybe he makes it seven. I wish he didn't refuse the offer. He said he's busy enough with Ethers and various science experiments as he heads Reformso, the group dedicated to scientific method and best practices. Purity.*

Poorly aging Janet scratched her head for a bit looking at Debbie. "You're over fifty. You told me you had a lot of plastic surgery. Can you give me your surgeon's name?" Janet looked over 50. Debbie still looked in her 20s. Esther recognized some of Debbie's nonverbal seduction beyond the innocent girl voice. Esther found she enjoyed the effect on Janet.

Debbie said coyly, "Janet, are you married or in a partner exclusivity contract? Want to see how good my surgeries are up close?" followed by that Debbie smile. "Want me to connect you to them? You do a good job on my daughter, I'll give you whatever you want for free." She licked her lips in seductive grin.

Esther noticed John was staring at Debbie, too, until he interrupted,

"Janet, stay focused. Yes, your daughter's body looks more like hers and not yours. It was not informed consent. We gave up so much of our genetic inheritance when we had our children. Which would you rather have, your daughter with your body or Debbie's over there? A world-class fashion model. Which body would your daughter rather have? Call her and ask, here and now..."

Esther now interrupted, "I'm very proud to have Debbie's body. It has served me well. But you're just talking about the outward appearance, bones and other tissues that form her shape. These are just measurements. Numbers. Proportions and ratios. Do we share the same internal organs, like lungs, kidneys, and hearts?"

The group there started to murmur. Esther's siblings Melanie, Shelly, and Rachel attested they liked their bodies and they were serving them well. Melanie observed, "It makes a lot of things simple and easy. Clothing is very easy. No one has any reason to be jealous of anyone's body. It probably saves a lot of conflict." Martin gave his peculiar testimony that Esther had a great body, and the Talents all laughed again, while the Normsos showed great confusion or concern. Josh kept a serene face in the commotion. Janet was still stunned while John had regained serenity. Esther wondered if Janet was in a sort of emotional overload, unable to process the disgust, envy, admiration, attraction, and sheer wonder at the results of raw genetic power. The stun of emotions resolved into fear on Janet's face. Esther noticed fear there, not love. The image/memory imprinted in Esther's memory, much in the same way Alison's face of fear had also imprinted. She supposed that human genetic engineering was always and would always be a cause for fear.

Martin suddenly put his phone in Esther's face, ending her observations.

Lucy: [This needs to stop. Change the subject to neuroplasticity. Janet held out on me the longest. She didn't want to share or let me take charge of Talent biology. She's been afraid of us from the start, and only consented to have a Talent child out of scientific curiosity. It became known among the Parentso doctor holdouts that my father was the spymaster the European Union sent to investigate BGC. Talents have the right to own their own biology, not their parents. I will tell you everything someday.] After a moment Martin took the phone away and typed in a message while Esther changed the subject.

"Okay, everyone, Talents like Debbie's body. We will look beautiful and sexy well past menopause; we should all be happy. We need to talk about my brain surgery. Neuroplasticity."

Janet recovered from her fear paralysis by closing her eyes. She took a moment to regain her nerves, swallowed, nodded her head, and continued, facing but not looking at Esther. "Yes, we get back to this concept of neuroplasticity, the ability of the brain to 'rewire.' Readjust. Our theory so far is that beating back the mental genetic health problems was accomplished by solving the neuroplasticity problem. Talents have an excellent history of trauma recovery. You are not the first Talent to receive eye and ear implants. You will go through a period of adjustment as you relearn how to see and hear."

"Okay, how long will it take?" *Forever it seems with my dad. Poor Ken. Abusing alcohol to deal with PTSD. He must be reliving his killing of a man with his bare hands.*

"Less than a year. By then you should have complete control of your new eye and ear and finger functions. But that's less important than the real recovery, the part that is really interesting." Everyone became extremely quiet. They all seemed to know this moment was coming, and why they were all crowded in that largish recovery room. The change in social disposition came on cue at the words "real recovery."

"The eye and ear trauma are nothing compared to the real trauma I am experiencing." Esther began to cry. Each of her loved ones came over and took turns giving her a hug. They cried along with Esther, except for her mother. *She still feels shame.* Debbie smiled at her during her turn. The same smile that Rachael said could sell millions of consumer products—the one that Esther could do too, which she now practiced back to Debbie, who nodded in acknowledgment. Esther's sadness dissipated. She suddenly remembered that Debbie had nearly died too. Esther saw Debbie's expression change to sympathy as she put one hand on her heart and another on Esther's. *My heart is palpitating, and my skin is shivering. Debbie makes me so happy. I feel I don't have anything to worry about Elsa. That she is still alive somehow, despite being cremated.*

After the ritual, Janet continued, now frowning at Debbie who didn't leave Esther's side and didn't stop smiling and making Esther smile. "Yes, you feel the trauma now, but Talents don't suffer from anything like post-traumatic stress disorder. You will return to your normal happy self. We have no cases where there was a need for medication or therapy, or where anything like suicide or drug or alcohol abuse occurred among any Talents who experienced any type of trauma. Your painful grief at losing a close friend should flatten out in about a month. The memory of being shot and being in the hospital will be just that. A memory. You won't be reliving it over and over."

Elsa, just a memory? Esther cried so much more now, facing down towards Debbie's hand on her heart. "Sweetheart, you have a good cry over a lost close and loved friend. It is good for the spirit. There is no shame in honest grief."

After a few minutes and more hugs and heartfelt expressions of "Oh, Esther, I'm so sorry about your loss," Josh decided to speak. "Everyone, I'd like you all to leave, except Martin." Some of the adults seemed confused by the request at first, but they all silently left. Josh closed the door.

Martin spoke first after looking at Josh. Esther guessed he and Josh had discussed what they were going to say to her. "The entire world Talent population saw what happened, live. They all send you their love and respect. You are not just their queen, priestess, lover, model, and entertainment. You are our hero and heroine. Herosa, they call you. Champion."

"A hero for taking a stupid risk and nearly dying? Having my best friend killed?"

Esther started crying again with her eye closed. She wanted to bang her head hard but couldn't do it. Something had to relieve this emotional hell of pain. The painkillers didn't help. She switched between shame, disgust, despair, self-hate, and acedia (the need to feel nothing at all).

When she opened her eyes, Josh was gone and the lights were low. She looked at Martin and felt a little lust stir. He had the look he was feeling it too, and winked it as agreed signal. [Kiss me.]

They made out for a little while. Esther's situation didn't allow them to go much further despite her desire. She pushed him away. The last thing she needed was a Peakso. She blinked this to Martin and told him [I am too tired.]

Martin nodded and decided to switch to verbal communication. "Before you go back to sleep and the surgeries start, there are a few things you should know. The Talents have analyzed the film footage exhaustively. Do you want to hear their conclusions? Is now a good time?"

Esther blinked to get this over quickly. "Okay, what do they think happened?"

"Well, we had the main camera fixed on the chancel, including the pulpit where Nate was standing and the lectern where you were standing and various videos from the haters' phones. While you were speaking, Nate pulled out a small 22LR pistol to shoot you, aimed at your head. I caused a distraction that affected his aim, which caused the bullet to hit your eye and nose instead of your brain."

"You saved my life then?"

"Maybe not from this particular event. A pistol shot is pretty iffy. Anyway, he fired a second shot which was the one that took off your left finger as you spun, the finger deflecting the bullet and causing the ricochet into your arm and stopping inside your left ear. Fortunately, your moms arrived just soon enough to bind your wounds and get you ready for an ambulance to take you to a hospital."

"I don't understand. How is that possible?"

"What I think happened is that you noticed Elsa coming in through the door to your left. Your body was automatically turning to see the movement out of the corner of your left eye when the first bullet hit. You were intending to turn your whole body to the left and maybe that caused the spin. Anyway, you lost balance, fell down, and hit your head on the way. The bigger they are, the harder they fall, so to speak. I had managed to turn out the lights before the first and second shot, further affecting his aim. Nate walked over to the lectern to try to finish you off when Elsa intervened. That was when they shot each other dead, nearly simultaneously."

Esther began to cry again. Martin stroked her hair and found some tissues to wipe down her face.

Martin continued, "You can watch the video if you want. The police are going to want to talk to you eventually. They've talked to all the other attendees, but they haven't said much. Don't tell them about the Talents or the video, or I'll get in trouble."

Martin put his phone up to her face again.

Lucy: [You cannot talk about us. I know I don't need to remind you of your promise, but I am reminding you anyway. I cannot stress too much how important this is. Martin gets it. He and Felicity have already created a fake story for the Parent spies still lurking around the Schools and for the kids at the church to tell the police.] Martin took the phone away at her nod. Esther was not involved in the complex workings that Martin and Felicity undertook to disinform the Normso and Parentso spies, who tapped into their alternate fake reality that mimicked college student behavior. They lately added various failed experiments on the hackable system, something Martin called misdirection and disinformation.

Esther had watched some of these videos. Girls were always giggling and talking about hawt boys and their crushes. Guys were always talking about video games, sports, anime, and the latest sci-fi superhero movies and TV shows. Both sexes talked about science projects and social justice and diversity, equality, and inclusion. All of it was completely fake. All mimicked from hacked campus cameras and social media accounts. They only thing they didn't mimic was social media. Talents didn't do anything on social media, real or fake. The exception was the Intalent Boardso discussion groups, many of which were moderated by Talents like Lucy and Josh. These were nearly all about discovery and creation. Discussions about politics, defense, and economics were left to Cysso, who had their own private discussion boards at this point. If Talents had a secret society, Cysso had a double secret society.

"Okay, I'll watch the video later. I want to know why I'm even more popular with Talents. This Herosa title."

From the corner of the room came the voice of Josh. It seemed he was there the whole time hanging in the dark. He stood up as he spoke.

"You found a truth, Esther. An important one. Perhaps the most important truth."

He walked over to her, and it was clear from Martin's startled expression he hadn't noticed Josh was there either. Esther thought she should feel creepy about the unexpected appearance but didn't actually feel creeped out. Instead, she felt immense relief. She felt the joy of an immense burden being taken off her, that her guilt over Elsa's death was a useless, vain obsession.

The room was quiet for a little while. Esther studied Josh's face some more. *He means it—my bravery did something, meant something extremely important to the Talents. Elsa did not die in vain. Her life was not wasted. I must come to understand that meaning.*

She closed her eye. *Talents don't know I'm a Normie. I am Normie on the inside. I am more like those Out-Talents in the videos: lustful, manipulative, dominating, enterprising. And here I am their queen, their diplomat.* Esther paused and collected her wits and purpose. *I am the mediation that brings peace. Blessed are the peacemakers. I am a child of God.*

She opened her eye. Josh's face changed into a serene smile. He squeezed her hand again. "Think about your new life. One with Talent prosthetics. John and Janet will be training me on them, so we will see each other from time to time as needed. They intend in the long-term for me to take care of you personally. I will be your permanent doctor. You should rest and contemplate. Have no fear about your impending surgeries. You have the best of care."

She thought about the prosthetics she was going to receive and keep receiving. So much of Parentso and Talentso resources would be poured into her body. She didn't think she deserved it all. She would become a Talent creation as well as a BGC creation. Martin would own and use her body parts, making her part of TOS and Intalent, the leader of a cybernetic society that she converted, was converted by, and through which she would convert the Normsos enough to stop them from killing and enslaving Talents.

"I'm ready for the operations."

Josh spoke evenly, "Goodnight Esther. I will stay on for a few days with you during and after the operations."

Martin spoke firmly, "I'd like some time alone with Esther."

Josh nodded and left, this time with Martin watching carefully to see him out.

Martin climbed in the hospital bed, and they cuddled.

"Wife."

"Husband."

<I love you>

CHAPTER FIVE

CONVERSION WITH KINDNESS

[A few days later]
A private rehab facility outside of Lexington, Kentucky

ESTHER AWAKENED and tapped her new finger with her thumb to turn on her eye-screen. She heard a voice in her head speaking Japanese in a girl's tone. *Kawaii means cute. Yoshi's obsession with J-pop, I think. Why did we make him 'inventor?' If this is what Talent adolescence is going to be like, I think I'm going to hate adolescence.*

What is adolescence?

"Sakura, what is adolescence?"

J-popkawaii/%**Japanese**: "People aged from 15–18 develop more interest in romantic relationships and sexuality, go through less (sometimes more) conflict with parents, show more independence from parents, have a deeper capacity for caring and sharing, and for developing more intimate relationships. They spend less time with parents and more time with friends, and they feel a lot of sadness or depression, which can lead to poor grades, alcohol or drug use, unsafe sex, and other problems. They also learn more defined work habits, show more concern about future school or work plans, and are better able to give reasons for their own choices, including about what is right or wrong." And [visual text.]

"Sakura, repeat in Tesp."

J-popkawaii/**%Tesp**: "repeat" and [repeat.]

"I can't make out the video or noise in my head." *The video is just on, no blinking. No need to keep my eye clean and moist. I can make out something moving. It must be the cursor controlled by my thumb on my prosthetic index finger.*

"I am here in the room, Esther. It's going to take time." That was Rachael-mother speaking into her normal ear. She used her real eye to discover she'd been moved to a smaller room. *I am still soaked in fentanyl.* Debbie-mother sat at her other side and smiled tenderly, putting Esther at ease. "Give it time, sweetheart. Your brain will figure it out."

"It's weird having a video in my head and vision in my head as well." Esther worried for a second that she would get sick because of the incongruence. She played with her finger-mouse and concentrated on identifying the cursor while her real eye was closed. She asked for and received medicine for her nausea. Debbie told her it would go away naturally.

Simultaneously/J-pop: "Testing, testing, testing." /Debbie: "Can you process two sounds and two visions at once, daughter?" Esther looked at Debbie with her real eye and what might be a pixelated video of Martin at the same time.

"This is amazing, I love it. Yes. Yes, I believe I can."

Practice.

#

[Twelve days later]

My new ear is improving faster than my eye. I can handle two conversations and two visions at the same time, the way a chess master can play twenty games of chess at the same time.

J-pop/%Tesp: "Testing. Do you hear me?"

"I hear you. That's a dumb question as I have no choice but to hear you." Esther contemplated that a Normso looking at her right now would think she was talking to herself in a one-sided conversation in a strange language. Debbie and Rachael were providing 24-hour medical and rehabilitation service to Esther, living in the room with her. While Esther conversed with the voice, she was listening to music in her other ear while reading a book with her real eye and searching on the Internet with her prosthetic eye, brain multitasking a four-way consciousness, expanding neuroplasticity to its limits.

Voice/J-pop, presumably generated by Martin, but could be anyone in Cysso: "Good. How is the video?"

"I'm adjusting. The switch between camera mode and computer mode in my new eye is still awkward." Esther considered that speaking out loud was heard by the device in her ear and transmitted to the Voice in her head and the voice in her head.

Voice: "How is the practice with your fingers?"

"Much better. Whose voice is this? It still sounds like Japanese J-pop kawaii. Tell Yoshi to grow up." *Of course, it's Martin.* Esther felt heart pangs and lost her four consciousnesses.

Josh/Sakura: "It's a computer voice. No one is talking to you. We are working on different voices. The Tokyo School wants robots with professional voices. They want to replace all labor with robots. I am typing in the messages for now. It's me, Josh. The computer voice is called Sakura. She was sampled from a popular anime voice actor, not J-pop, but still kawaii. Close guess." *Technically it could be anyone. It is a text-to-voice system, so it has to be Martin. My own thoughts in my head are close to what this "sounds" like.*

"Okay, Sakura, I'd rather listen to Martin or Josh voxplay, if you don't mind the sampling effort. Not that I don't like the sound of cute Japanese girls. Can't I just select what voice I want? Can I mute you?"

Martin/Sakura: "Yes, we can program that. I mean, I can just ignore your choices, you know that."

"Okay, I don't want you waking me up accidentally."

Martin/Sakura: "I'll program a do not disturb mode then. You are still 'on' though."

"I hate waiting for a whole sentence to pop in after a pause while you type it. Why not just speak directly? Why do this at all?" *Now that I think of it, does a computer generating spoken language compose a sentence before it speaks?*

Martin/Martin (real-time): "Because it's cool. Because it leads to other stuff. Because we enjoy doing this stuff. We already started a new translator; you will hear every language in Tesp. You're getting faster at the finger-mouse, I see."

"You watching me watch? Make me a glove so I can use my whole hand. Make me two gloves." *My finger can just be a battery and transmitter this way, kinetic fingers with spoken/text outputs. I learned kinetic communication with Martin when we were together. I miss that. I miss our weekly lovemaking. What am I going to do?*

Martin: "Yeah, is that okay? Me watching? I see your screen as well as hear everything you hear. Plus, I have the cameras in your room. There is a member of Cysso observing you at all times. You can access these cameras, too, if you want to look at yourself."

This gave Esther a thrill. She switched around different cameras in her cyber-eye, while listening to and looking at Rachael talking to Debbie about her fentanyl dosage. She had a camera cyber-eye and her real eye viewing her at the same time, while neuroplasticity helped her "make sense of" how her senses worked. The camera was zoom adjustable with her finger-mouse. "Give me multiple cursors for my two hands." *Lucy confirmed all Talents are ambidextrous with lightning reflexes. Genetically, we could all become master pianists and violinists with practice.*

Martin: "Okay. In the development queue."

"What's going on in Talent land?" An AI summary and the current video Ether downloaded. She would view them later. *They don't need me for my magazine and TV show anymore. Josh runs both from the Estate Labfarm. Josh and my Sibsos.*

Martin: "Expansion. I think Talents are pretty much done with living in bunks at tight Schools. The expectation is emigration to a Labfarm just after turning fifteen. Each School has started one. Your Estate in Kentucky is connected to Chicago Science. Sort of a short plane flight. Circlesos are living in houses together. Smithy has planned a massive installation in Wyoming using all new Talent materials and automated construction."

"I need another nap. Space is tight?" *My body is healing, but I'm still on fentanyl. So sleepy.*

Martin: "Yes, and only getting worse. We live like rats in warrens. Everyone is planning to dig down and make bunkers out of our Schools and Farms. Nuclear survival. Smithy is on a land shopping spree, looking for coal and geothermal rural areas. The plan is still a coal-based society. Coal for materials feedstock, not burning. We will build everything out of carbon and carbon-based nanomaterials."

Esther found a *do not disturb* icon on her screen, selected it and fell asleep. She woke up and talked to her ear.

"Martin, you there?"

Josh: "No, it's Josh here now. Actually, Martin could be here, and we wouldn't know it." *It's Martin alright. Josh would never say something like that.*

"What did Martin do at the church? He talked about the shootout. What really happened?"

Josh: "He overloaded all the electronics and burnt the church down. The Antitemperance society all fled; Nate's friends didn't stick around to finish you off. I suppose your speech talked them out of killing you."

Martin pretending to be Josh is quite funny. I didn't think my speech did that much. Maybe they thought I was already dead.

"He saved my life. I don't think anything less than burning the church down would have saved me. I can understand why everyone panicked and fled. I agree, one of Nate's buddies would have tried to finish me off. What's happened to all those people anyway?" Esther changed the camera view to the hallway where six students camped outside in the clinic corridor. They had been identified as present at the church fiasco.

Josh: "The police questioned them all. They just say Nate pulled out a gun and they all ran away. Just like they were taught in school. Someone pulls out a gun, run for it. They went to Elsa's funeral but not Nate's. Nate's family moved out of town."

"I feel sad I missed Elsa's funeral." *Of course, but how long?*

Josh: "Yes, you've been hospitalized for four weeks. I'll send the video of it."

"How much longer on sedation and recovery?" *I hate drugs. I can't tell time anymore. When did I first recover? I'll figure it all out later. Need to practice. Need to reprogram my brain.*

Josh spoke now in live audio to Esther's cyber-ear (Tesp. Tear), "Stop pretending to be me, Martin." Esther giggled.

#

A new recovery location

Josh, Rachael, and Debbie took over her care using telemedicine advice from various doctor Parentsos. Her new room had two guest sleeping benches (for Rachael and Debbie) and a TV system and all sorts of bed controls. She still had a catheter in her arm, but she occasionally got up to go for short walks surrounded by her students and held up by Debbie. She was stiff and weak. Josh visited one day a week, inspiring Martin to play the prankster. Esther thought it was silly, given Josh made zero IOIs (indications of interest, pronounced "e-oys"), a now popular slang for subtle flirting among Talents.

She was walking with Josh holding her hand when Josh interrupted with "How's it going babe?"

Esther giggled, nearly making a misstep enough to fall over. "Hey, I'm concentrating, babe."

Martin said, "Sorry Esther. I was pretending to be Josh, testing out the sampler. Seems it works. Could you tell the difference?"

"Maybe. Maybe not." *Martin is funny. He is pretending to be Josh as well as Josh: real and virtual life versions. He seems unconvinced that IRL Josh is not IOIing me despite the spy cameras everywhere.*

Esther laughed now at her own humor. She had to admit to herself that Martin's tricks amused her.

"Let me come up with a way so you know for sure it's me, no matter the voxplay or textplay," said Martin.

"Just communicate with me in voxplay."

The real Josh holding her hand in the hallway spoke in her bio-ear, "It's good that you are laughing. I'm going to reduce your sedation some more." Now that she was recovering, his visits were mainly for walks and talks about upcoming Ethers, which had switched to conversations about Talent prosthetics, neuroplasticity, and cyborg-ism (Borgso) in general.

"I hate sedation. Will I have to overcome addiction?"

"Other Talents have had accidents and recovered without addiction complications. I'm not worried." *Because we love each other. Kindness is the best cure for addiction.*

"I have too much to do. I need out of this place. Get me out of here, Josh."

Esther considered her new physical reality. She was "with" Debbie, Lucy, and Rachael in her Tear and cyber-eye every day. She had allowed listen and camera mode on her for all her family and Martin's Cysso, what she dubbed circleawareso. Only the Twins had the ability to create privacy mode for her. This level of intimacy with everyone was welcome and comfortable to Esther. She reflected that Borgso was only feasible in very high-trust societies.

Josh nodded to her and helped her into her bed. "I think you are ready to leave this clinic for home care. You are walking around fine." Esther looked at Debbie, who was awake while Rachael slept, and Debbie nodded as well. "Yes, let's take our girl home, shall we?" Debbie carefully removed the catheter and replaced it with a fresh bandage. She shook a small medicine bottle labeled ibuprofen and smiled at Esther, who felt immediate relief that the fentanyl brain fog would soon go away.

Josh spoke rather loudly, "Esther you are still on sedation. So, take it easy." Just then Rachael woke up and sat up. Esther got up from the bed on her own and looked down on her mother now standing up. *She chose me to be more than a foot taller than her. Is she still happy about that decision?*

Rachael looked up to her. "You're recovering well, Esther. I am glad you are tall. Your cosmetic eye is not yet ready. The temporary one looks, well, it looks creepy." She dug out a pirate eye patch from her lab coat and put it over the creepy eye as Esther bent down to receive it.

Josh spoke from behind her: "The nose, eyelid, and ear patch are mostly healed." Esther used her cyber-eye to access a room camera and zoomed in on her pirate face.

Still too pixelated. Josh handed her a T-pad for her bio-eye to view a snapshot from the camera. The bio-eye (looking at the T-pad camera vision of her) and the camera-eye view matched (except the pixelation).

Esther admired the nearly healed damage to her face and resisted the urge to pretend to be a pirate. *Aye Jimboy. Why shiver me timbers.* There was still a pad on her ear, which had a thin wire coming out for wireless reception. *I got turned into Medusa for my hubris. Will I be able to kill people with a glance someday?*

"Can we go now?"

Josh studied her carefully for a few moments. "Yes."

Esther walked over to and sat down at a table with a large mirror and took out her creepy-looking temporary "cosmetic" cyber-eye (which she referred to as her glass-eye not made out of glass, designed for appearance). She then inserted the "camera-eye" cyber-eye system (designed for functionality). An eye-shaped bulb went into her partially empty eye socket, which was framed by what looked like thick glasses that wrapped around the back of her head. A power cord hung down to a necklace that held further battery power. She carefully put her glass-eye in its receptacle cleaning device and wireless charger. She would retain this glass-eye until the one with better cosmetics arrived.

The camera-eye system gave her much better resolution but looked strange. Her violet bio-eye looked out through a clear unmodified glass lens and her camera-eye on the right side of her face looked like a dark phone camera, with some protrusion for zoom capability. She flickered from her camera-eye vision to other cameras to Internet browsing and back to camera-eye, her vision merging and unmerging while her brain interpreted the dual vision correctly.

She found the mirror over her sink and brushed her shoulder-length hair so that it hid the wire coming out of her Tear and the head wrapping for her glasses/camera-eye. She put the camera-eye into control mode and flickered her Tear between room sound, music selections, Martin's room, conversations between her Circle at the Labfarm, and then back to room sound. The room sound control screen displayed in her camera-eye had controls for sensitivity (her hearing could be volume and ultrasonic enhanced, e.g., "dog whistle hearing"). She switched her vision from Tear control mode back to camera-eye vision control mode, testing the zoom function until deciding to set it to normal.

"Okay, ready to go."

Josh opened the door to the room to find six of her students waiting in the hall outside her room at the recovery clinic. They all stood up when they saw her, bright gladness on their faces, full of anticipation. Esther felt both encouragement and relief. "Okay, follow me back to my Estate in your own vehicles. We're all going to live there from now on. Don't bring anything. You'll get all new stuff, including clothes and electronics." They all nodded silently.

#

Back at her Estate she found an external tent camp set up along the walls connected to the gate entry system. Rachael gave her the update on her Tear. "They set up a sentry system with some building help from Ken and uh… Not sure what to call them."

Martin: "Construction Talents. Talents devoted to building materials and automated construction."

"Construction Talents, Mother."

"Your fellow students patrol the whole perimeter. Your father gives them some basic military drilling and training when they aren't at school or their odd jobs."

#

[A week later]

Martin: "The police are at your door."

Esther opened the door to the main house at the Estate. Rachael and Ken had escorted them around the Labfarm prior to visiting her. The two officers, Detective Jack and his deputy, Alice, had examined the various laboratories and other ground facilities, and had talked to a few of the Talents about their work on hydroponics, agriculture and food production, alternative energy, and animal medicine projects. Martin had earlier reported that it was all beyond their comprehension.

"Hello, Detective Jack, Deputy Alice. I'm Esther. Welcome to my home. Can I get you anything? I am at your service." They placed their coffee orders and Debbie went to the kitchen to make them as planned.

She guided them to the living area, and they all sat down. Debbie brought Esther the first coffee and winked at the detective, who was visibly startled. She walked back to the kitchen to make the other two coffees.

"Your other mother, Debbie, I take it. My records here show two partnered women, Rachael Stein and Debbie Robinson, about sixteen years now, and a recent commitment ceremony at a church in Lexington."

"Yes, officer. I also have my adoptive guardians here as well, Ken and Amanda. You can speak with me freely. I consent to a recording as well. You are also free to search the house. Talents have nothing to hide from anyone."

Martin: [Nice lie.] Instead of having to read a phone, text messages just popped up in her new glass-eye like movie subtitles.

Esther had offered to meet them at the station, but the detective insisted on inspecting her Estate, which was currently listed as joint owned by legally partnered Ken Rutherford and Amanda Keating. Greg had organized the formal change of ownership a few years ago when Ken had anticipated the police would someday inspect the arrangement. Local law enforcement officers were always inspecting survivalist communities for gun stockpiling and cult activities these days. Nonrental properties uninhabited by their owners was a red flag in the system. Ken was a well-established farmer, descended from generations of Kentucky farmers, and his partner a well-established large animal veterinarian. That they were there teaching Talents their plant and animal skills was the cover story. Talents wanted to improve food production technology to fill the world with healthy and delicious beef products with less environmental impact. They were currently developing cow feedstocks so that the animals would belch less methane. They were working on cow manure collection by automated drones for methane and fertilizer capture.

The detective glanced between Debbie and Esther a few times. Esther recognized the familiar Crushso symptoms on the officer's face, looked at Debbie who nodded, and realized she could seduce this man with some effort. She put on her best smile. "Whenever you are ready, sir."

Detective Jack coughed and regained focus. "Why do you think Nate shot you?"

"He was jealous of me and Elsa. We were lovers. Or he hated Talents. Did you look into his associations? Did you find any groups of people who want to kill or kidnap Talents to sell their organic resources?"

The detective blanched very slightly. "Who would want to kill Talents? That idea is ridiculous. You are a model citizen, Esther. The jealous lover explanation makes the most sense, doesn't it?" Detective Jack was trying his hardest not to stare at her and failing repeatedly.

"The church meeting was about anti-Temperance. Meaning anti-Talents." *Someone managed to remember to grab the sign during the panic. I have it now. I'm not sure what to do with it. I don't think I want to involve the police in my problems. That was Ken's advice. He told me not to trust the police.*

"Was it? We found no evidence of that. It was a regular Temperance meeting, according to the church records. Kids on a Friday night not drinking is a good thing." The detective seemed sincere about this statement.

He's a good man underneath, I think. The day is coming soon when I will convert authorities. Yes, he will be my first.

Esther had argued with Lucy for days about this eventual confrontation. Esther insisted that Lucy's father was a spymaster and knew everything about police interrogation. While Lucy didn't deny the claim, she insisted that Esther just do her best. She only had to follow her promise not to reveal Talent culture or other secrets to Normsos. Lucy and her father had discussed this at length and agreed that the best course of action was the simplest.

"So, no evidence of a conspiracy to kill me?"

Jack looked genuinely surprised. "No. Um. Er. Evidence? Uh. Everything burned down. The church was old and in disrepair. It's a good thing all the kids ran, but they should have dragged you three out and bound your wounds. I suppose they all thought you were dead. How's your recovery? I see you have a fake eye. Looks pretty good." He started looking nervous and flatfooted.

The new cosmetic glass-eye had arrived three days ago. The color shading was good, but she had to look people straight in the face. She turned off the screen to focus her attention. Flatfooted and nervous was an opportunity for direct questions.

"None of the people who were there have said anything?"

"They all gave the same story. They talked about the importance of not drinking alcohol, and how you gave a speech about alcohol as a guest speaker. They said Nate was jealous of Elsa. When she showed up uninvited, he broke down and tried to kill you both. Elsa and Nate exchanged shots and died. Esther, what we don't have is any explanation of why the church burned down. We found wreckage of fused out phones, d-pads, and computers. Do you know anything? Why would students drop their phones and leave them behind?"

Esther teared a bit at the mention of Elsa dying. The detective was startled and then looked embarrassed. Rachael came over with a tissue. *It is still raw and powerful.*

Esther exploded, "How would I know? I was shot and unconscious. While my bae was murdered." She started crying in earnest.

She noticed Jack scanning her for a bit and looking contemplative. She felt the lie went over well. All the recording devices were destroyed, but he wouldn't know the Talents had copies.

The haters who provided testimony (with direction from Martin) said they ran and dropped their phones when the guns came out and had no idea what started the fire. It was an old wooden church, and the congregation was thinking of building a new one because of potential fire hazards. Even the minister of the church there testified to this. The church admin said the fire was her fault for running away in panic. The minister said the insurance company fire claims unit insisted the phones had started the fire but were fighting the equipment manufacturers, who claimed this was impossible.

It is all a bit flimsy. Martin said his phone hacking program could never be used again on a scale like that. Janet said I would get over Elsa. I won't, I've kept her necklace. I am NOT a goddess. Tears. She gripped the star tightly. She did that at least once a day or whenever she felt extremely powerful or lustful. *Debbie and Lucy both recommend I take a new bodyguard for my power and lust drives.*

"I'm sorry. No, I suppose you wouldn't. You know, it would be a great help to us if you talked the other kids who were there into telling us something more. Could you do that for us?"

"I will talk to them. I can't promise anything." *The detective and his deputy are easy pickings. No, I won't do what they want. They will do what I want.*

"You take good care of yourself. Good looks like yours could cause anyone to be jealous. Now that I've met you, murderous jealousy is a much better explanation than your anti-Talent theory." *Oh, an IOI.* She quickly glanced to Debbie, who nodded.

"Yes, I understand. Jealousy can kill. Thank you, officers. Come by any time." Esther winked and Detective Jack smiled back. *He's a good-looking man, now that I think about it. Used to girls crushing on him, I bet.*

The police left.

Shortly after their departure, Esther decided to summon all the teens who were at the church to the new Estate auditorium.

While Esther spent over a month in the hospital and recovery clinic, Talents had been trying out advanced robotic construction technologies to manage the 95,000 Talents entering the Talent population system each year. By now, around 1000 Talents (15 and older) had relocated to her Estate in Kentucky. One of the first buildings these Talents built was this auditorium. As she approached the building finally completed, she admired the glistening diamond crystal sheen and the various architectural elements that vaguely reminded her of the Baha'i temple in Wilmette, Illinois, with its large round towering white dome. It supposedly took one month to build and was made completely of recycled materials and industrial byproducts, mostly plastic and sawdust. The audience room was a large circle, and she now walked to the center to a raised dais where she could be seen clearly by everyone. She looked up into the high dome and admired the detail produced by computer programming rather than hand craftsmanship. Instead of geometric forms as expected, Talents went with Mandelbrot fractals of various styles. The overall impression was that she had entered an alien spaceship.

The teenagers sat on benches made of the same materials as the rest of the building, and Esther thought for the moment that she too was building with recycled mixed with by-product. "Thank you all for coming. Thank you all for being quiet with the police." A modern sound system had been installed by Percy and Shelly, which also connected to their phones (and earbuds), producing a live text-captioning system for the hearing impaired, so to speak. A few teens were using their new Talent phones to see her talk, using the various zoomed-in camera placements. They sported new uniforms as well, dresses for girls and shirts and long skirts for boys. They were green and yellow, designed to make them stand out from the Talents who dwelt at the Estate, who wore mostly white. As usual, nothing was form fitted (sexy), and everywhere were pockets.

Congregation: "Thank you Esther." The teens spoke in near unison unprompted.

"Thank you for going to Elsa's funeral. Thank you for watching over me."

Congregation: "Thank you Esther."

"What are you all thinking?" She said this in the nicest way possible. "Tell me what you are looking for, what you are waiting for."

A male stood up. "We've decided our best possible goal in life is to serve you, Esther. Any way you see fit."

"Serve me? Why?"

A female stood up next to him and took his hand. "Nate tried to kill you with a cheap shot and died. The whole place burned down. You've come back stronger and smarter than ever from a head wound. Face it, Esther, you are a living goddess among us. Maybe if we serve you in this life, you'll get us access to Better Genetics. None of us could ever afford the place. If we want our children to have any hope of a future, we will need to serve you."

"Why not just work hard and save money?"

Another male stood up next to the female, held her hand, and spoke. "We saw and met with those doctors and Talents at the hospital. We still remember the pain of our phones shocking us and catching on fire. The world is changing, Esther. Faster than you think. We saw and heard how much these other Talents admired you. Some even called you their Queen and the other guy their King. We heard the way they spoke about you when we asked them questions. We're not as smart as you, but smart enough to understand that you are their leader. That's what we think. One day you will rule the world, Esther. With your husband, Martin, for sure.

We want you to rule the world, and we want to be part of it."

"What do you think you can do for me?"

Another female (Sally) stood up next to the man and held hands. *My new Followers orchestrated a response to me. They had a lot of time to talk while waiting for me to recover.* "Protect you. I worked closest with Nate and his contacts at the Antitemperance organization. I've been kept as a member at a distance. They are not sure of me. I would be happy to keep infiltrating them. The other people here want to be your bodyguards. They will think hard before trying to kidnap or murder someone protected by an armed, trained, and highly motivated group of teenagers."

The words goddess *and* queen *came up. I am starting a cult. I know a lot about cults. Do what thou wilt. Fine. There have been female cult leaders before. Nate's dream told me I had to do better than Elsa the next time. Now I have a hundred Elsas. It's time to make a New Covenant.*

"Your service to me is acceptable under important conditions. None of this goddess stuff. I will not be worshipped. You shall call me Beloved. There will be no cult of personality either. If you all are my Followers (which I will call any Normso who follows my leadership and commands without hesitation), then you will study, learn trades, and work here at the Estate. I don't need a hundred people following me everywhere all the time. Do you understand?"

Congregation, "We understand."

"We will practice kindness. If people are out to kill me, then Followers shall be kind to each other because you all will be risking your life for me. We make our time on Earth valuable to each other. There will be no drugs or alcohol or rude or mean behavior. You will not be permitted any kind of sexual activity among yourselves. When the outside world looks at you, they will say you are model citizens because you will *be* model citizens. If someone doesn't strive with all their energy to meet my standards, I will cast him or her out." *I will have them killed probably. Yes, a cult leader. Godlike but not a god.*

The first Follower spoke again. "We love you, Esther. Beloved."

Congregation: "We love you, Esther. Beloved."

"I know that you love me. Let us pray." Esther held her arms out wide, face full of compassion, reveling in the pure joy of conversion with kindness that was far more satisfying than mere sex. *I died to make these people mine. I have paid Debbie's price. Now I am their lord.*

The lord bless you and keep you;
The lord make his face to shine upon you and be gracious to you;
The lord lift up his countenance upon you and give you peace.

Congregation: "Amen."
"You shall serve me with all your heart, all your soul, and all your mind."
Congregation: "I shall serve you with all my heart, all my soul, and all my mind."
And I shall serve you too.

CHAPTER SIX
ZOOANTHROPOMORPHISM

[August through December 2060]
The Compound, Kentucky

LIKE ANY GOOD CULT LEADER would do, Esther renamed the Estate/
Labfarm her Compound, a permanent residence area for her 100 devoted
Followers who could protect her, her family, and the 1000 Talents living
there. Elsa's brothers trained them on handguns, rifles, drones, hunting,
and horses; and her father, Ken, would train them on basic military com-
bat, from both his years in the military as a soldier and his connections
to his local survivalist group and his associates on the Internet, who included many ex-military from around the planet, people who visited the
Compound as guest teachers.

Like most cults, Esther's concerns were always put ahead of other
concerns, and nothing less than complete devotion was acceptable.

Unlike most cults, a cult of personality was not permitted. They were
to neither imitate nor worship or idolize her in any way beyond keeping
approved nonsexualized pictures of her on their phones.

Unlike most cults, Followers committed to healthy eating, sport and
fitness, skills training, and volunteer work for poor and powerless people (e.g., shelters, soup kitchens, hospitals, tutoring with the latest Talent
teaching technology, etc.). They would not engage in degenerate behavior

(e.g., bitterness, rage, anger, brawling, slander, malice, promiscuity, greed, obscenity, foolish talk, coarse joking, or limbic abuse) but would rather "become children of the light," serving a nondivine lord and all her purposes, usually summed up and verbalized as "kindness."

Like most cults, there was a sexual aspect to her expanded community. She had tested her Followers on the Circleturbo but found everyone to be idiosyncratic. Talent bodies not only shared a male and female "ideal shape," they also benefitted from chosen sexual traits that "gave the most pleasure the most easily," as Lucy tried to put nicely. Nor did Talents suffer from any form of "performance anxiety" or period of "sexual self-discovery." Esther wanted her Followers to be happy and not frustrated, but also to be motivated. She promised she would match everyone with a suitable spouse when the time came, but for the time being they would sex segregate and could selfturbo in the bathrooms if Circleturbos weren't working well enough.

Like most cults, her Followers were told they couldn't leave, with few exceptions. They could visit family and live at home. A few were allowed to take jobs to acquire certain skills. The Compound, transportation routes, Shelby High, their homes, and work locations were registered "Okay areas." Their Talent-issued phones would send an alarm if they went outside those areas. The Followers also wore a fixed thin diamond ring around their necks with an embedded tracker that was charged during their sleep and was nearly impossible to cut off. Martin had installed GPS tracking drones that could hunt down and incapacitate any Followers who left approved areas, and Esther organized a demonstration of the system to discourage runaways.

Their phones, workplaces, and living spaces were also set to have microphones on all the time. Cysso created an AI dissent detection system which also looked for encoded/private language and idiom habits. Followers had to learn and speak Tesp as well. When outside the Compound, their phone mics had to be active (e.g., not put in a pillow), with 30-minute sound checks. Esther made clear that any dissent would not be tolerated. Followers were given set responses to questions from outsiders about the Compound.

Beyond defense training and related activity, Followers worked the farms and the latest Talent construction equipment, operating prototypes of Yoshi's new 3D nanoprinters, which included managing the shipments of coal, plastic, and sawdust that served as both feedstock and energy source. Days were long and busy, and her Followers grew tough and disciplined.

#

Esther continued her daily breakfast conversations with Debbie, who was currently living monogamously with Ken, sharing another bedroom in the main house. One rainy morning in November she decided to have a sanity check with her over breakfast made by Sally, who had effectively replaced Elsa as her friend, lover, and bodyguard. Esther admired Sally's fanaticism and the fact she kept attracting blondes to her. She looked at her blonde mother sitting across the breakfast table eating her eggs, toast, and boiled meat and veggies.

"Mother, what do you think of my cult?"

"Daughter, I like it very much. I am very impressed. Your Followers are happy, devoted, and fruitful. I'm going to help you with rewarding them." Debbie got up from her seat and walked over to Esther and rubbed her back while she sat on the kitchen stool, contemplating her coffee, like she did every day.

"Thanks, Mother. I told them to worship God and not me. I make no declarations concerning divine providence. I can't think of any other options. I need them and they need me."

"Do you believe in God, Esther?"

"Not yet. I might. What about you, Debbie?"

"I did. I believe in *you* now." The "you" came across as remarkably sincere, to the point of worshipful. Esther thought it would have been better to see the expression on Debbie's face when she said this but made no effort to turn around as her back rub felt so good.

"I am working under Martin and Lucy's advice. My cult must not appear like a cult. I think I'm doing a good job."

Sally (who was cleaning up the kitchen) interrupted, "Your cult is awesome, Beloved! We're so happy here."

"Would you die for me like Elsa?"

"Yes, I wouldn't hesitate. None of us would. The world sucks outside of your Compound. We live in a happy place under your wise and generous rule."

Debbie kissed Esther on the back of her head and hugged her from behind, putting her mouth near Esther's Tear. "Very impressed. How about you, Martin?"

Martin: "You do what you need to."

"Martin's okay with what I'm doing."

#

PASS

Martin was in his private computer lab with Felicity, wearing his external headset. The Twins now spent the majority of the day in this room sitting across the computer table from each other with bare feet touching. When not sitting working on cybersecurity, software projects, and AI systems, the two would engage in their acro dancing and wrestling fitness activities, maintaining a buff, lean appearance.

Yesterday they had ventured into the common hallways to inspect the School until a Parent physically detained them to threaten their control over the School. He was shot in the neck with a tranquilizer dart from the latest drone activation system. Martin distracted him while Felicity organized the shot. Demonstrations of automated drone control systems were tested on hostile Parents at all the Schools over the year. They were objecting to their children disappearing to the Labfarms instead of attending local universities or working in family companies. "You can't stop me from seeing my child," was the usual complaint. Martin would give them a view of their simulated child on a computer screen, saying, "Here I am." "I'm going to stop funding the Schools," was the other usual threat. "You have some better way to dispose of your money? Hedonism?" was the usual response. It had occurred to Martin these threatening Parents had achieved negative utility, parasitism; Talents were healthy organisms that disposed of parasites.

Martin hadn't decided on whether or how to tell the Parents about the missing Talents who all seemed to have in common, from the videos, a missing recommendation from the intense sales and marketing process at BGC. Talents had been reclassified by Memeso into Intalentsos (those at the Schools and Labfarms, roughly 94% of production, for all of whom the Parents took all the recommendations), Dissentsos (those at Lucy's Paris containment and study area, 1% of Talent production), and Outalentsos (5%).

Memeso had spelled out castes within the Intalentsos. Cysso was largely at PASS, but a male and female pair now existed at each Labfarm and School to administer the local networks and related systems of hardware and software, lending to each Coxo the ability to tranquilize dissenting Parents. These two people at each location seemed to pair up well; with Lucy's approval, he had allowed them to pair-bond but not produce children.

"Martin, I have detected another anomaly at Esther's Labfarm."

"Esther has already noticed it. There is a sub-sub-caste of Talents who surround Josh, including all her childhood siblings."

Felicity tilted her head, looking serious for a rare moment.

"Send me your list."

Martin printed out a copy of his personal anomaly list and handed it to Felicity.

Anomaly List

Cysso—the bureaucracy is nearly all Martin's out-family.

Circle of Six—precocious Talents volunteered for central executive leadership.

Reformso—at least two Talents at each location, organized by Josh and Lucy.

Preppers—less intelligent Talents. Keep to themselves. About 10 at every location. Pair-bonding monogamous hets. While not showing psychopathic behavior, they mirror elite military training drills and exercises. The women keep up with the men by taking steroids for muscle mass. None exhibit standard side effects from steroid use. They want to operate all the internal drones instead of Cysso. I've decided to give them local defense powers under direction of their Coxos.

Dissentsos—1% of Talent population currently moved to Paris at the age of 12.

Josh's Circle—a group of 30 Talents at Esther's Compound who do not engage in Circleturbo and are practicing Christians.

Juan—introverted, no Circles. Blonde hair, blue eyes, black skin. At Mexico City Science. Orphaned.

Lucy—introverted, a spy.

Included in the printout were the names of all the Talents. Martin had started files on all the oddballs.

Felicity read through his printout, nodding her head from time to time. "Josh's inner circle agrees with my list. They declare their loyalties to Esther and Josh, but not you. It seems you have a rival, bro."

"Rival for what? I've told every one of them if they want my job, they can have it."

Felicity looked upset at his declaration. Martin read his daily newsfeed on his "Piss me off" app. More proxy wars, epidemics, useless promises from politicians, worries about what Talents were up to.

#

[On a snowy day in December]

Esther [camera-eye computer input]: [What are your plans, Bigwig, for your rabbits?]

Martin [text on computer screen]: [Seriously, *Watership Down*?]

Esther/Felicityvoxplay: "The big bad Normies are going to come and extinguish you all, they will fill your rabbit holes with poison gas."

Martin/Esthervoxplay: "You don't think our Parents can protect us? Mrs. Frisby?"

Esther [text to voice/Martin]: "No, I am now part mouse and part *Rats of NIMH*. Animal intelligence enhanced by technology to the point of moral consciousness. But the children's book didn't discuss rat vision."

Martin [voice/vocal input, computer screen output]: [No? Our Parents are rich and powerful and under my thumb. Explain rat vision.]

Esther [computer screen input to Sakura voice output]: "Normsos have rabbit warrens too, but they are stocked with munitions. What have you got? Drone dart systems? Carbon sinks? Darts and sinks. Not very scary."

Martin: [Carbon sinks are more useful than you think. Those and garbage bins. Normso waste is our gain. Again, explain rat vision.]

Her Compound had recently added a dumpsite for nanoprinter feedstock. A special "Incinerator" memesoed "Gehinnso" (based on the Hebrew word [not the Greek *gehenna*] for the place where they burned trash outside of Jerusalem) "burned" or electrolyzed (purified) garbage back into essential elements and stored them in vacuum tanks organized by individual (periodic table) elements. Talents were working on advanced materials based geothermal power technologies (tapping into the Earth's crust) to power the Gehinnso, the "fires of the underworld," Esther liked to muse, or hell power.

Martin and Esther continued the conversation using each other's voxplay.

Esther: "Rat eyes move separately from each other. My brain has finally rewired. I am used to looking at unrelated visual stimulation and an unblinking computer screen inside my head. I don't get sick from it anymore either."

Martin: "I'm sure. Why are you and your Circle helping dying animals, by the way? I do not want rat vision. I have twenty distinct computer monitor images going at once. I can watch them all at the same time. Let's go back to our original voices."

Esther was in her bedroom now in bed naked with sheets and a blanket covering her. Sally was giving her a foot massage from the edge of her bed while managing the prosthetic sex doll that was making love to Esther. "We help the dying animals because it justifies my access to the gene cameras and stem cell research required to cure the disease. If I make a mistake, the animal was about to die anyway. The animal is heavily sedated. Better than a bullet to the head and a trip to the animal processors for their collagen to be turned into glue. I think in the long run, we may need to challenge Better Genetics for supremacy. Lucy favors that opinion. I suspect that's what she was created for."

Martin/Martin: "That is *not* a popular idea. Talents all seem to love Better Genetics. I'm quite serious about this. Why would an organization create someone to overthrow it?"

Esther laughed and then Martin laughed. "I don't know. You are right, no one wants to help her compete with BGC technology. Everyone thinks we will merge with them eventually. I think we need to conquer them with soft and hard power. All the more reason to keep our plans secret."

Martin: "You're a very dangerous person. You know that?" *She has to be dangerous, and I have to make her dangerous.* "I am making you very dangerous. You may call yourself and behave like a Normso, but you still have a Talent brain and body and an entire civilization to back you up."

Esther sent an image of an apple. "Take a bite. Seriously, not a game." *She says this quite seriously. It is not a game.* "You've got to be kidding me; it is not a game."

Esther started shaking. She made the usual clutching of the sheets with her hands to signal Peakso. He zoomed out to watch Sally lick her curling toes. Her genetics allowed her to peakso 20 times a session to his one; she occasionally passed out from the pleasure. He considered this ability might come from her "Near Death Experience," too, the notion that she had "let go."

Sally: "She passed out." Sally stopped the foot licking, yet another erogenous zone discovery. Ears, fingers, inner thighs, nipples, multiple vaginal locations were all "Peakso capable," according to Esther. "Boy, Better Genetics knows how to have a girl have fun. I mean, uh. You know what I mean. What a girl wants? Am I sounding stupid? Didn't ancients think orgasms were something like death or something? She says some weird shit when she sleeps."

It was only 10 seconds later that Esther resumed the conversation and Sally restarted the sex doll per prior instructions.

Esther: "Do you want to survive or not? To survive the coming war, you must know evil as well as good."

Martin: "Is this what you learned from dying?" Esther had chronicled all her experience from the age of 0–15.5 with Martin in her diary, titled *Living Beyond Good and Evil.* She even detailed her experiences with him in bed. Martin had reciprocated with his life and all his experiences and his experience with her in bed. They were working towards brain fusion. The mental intimacy was necessary to Esther, and Martin found it enjoyable.

Esther: "I lost my fear. I am not afraid to do what needs to be done to save us from dying. If we are not very careful, we'll provoke more Normsos into killing us. We must keep our secrets from the other Talents. Our actions will not be popular." Martin had not recontinued her 24-hour reality TV show after her recovery. When she appeared on Ethers with Josh, she only spoke the words given to her through her Tear. With Josh taking over Ether production, they were less focused on her life and more on the latest scientific breakthroughs and other Talent success stories.

Esther: "While my Estate has become a cult Compound, the Schools and Labfarms are now rabbit Warrens. It's a question of time before they come for you. You must bite the fruit and pay the price of knowing evil. I cannot protect the Talents without your help. We gain the knowledge to become beyond good and evil."

The lawless one. Her own laws. Her obsession she is the Anti-Christ and not just an anti-Christ. I married a religious nutjob.

Martin: "You see a war. You see a need to protect both sides. Talents do not see a war. Talents see a bright future for everyone. You are corrupted by Normie. What you ask is unthinkable. You are corrupting me." Martin felt choppy, like he was resisting temptation. He thought he already took his duty as King seriously, protecting and serving his people to the best of his ability.

Esther: "The Talents must see the invisible war. I want to create a Student United Nations from Memeso. You will nominate me as its official Ambassador. The SUN will shine a light on humanity."

Martin: "Why? Why do we need a SUN and why do we need an Ambassador? The Talents all love their own countries. Or so I think. Do I particularly love America? Yoshi seems to love Japan."

Esther: "Talents love Talents, not their countries. Anyway, by making me official Ambassador, I will have clout with Better Genetics. I think we need this to get them to cough up their client/Talent list."

And there it was. The idea they were looking for. Martin and Esther finished and turned off the machines. During his refractory period Martin reflected that Cysso was a proper and improving economic and defense system. That Reformso was scientific unity. They shared a high-trust moral and ethical system. A diplomatic core was the logical next step. *SUN. We are turning into a nation.*

Esther/doll was lying next to him. The computer image on her face was that of near complete sexual contentment. The doll reached to him and held him. She liked to cuddle after sex, the doll's artificial skin simulated softness and warmness. Their sex dolls, human (robotic) prosthetics with simulated sexual organs, didn't use the romantic immersion AI personalities and graphics popular with Normsos. Instead, they connected to each other with roomspace cameras, VR headsets, and haptic facemasks which created a computer simulation of each other's bodies and faces. The dolls themselves simulated the physical movements of the distant partner with about 0.1 second latency. They couldn't kiss (properly) or otherwise touch each other's body with their heads, but the hands had functionality when they added haptic gloves, which Esther and Martin always wore during sim-sex.

The apple was still 1/20 of his VR screen space; the icon sat in the corner, him staring at it. It was minutes before Esther broke the silence. They still lay in a cuddle, sexually exhausted.

Esther: "The apple, Martin. Newton's fruit. The Garden. The scientific revolution that accelerated humanity. Gravitas. Bite it. Asexual manhood into asexual scientifically reproduced mankind. Let me make you a promise then. A personal covenant."

Martin: "What can you promise me that is worth eternal damnation? By us keeping secrets, we violate the Talent transparency which makes them so happy."

Esther: "The promise is extremely simple. We keep our Talent conspiracy to two. By just *you* biting the apple, you protect all the other Talents. I will approach no others for help except those we both agree to let join our inner circle. A circle of two. We are both sexually bonded; we are information bonded. We are cybernetically bonded. We are religiously bonded."

Just then Felicity popped in, standing by the bedside with her typical teleportation flourish. She never liked his private communications with Esther. The VR sex pod in his bedroom was private and soundproof to the outside, but Felicity was inside the system by default. She looked at them briefly then teleported out.

Martin: "What is with all your religious imagery? I appreciate your experience with religion, but it is still a hoax to me. Lucy agrees with me. No God, no immortal soul, just truth against the darkness of space."

Esther: "Then my metaphors are a powerful tool of persuasion."

Martin: "I am going to regret this decision. I know it. Knowing evil. Beyond good and evil. What an absurd notion."

Esther: "Well, you'll be alive to regret. Which is better than dead. You'll have saved your friends as well. Some Talents *must sacrifice* in order for the others to live. Sacrifice is a virtue too, the greatest kindness. I am prepared to sacrifice everything, but I cannot succeed alone. I have to have your help. Just... you must give it to me. Why do you get to be selfish when I am not?" Esther's face became angry and frustrated.

Martin: "You don't stop, do you?"

Esther: "Don't you feel the need? To live. To procreate. To survive. To advance science. What are our lives for? Die in your rabbit holes. Wait for them to invade and drop missiles and gas you out. Your Parents cannot protect you forever. Watch them wither and die. Will Talents then come out of their holes and become politicians and judges and policemen and soldiers and live among Normies? To be picked off one by one?"

Martin: "Nobody wants those jobs. Nobody wants to live among Normsos."

Esther: "We are here to re-create the world and refound civilization. You know it in your heart. You've been told it from an early age."

Martin: "When did we go mad? What is our goal? Our endgame? What drives us?"

Esther: "It ends after we complete the Better Genetics mission. We clean the entire human race of genetic sin. We stop all violence and disease and want and destruction of the planet and everyone becomes naturally happy, peaceful, and kind. We turn all human life into Talent life."

Martin: "It's not possible. It's insane. You'd have to conquer the world to do that. The Founders are hippy idealists as far as I'm concerned. How would you conquer the world without destroying it? There are twenty countries that have nuclear missiles now. No one is conquering the world."

Esther: "Like the Romans. One step at a time. One step at a time, you conquer the world."

Martin: "World conquest. A two-person conspiracy. This direction can only lead to unspeakable acts of evil. The world does not want to be conquered. It will resist to the very end. It's not even possible anyway."

Esther paused. Calmed. Relaxed. Then said: "Then give me your sin. I will take it all. I will do it alone."

Martin: "No, it doesn't work that way. No, if I'm going to do something evil, I will own it. Talents own their misdeeds. That is our way. No passing off anything."

Martin stared again at the apple image on his computer screen. He brought up Genesis 2–3 into vision as a simulated document and read it.

Martin: "You bit the forbidden fruit then? A talking serpent beguiled you? We will be like God, knowing good and evil?"

Esther laughed for a while. "No. The curse on Adam and Eve is no more. The suffering in childbirth and working the land stuff is coming to an end. I will crush the serpent head with my heel. We are going back to Eden and eating from the Tree of Life this time. The flaming sword zooanthropomorphic cherubim have gone, and the way is open."

Martin brought up on his VR vision an artist's depiction of the strange being described in Ezekiel with animal heads and wings and felt a shiver followed by goosebumps. He had thought intellectually as a 10-year-old that it might come to conquering the world. Thinking back, it seemed like a silly childhood expression and fantasy. He thought about the paradox some more. Talents wanted to control the Earth's environment but were opposed to violence. A Boardso discussion group had sprung up around this subject. He reconsidered Marcy's comment that power IS violence. He thought perhaps he was lucky to have a co-conspirator who recognized the need for violence on at least an intellectual level. Felicity had become instantly angry at the whole subject. Martin relaxed and thought through Esther's arguments.

Martin: "Okay, let's try to conquer the world. If that's where you think this is all heading. You and me, we conquer the whole world together. You Normso and me Talent."

Martin accepted the apple by making a save file of the graphic. A deep chill came over him that lasted about three seconds. He felt nervous and crazy. *Esther is mad and now I am mad.*

Martin: "What's the next step, would-be world conqueror?"

Esther: "Thank you, Martin, my love. That wasn't so hard, was it? The SUN. Start making commercial products to wipe out Normie industries as Smithy has foretold and planned. Let's create our own personal language using a euphemistic vocabulary to disguise our intentions from both Talents and Normsos. I want to know for certain that I'm talking to you. I like zooanthropomorphism."

Martin: "My love, the attributing of animals with human-like traits to humans?"

Esther: "Yes, from now on I am Frisby, and you are Bigwig. Two anthropomorphic animals concerned with extinction."

Martin: "I'll create several word and sound alerts. Just say 'efrafa' for my immediate attention."

Martin signed off and Esther removed her VR equipment, handing it to Sally. She removed the sex doll from the bed, replacing it with her body, until Esther was sexually satisfied and fell asleep.

#

[New Year's Eve 2060]

Esther was in her bathroom inserting her glass-eye. It took about a minute to get it right. If she made any mistakes, she was rewarded with unbelievable pain. She still got up for daily morning swims with Debbie and was getting her swimsuit on when she decided to patch Martin.

Esther: "Efrafa. These batteries are not going to cut it, you know. I have to switch out my eyes four times a day and plug my ear in during my afternoon nap. These are not fun activities."

Martin: "Energy density is the big one. The only long-term option you have for your eye is the camera-eye, where the power cord plugs into your eye prosthetic and runs down your back. Tell me where you want the big battery to end up."

Esther: "A shoulder holster then, like James Bond assassins."

Martin: "The guys in Seoul think they can get a full-res glass-eye monitor to you in a year. There are heat and power issues, too. You will get a new glass eye with the color and iris pattern matched a little better. Tokyo is working on the dilation system. They want their robots' light sensors to dilate, too. Otherwise, they look like they are staring all the time. Good stuff, Frisby." *Love.* "Love."

Esther: "Is the tracking impossible?" *Love.* "Love."

Martin: "All we have for you is two recommendations. You can practice turning your head, so you always face people straight on. I would recommend that first." *Love.* "Love."

Their conversations were now permanent tags. "Love" had become a call sign, the kinetic communication <F9> sending a heart emoji. L

Esther: "Already started with my parents." L

Martin: "Janet is working on muscle reattachment, but that requires a permanent base implant, something a long way off. Is it really that important? It means regular surgeries." L

Esther: "No, I hate the surgeries. I can learn to turn my head." L

Martin: "I've been reading books on linguistics. I want to go beyond zooanthropomorphic euphemisms into mixed-language sequences, a rotating pig Latin–type structure, use non-keyboard characters such as glottal stops and clicks, and incorporate tonal and beat features too. Sound fun?" L

Esther: "Okay, yes." L

\#

[*Five months pass*]

Over time they developed a dynamic private verbal language called Babel. The language was keyed on a word that started a new rule set that only Esther and Martin knew from personal interaction and history. They used some rare and dead languages to spice up the vocabulary. As the language kept evolving from random contextual inputs, Babel became impossible to teach and impossible for a computer to decode. "Harder than Navajo," Esther described it.

The evolution of Babel gave them the assurance they were talking to each other and not someone else's voice/text/computer hacking. While Felicity was his obvious choice if he died to pass true-root (ultimate computer control) to, he secretly decided to give it to Esther instead. He did not want his sister to experience his corrupted evil role in attempted Talent nonviolent world domination. Martin got what he needed, an encryption system with a socio-organic "random number generator" that was both unguessable and impossible to sequence. The language was verbal; it had no written form. That would make it hard for Felicity's AI to grind as she was in the room with him and could hear him talk while recording his conversations. She made no comments about trying to decode Babel.

Talents meanwhile had started taking regular vacations where they spent a whole day in isolation, typically with zero electronics contact. During these rest periods, Talents were encouraged to use brain areas they never ordinarily used. Esther felt the need to compose poetry during her time off and made several compositions, each of which improved over the months passing by.

She was lying in bed alone in the afternoon when she mustered the courage to contact Martin and deliver her favorite poem.

Esther: "Efrafa, I've written some poetry you might enjoy."

Martin: "Please, I hate poetry."

Esther: "I think why James Calhoun's NIMH utopias fail is because of fear. Rats are the most successful mammal on Earth after humans. They know nothing but fear. Take that away and they die." Esther wondered why author Robert O'Brien turned Calhoun's mice into rats in the kid's book, while keeping Mrs. Frisby as a mouse. *Calhoun, mice of NIMH, O'Brien, rats of NIMH.*

Esther was referring to a popular Talent Boardso discussion about whether Talents would die out because their lives were so easy, the notion that utopias always fail, which Calhoun tested in a famous science experiment where the mice all die out despite being given unlimited space and food in mousetopia.

Esther, like any good Normso, enjoyed spurious arguments. Martin responded: "No, they died because humans built their utopias and not mice. The mice didn't like the *human* notion of a utopia. Mice perversely enjoy living in fear and desperation, just like humans. That's why both species are so successful."

Esther laughed. When one of them laughed the other laughed.

Esther: "Most Normsos don't live in any actual fear. No real threat of wars or famines or plagues, just entertainment that titillates and news from obscure parts of the planet where nobody ever goes and the occasional terrorist attack. Their biggest killers are car accidents, drug overdoses, and suicides, yet they drive cars, take drugs all day long, and seem to have no fear of death. Hundreds of years ago, everyone died of everything all the time. The Scientific Revolution used invention to beat back death, and humans create synthetic fear to fill the existential void."

Martin: "Okay, Randroid."

Esther laughed so Martin laughed.

Esther: "Making fun of my android condition already? And Ayn Rand?"

Martin: "Yes. Enjoying it too. We need to have IRL sex together. We are together always but not really." L

Esther: "Yes, we need more sex together. I have to fly to you though, and my Followers need me." L

The conversation ended up here every day. They knew they were body bonded, but clearly they were also love bonded, and not being together physically was going to drive them nuts. Esther needed to change the subject quickly before she lost control.

Esther: "Suffer from my scary poetry. The poem is called *Frank Herbert*." She cleared her throat.

I must Fear.
Fear enhances the mind.
Fear keeps us from death and total obliteration.
I will accept fear as my source of survival and make rational
    decisions because of it.

Once fear fills me, I will find a path that leads to the safe
replenishment of heavenly life.
Those who live without fear shall die out.
Only I will remain.

Martin: "Your dark side makes me afraid. It means I find my dark side."
Esther: "You know what your dark side is already. The Talents must learn fear of Normsos and Normsos must forget fear of Talentsos. That is our diplomatic posture."

#

Esther continued to participate in farm animal experiments. While she had lost the obsession with death and personal mortality that characterized her younger years, she felt an urge to keep exploring death's boundaries. Martin would tease her about her dark side, but she wouldn't mind. She wanted him to see it.

One day a week she had taken to driving to Rachael and Amanda's place for breakfast, after which she would test herself on her learning progress to becoming a veterinarian.

One bright Monday morning after testing, she decided to push the envelope of death a little more.

"Mothers?"

Submissive Amanda now took a complete backseat to dominant Rachael during conversations. She had awkwardly told Esther she was relieved s/he had given up the whole trans phase, including completely giving up men's clothing and both-gender vocabulary. Esther got upset and told Rachael it was better that Amanda did not speak to Esther anymore. A further rift in their relationship started when Rachael had stopped using the implants that gave her a feeling of being in love and lusty (ludos and eros) at the same time. The two had stopped making love immediately. Amanda had asked Esther to tell Rachael to start using them again, but she refused. Esther didn't tell her why, but she wanted to find out what happened without using them. Amanda had grown bitter and frustrated. Amanda had something Esther now wanted. The fact that

Esther was using artificial sexuality and petty revenge and manipulation as leverage was not lost on her.

"You don't call me Mom anymore. That's alright. What new thing do you want to do?"

"I want to be the one that kills all the animals. It's important to me. I've killed plenty of rabbits and deer while hunting and farm chickens for meals. I want to euthanize the other farm animals we put down. I want to kill our pets and slaughter them and smoke and salt them for later consumption or turn them into leather and glue. I will train my Followers as well. We need to get used to killing things. Veterinarians get used to killing things."

Rachael came very close to blanching and hesitated just a little, squeaking, "Okay." Amanda threw up her hands and stormed out of the kitchen; a faint "bitch" came from the hallway.

"Please don't think I'm death obsessed or emo. I am still the bright, happy, healthy girl you dreamed of having." *Bright, happy, healthy and beyond good and evil. I just need to practice an evil laugh to complete my self-caricature.* Esther started evil laughing. "Bwah-hah-hah-hah-haaaah."

"Your lying is perfect, it seems. Death has changed you. You are a more serious person now, or maybe you are just growing older and losing your childhood idealism and sense of immortality." Her mother got up and came over to give her a hug and cried a little. "You have a cult at your Compound. Supported by Ken and Debbie. You are building and training an army. What has BGC created? Would I have accepted you, only to find you would create a cult?"

"I'm a scientist, Mother. For now, we find a cure for Alzheimer's in animals by the time I turn eighteen and go to Yale like you did. Josh thinks we'll be done by then. In the meanwhile, I need to keep my Followers busy and used to killing. What good are soldiers who are afraid to kill? We practice on animals." *Like any good serial killer, we must start with killing animals.* Her mother's hug tightened.

"I don't know what I created anymore. You are wonderous and scary. I suppose a near-death experience can't be ignored. I decided long ago my love for you, Esther, would be unconditional. Nothing will change my mind. I will do everything and anything I can to help you cure this animal disease and share it with the world. We will show the world that Talents are kind, despite this dark side of yours."

Esther smiled. "I still love you, Mother. You have had a wonderful life. Horse breeding, a strong, happy family, and now participation in a cure for Alzheimer's. My life will include brain research and protecting the people I love."

"Those accomplishments mean so little to me now. I have been mother to *you*. The only accomplishment I really care about. Be kind to us Normsos. Make me proud of my decisions. Make me proud of my life. Be a kind person."

"I will try. I will try," Esther cried finally. She got off her stool, breaking her mother's embrace, and bent way down on her knees to talk to her face-to-face.

"Do you want to go back on the artificial sexuality implants or stay the real you?"

"I have a choice now? Your experiment is over? Amanda is frustrated and bitter. Is that what you wanted to find out? I don't desire sex, but she does?"

"Well?"

It had occurred to Esther that talking Rachael into this arrangement, synthetic gay, a now popular product being sold by the Davos business empire to boost Registry sales, should be reconsidered. Esther didn't want a sort of "complete control" over people's lives. Just the purpose and will of their lives. Telos. She had decided to use God as her measure or role model. She wanted Rachael to choose her sexuality with informed consent. It was her rebellion against Debbie choosing her own sexuality without her consent. There was no "reverse gay" product available. Maybe she would find a brain surgery that would disable the part of her that was "turned on" by sexy women. Her life would be a lot simpler to manage. She stood straight now, thinking and waiting for her mother's decision patiently.

"I'll go back on. I won't ask what purpose you had. I do it to make Amanda happy. I don't want to live with a frustrated crank."

CHAPTER SEVEN

CULT TECHNOLOGY

[July 2061]
The Compound, Kentucky

ONE BREAKFAST MORNING after swimming with Debbie and Sally, Esther decided to hold a voice videocom meeting with Ken, Lucy, and Martin attending.

"Debbie?"

"Yes, sweetie."

"Besides having a hundred bodyguards, what should I do with my Followers?"

"Do whatever you like, dear. My only suggestion is to add a lot more."

Lucy: "I agree. We need an army to protect you and other Talents. We can't just use hired Normsos."

An army?

"An army?"

Martin: "I agree."

"Have my Followers proselytize?"

Lucy: "I don't see why not. I really don't see how we should limit our imagination to men forming cults. There are many examples of women cult leaders. Your women are probably going to be more successful at recruiting and your cult has a lot to offer people. A lot of people these days are sexless, without families or the hope of families, and economically dispossessed. Promise them regular work, sex, and Talent children for families. The rest of society is not doing these basics anymore. Everyone is atomized when people long for community. Provide them that community. It's working for religious people. I cave in on that point."

Debbie offered, "We can handle volume. We have no lack of space or funds."

By your fruits you will know them.

Esther often reflected on the meaning Matthew 7:16. *If I am a false prophet then I will produce thorns and thistles. So many organizations out there produce nothing but anger and hate and destruction. I should produce peace, love, and creation. That is what I want. I am lawless like the Anti-Christ but not a false prophet.*

"How can we build an army without the government interfering?"

Martin/%**Babel**: "Working on it. Um. Marcy has a whole bunch of ideas. We have access to a lot of systems, it seems. That's my job."

Lucy: "You guys and your private language. What did he say?"

"Just how beautiful I am."

Debbie laughed.

Lucy: "You and your secrets. The Boardsos have come to accept you two have secrets. They understand that's your job. I won't pry. Power means we exempt ourselves from our own moral system, it seems. Talents seem to understand that."

#

Esther organized her Followers and explained their new mission. She selected those Followers with good looks to reach outside to those lacking prospects. "All those who were in distress or in debt or discontented." 1 Sam 22:2. It worked for King David. She would beat his 400 number. They were allowed to recruit members with the following promises:

1. They would always have work, albeit some of it potentially dangerous.
2. They would be given an appropriate pair-bond once they proved worthy.
3. They would get a Talent child.
4. Esther would be the legal parent of all their children, a financial commitment.
5. They would devote their lives to protecting Esther and other Talents, even at the cost of their own lives.

It was explained that alcohol, drugs, and promiscuity would no longer be potential lifestyle choices. If they had those elements in their past, Esther would forgive them so they could be "reborn," as she called it.

They didn't know about the permanent tracking collars and Talent phones and that they had made a one-way life decision.

Esther conferred privately with Lucy about this practice one morning in her bed.

Lucy: "You've collared them like animals."

Esther: "Humans *are* animals. They have to prove they are better than animals, that their consciousness can beat their lizard brain animal instincts to kill, eat, and fuck."

Lucy: "They have no pay, they are slaves."

Esther: "Bondservants. Not slaves. I take care of all of their needs and treat them well. If American government and society fails to provide them spouses and healthy children, then it is a failed system. I give them quality food, clothing and shelter, the promise of a family life, and a goal: keeping me alive. What does the American system offer? Drugs, alcohol, and promiscuity, and other forms of limbic abuse coupled with debilitating debts. What is slavery? Is debt slavery not slavery? How can one call himself free under the weight of crippling debt and no prospect of a family? Only the rich and powerful are truly free in this country."

Lucy: "It's a one-way decision. Some people don't like that. Is it not indentured servitude?"

Esther: "Short-term slavery. They earn a place in society. Let me think more on it. I'll come up with an experiment."

Technically speaking, the GPS diamond collar/necklace systems registered when a Follower was outside acceptable coordinates and dispatched a drone armed with tranquilizer darts while two other Followers were sent to collect and return the body. That was the current policy that was explained once a new Follower was converted, reborn, and collared.

One new Follower, named Ben, sought to cut off his collar while at his parents'. He thought that would give him time to escape since it would be a full day when he was expected back. With the loan of a car and money from his parents, he drove to Texas and worked a farm job there.

While he was there, he compared the money he was paid and the food, clothing, shelter, and amusements he could afford with the quality of the food, clothing, and shelter of the Compound. He compared the company of his coworkers with the company of Esther's cult Followers. He compared the financial situation of his coworkers (all deep in credit card and school debt) with his financial situation—no debt (Esther/Smithy paid off whatever debts people had upon joining). He compared the lifestyle of his coworkers, weekends binging on weed, alcohol, and hookups or some combination thereof. Their week was spent contemplating a weekend of "fun." That was living a "best possible life," according to TV and magazines and all other entertainment. He asked his coworkers what their hopes for the future were. A nice-looking submissive/devoted/empathic personality sex doll was their answer. Few thought they'd win the Better Genetics lottery. Few were motivated to have kids the old-fashioned way. No one wanted to risk cohabitation and its inherent financial penalties without any compensating upside.

What Ben didn't know was that his collar sent an alarm when he cut it off and that Esther decided to let him go, based on Lucy's comment. Martin was worried he'd blab, and Lucy suggested that they just be honest about the whole situation, that her Followers were slaves. Esther was insistent that bondservant was the better word, being contextual on whether labor was paid, unpaid, or serving debts. There was no point in giving cash to her Followers as there was nothing to buy with it except forms of limbic and planet abuse.

She reasoned with herself. *Did Jesus pay his Followers? Moses and Jacob worked for men unpaid to "earn" wives. I give not only spouses but children. Children are the pension plan. My cult will take care of the widows and orphans, the unfortunate ones. Religious leaders and organizations used to collect money for their upkeep, not the government. I am both their prophet and their government.*

Ben lasted two weeks. When he came back, he spoke briefly about the situation, asked Esther for forgiveness (given), and nobody tried to "escape" again. The collars were hereafter thought of as protection, since drones could come to their defense quicker and more reliably.

#

Martin in the meanwhile explored the concept of what Marcy called "entryism," the notion that people, "entryists," join organizations just to wreck them. Entryist success stems mainly from their ability to lie. They had to lie about their reasons for joining the organization and had to lie about other members through gossip or slander, to discredit them and turn cohesive organizations into factions.

"Diabolos, the Devil. Translates as accuser/slanderer, to throw across," was Esther's comment about Martin's project. If Satan was the god of lies, then the Devil was the god of false accusations and gossip.

Martin stuck with calling them entryists. Well-run organizations had to neutralize entryists as quickly as possible.

Felicity and Martin regularly discussed their plans with Marcy in their chambers once a week. An important strategy meeting went as follows:

Martin said, "I can see how the violet eyes prevents entryism in the Warrens. We have one record of a randomly generated person with violet eyes attending a School and dropping out quickly after discovering various basic health problems and not being able to keep up. I fail to understand why people would voluntarily become slaves to Esther, putting her life above their own lives."

Felicity nodded her head in agreement.

Marcy looked as if she was considering an answer and then spoke. "That's sort of the normal state of nature. It's the essence of kingdoms and empires. Power is clear and stable. To disrupt that situation is civil war, and those can be nasty. Anyway, let's focus on keeping entryists out of Esther's growing cult."

"I've got AI monitoring all their communication. It's not hard to figure out who they are. Glowies is another slang for entryists. These people glow. There are three there now, one working for the FBI and another for the State of Kentucky. The third one works for some sort of antislavery, cult-busting NGO. They snuck in their own comm devices and thought they had the phones I supplied turned off, although that was just a mimic. One tried to abandon his phone, but the GPS system noted the device alienation between the phone and collar, which caused an alert. One guy left his Talent phone in his barracks and walked out to the forest with his FBI phone. I don't have a recording of that conversation."

Felicity signaled: [What should we do about them?]

Marcy as usual suggested, "Let's see how you smarties work it out."

"Well, with the Parent spies at the Warrens, we have their kids as hostage, effectively. We can threaten them with alienation. A lot of Parents still hate me for that. But you said that's normal with power. People tend to hate those in power. Envy."

Felicity signed: [These entryists. How can they possibly hope to wreck Esther's organization? Smithy has created faux bank accounts and taxes to simulate payrolls and paychecks. The Followers don't do any crimes. They can't lay false allegations because all conversation is in evidence.]

Marcy signed back. She always seemed to keep pace with Talent efforts to communicate with each other so that Parents couldn't comprehend them. [One day, they might have to commit Normso crimes. We must prepare for that. Martin, I believe, wants to conquer the world someday.]

Felicity: [No he doesn't.] "You are *not* planning this are you? You are no better than Smithy. I think all communication about Talent supremacy should be banned. It's disgusting."

Smithy had learned not to talk about it around her. She knew about his growing circle of friends who thought as he did.

"It's a lie, Felicity." Martin had learned to lie to his sister. "I just make sure these three entryists are not aware of any crimes. There's nothing to report to their masters. They are witness to all the science projects going on and take turns doing guard duty outside the main entrance. They haven't made private security illegal. Talents are functionally rich kids offering handsome ransom payments to professional kidnappers." This was one of many cover stories.

Felicity: [But they are aware of the discrepancy between Simulated Reality on the Internet versus reality on the Intalent which includes eyewitness testimony. The Talents at the Compound don't behave like degenerate college kids like in the simulation. They don't talk about their next score and so on. They've seen the Circleturbos.]

Marcy gave a strange tell on her face, passive and blank instead of happy. She had taught Martin to look for subtle changes in people's emotional state. The three played poker from time to time to practice that passive blank look.

"Wait a minute, Felix. Felicitas. Happy go lucky. We do have children as hostages. Look at Debbie's list of sex conquests, those who got lucky."

Felicity had names and high level Registry access from Marcy. She ran a search for government and NGO spy handlers, trying out the various titular euphemisms organizations had for this particular vocation. "Intelligence" something was popular. Sometimes "outreach" or "coordinator." She even found an Intelligence Outreach Coordinator at one major NGO.

Martin considered that this was poor organization on their part to let members, who were responsible for spying on Talent organizations, have Talent children, the subverters being already subverted. But then they didn't know the level of control Martin had over the Warrens or the private agreements Esther made with them. *Honeypot* was the spy word. Debbie and Esther were the ultimate honeypots.

He gave Marcy a hard look. She was still poker faced while Felicity worked.

"What's going on, Mom?"

Marcy said, "It's already done. Voxplay Esther has already told them to convey that the situation is normal. Simulated reality still holds."

Felicity stopped working and looked up at her mother in complete frustration.

"They can still defect without our knowing. You don't know that for sure, Mother."

Marcy's poker face converted to a broad smile and a nod.

Martin thought for a bit and contacted Esther with a plan to turn her glowies into double agents.

#

Esther brought the three entryists into her bedroom, a girl and two boys. She signaled and they sat on the end of the bed next to each other.

"I understand you have other employers. Don't lie to me." She showed on her T-pad the names of their handlers.

"You must declare your loyalties now. Me or them. My world or their world. Which world is better?"

The girl working for the NGO spoke first. "What would you have me do?" She looked really worried, yet at the same time infatuated with Esther.

"We have your voxplay, your communication information, and we will hack your comm devices. We will send your reports. You will confirm them when necessary."

The guy working for the FBI also looking infatuated spoke next, "Easy peasy. Do we still get, uh, a pair-bond partner and a kid with you? What if they pull me back suddenly?"

"I've already taken care of that possibility. And, yes, to the other questions."

The guy working for the State of Kentucky spoke. "You have? How? No, don't answer me, I don't want to know. For God's sake, I trust you."

"Do you love me?"

The entryists answered, "I love you, Beloved."

Esther delivered the ritual response, "I know that you love me."

CHAPTER EIGHT
TAXATION AND REPRESENTATION

[July through December 2061]
PASS

MARTIN HAD INSTALLED the new holographic system that allowed Smithy and Yoshi to sit at the small table in his room. Martin's hologram was sitting in their rooms as well. They were now high resolution and real time, based on both Lidar and 360-degree camera placements. He immediately thought the VR goggles was a better alternative.

The men tasked themselves to create an advanced Talent-only economic system that was fair and efficient and evolved from all the systems and experiments the various Schools had tried so far. Cysso had processed the chatter on the Boardsos, where the general agreement was that Talents would trust the Circle of Six and the Coxos to decide on a fair system. The three men of the Circle of Six had formed an executive subcommittee.

Martin began the meeting: "What do Talents see themselves as?"

Smithy snortled: "Mathematically speaking we are a cybernetic-accelerated people. I predict the full cyber-singularity to be completed in a couple of years. Already our sexual behavior and reproductive system is cybernetic, and most believe our genetics were cybernetically generated. Now that Talents have mastered the basic science skills and have mastered all Normso current technology, the rate of inventive successes will accelerate. We have no "drag" on the economy outside of self-defense needs. Our focus should be unity with ample encouraged outlets for dissent. Anarchic totalitarianism. This is possible because of near total mutual transparency. Who watches the watchmen? Everyone does. No one watches Martin, who controls the access to Esther. This is a stable system as no one seems interested in what you two are up to. Absolute power in exchange for absolute freedom."

Yoshi seemed pleased: "We stick with the original game plan. Martin and Felicity master cyberspace, Smithy runs the economy, and I run the industry. Esther and Lucy will keep setting social standards and ethics via Talent-specific biology, while we create a justice and tax system to support these standards and ethics."

Martin commented: "The local government model is working well, the Schools and Labfarms seemed to have generated good Coxos with no dissent. Each Warren has a good measure of autonomy but defers to our decisions in implementation standards. We stick with the Coxo model so leadership is thinnest. All Warrens will run on Cysso AI based on Smithy's mathematical efficiencies. Yes, cybernetic society is the right word." *Warrens* was now the collective term for all Talent-run institutions, since they all were digging underground for growth space.

#

Martin invited a pan-meeting of the Coxo higher aristocracy (the 50 largest Warrens, not including the hundreds of smaller Schools nor the rural Labfarms popping up everywhere). He wanted a formal political organization (the SUN) before he could work out an acceptable monetary and justice system. All Talents were invited to the meeting to observe, but few went. They just waited for the Ether that Esther would produce afterwards.

After a considerable discussion about Science and Society and what really mattered in their world government, they agreed on a first principle for Talent government:

All Talents have a voice. All Talents must give a voice.

The tangible outcome was a mandatory polling system. Once a week, Coxos would publish polls and Talents were required to respond to them. They would work out a penalty for nonresponders through the soon-to-be-built tax and justice system.

Polling questions had two major requirements. Talents had to state a preference and state a level of interest in the preference. The first polling questions were centered around what Talents considered to be the biggest problems in their society. The polling questions were universal and decided upon by the Coxos. In a short time, Martin created a rotating polling committee of 10 Warrens' Coxos to work out the final drafts, which were then approved by all the Coxos.

The first poll was utilitarian in nature.

Are Talent disputes a problem?

There was a 1 to 10 rating, with 10 meaning a big problem. The tag questions were: 1 to 10, does this problem need solving now or can it wait a month? And for every polling question: 1 to 10, does this problem matter to you? It turned out to be a problem for about 10% of Talents, but it could wait.

The second polling question was cultural/utilitarian.

What do Talents think about using Normso labor inside the Warrens?

Talents were uniformly against it. Through a series of related polls, it became clear that Talents would prefer to do all menial labor versus having to deal with Normsos creeping around the place. The agreed-upon vision was that Talents would eventually automate all menial labor, so Talents didn't have to do the work either. Martin reckoned BGC had built Talents to have some sort of natural disgust for Normsos but couldn't reason how this was possible. Talents generally agreed because of their lack of psychotic personality traits, no one would "get off" on abusing Normso "lessers," let alone see them as "lessers."

The exception was Smithy's tiny Boardso group of Talent supremacists. The pattern was easy enough. They were Cysso members most exposed to Normso research. Yoshi and Lucy were also active on that Board. Esther wanted to condemn it, but Martin wanted to observe who joined it. Marcy told him to use that hate later for his advantage. He would need it. Regardless, the universal agreement was not to use Normsos as servants in the long term, with Esther's cult and Yoshi's relations the noticeable exceptions.

The third polling question was socioeconomic.

What do Talents see as a proper division of menial labor?

Equal. All Talents must engage in the same amount of menial labor. No one wanted rich or poor Talents in their society. They were all sick of this dichotomy that drove their Parents crazy. The point was to get rid of menial labor and menial jobs. Rich Normsos loved to have menial labor so they could consume huge amounts of resources. This drive to overconsume was considered to be genetics driven. Since Talents were naturally happy people living in a happy society, massive resource consumption was considered a crime against the environment and an unhealthy abuse of the human limbic system. Talent normal food was delicious. They had a satisfying group sexual experience. They were promised a proper pair-bond partner in the near future. Their simple ambition was to understand and explore the universe.

With these poll results in mind, Martin, Smithy, and Yoshi worked out an internal Talent tax/currency system and named it the Menial, sort of like how Normsos would use the word *dollar*. At the age of 15, all Talents accrued a weekly debt of Menial work measured in hours. The Coxos estimated all the menial work required to operate and expand their Warrens and rounded it to one day a week. Talents universally required only five hours of sleep and about one hour to do basic grooming, dressing, and eating, leaving 18 hours for menial work per week. One Menial was one menial work hour.

Menials included the whole variety of nonacademic and nonscientific work that needed to be done. Cooking, cleaning, mending, building space, plumbing, haircuts, teeth cleaning, teaching underclassmen, early childcare, outer defense, supply exchanges with Normsos, moving stuff around, all stuff that nobody necessarily wanted to do but had to be done. They could listen to their earbuds the whole time if they got bored.

A weighting system was developed to even out the workload, since some menials were more menial than others. Building space was the most dangerous work and could get up to 2:1 ratios, meaning you only had to do it for 9 hours instead of 18 per week. Cooking and cleaning was more desirable work than construction and ended up around 0.8:1 ratios. Teaching was the least menial work, and resulted in 0.5:1 ratios, meaning you had to work 36 hours a week teaching lower-level students basic math instead of 18. Childcare and breastfeeding went off the chart and were judged to be recreation activities. Felicity and Smithy optimized a fair share of the time and offered reverse Menials (payments) for breastfeeding induction (recognizing that their genetics made this a pleasurable activity and that there were more women willing to breastfeed than babies to be breastfed).

Talents could trade Menials, and Menials were given out as punishments or compensation for wrongs. For instance, if you accidentally hurt someone, you could offer one Menial as compensation, meaning one hour of labor debt would move between their accounts. Talents could not accumulate more than 72 Menials. They were punished with more Menials if they tried to shrug off work and ostracized until they brought their balance back below 72.

This system got rid of banking, interest, and capital accumulation. You *had* to work. Everyone had to do something every week unless they got sick or injured, which was considered the only excuse to accumulate 72 Menials.

The actual real-world finances with real-world dollars were still handled by the Warren Coxos. Cysso TOS was refooted on the Menial system. The Cysso Talent Bureaucrats were not allowed to trade Menials, since they were the virtual bank. Economics could not inflate through a government money printer. There was simply work to be done.

Crime was meaningless since property was meaningless, so the justice system had to cover only accidents. Talents were hurt because of other Talents' mistakes. The most challenging situation was the extremely rare accidental manslaughter (such as a lab accident).

Initially, the response to manslaughter was to involve a lawyer Parent who acted as a temporary guardian while the Talent left the school to face Normso punishment. The problem was that these Talents never returned. The anti-Talent movement got them, or they were raped and murdered in whatever disciplinary institution they were sent to (if they didn't go missing presumed kidnapped). Talents were physically tough and could take a beating, but they rarely learned how to fight besides wrestling and fencing. Esther's Ether about disguise while serving time helped only a little, as the local detention services lacked trustworthiness about secrets, and judges sentencing Talents to government detention didn't seem to care when the Parent went crazy about losing a loved and promising child. Martin decided the simple solution was to not involve the outside at all. Parents would not be informed their child had died, and a close body double would be procured for visits, with AI simulating the rest of the Talent's existence.

Cysso devised more polls to decide on administrative punishments, starting with manslaughter, calculated at 6500 Menials. A year of menial labor. They still accrued the 18 hour a week tax during this time as well. The responsible Talent had to carry the dead body to the Warren Gehinnso to be consumed and atomized.

At the opposite end of the crime spectrum was lying. If there were just two parties involved in a domestic situation, usually differences were worked out and judged locally, resulting in a Menial trade. Lying in a group context, say a science project, was considered a major crime and could quickly rise to SUN level and receive statutory Menial punishments. Adjudication came from rare situations where lying couldn't be independently established, and parties didn't back down. Talents assembled from other Warrens formed a temporary jury. Jury duty and even the judgeship for the trial became a Menial. Lying incidents fell in half each month and were expected to approach zero by the end of the year. After a month of functioning under the Menial system of commerce, taxes, adjudication, and punishments, the biggest polling complaint became polls themselves. Crime was gone, along with accidents and disputes.

Martin next returned to the question of central government. While he was nominally King and Esther his Queen, they wanted to clarify what that meant in terms of authority and responsibility. As King, his primary authority and responsibility was Warren defense, the preparation against future violent attacks on Talent collective property and people and the inter-Warren cooperation concerning defense standards and practices.

As Queen, Esther proposed that in addition to being Ambassador to

Normsos, deciding how Talents would interact with Normsos, and setting various other cultural and behavioral internal standards for Talents, she would be their official Ambassador to Better Genetics. Their authority/responsibility was quickly ratified with no dissent. Polls stated that "they are doing a great job so far" and "I'm glad that someone wants the responsibility."

The Boardso discussions about formal ratification centered around why only Esther or maybe Lucy wanted the job of Ambassador to BGC. Esther and Lucy made it clear they decided between themselves that Esther would take the title for the time being as they believed Esther had the closer relationship already and given that her genetic inclinations so far appeared to be unique among Talents. She reasoned that Talents needed champions, and that she and Martin had been preselected to take on these specific leadership roles.

Esther had proposed rotation and a system of recall for her position, but the polls returned that it was efficient for the one person who actually wanted and was suited for her "awful" job to focus on what was surely a complicated and specialized affair. Talents favored stability and order. Their government would be "agreement capable" as outsiders wouldn't be able to bribe or sneak around the system or wait it out for a friendlier government. Esther and Martin were Leviathan in the Hobbesian sense of the word. They were "Us" or "Talentkind" and were Law. Coxos had regional powers specifically delegated by Martin and Esther. The Coxos determined not only outbreeding practices but specific defense measures, trading practices, and direct involvement with Normso purchasing and later, when Talents created marketable products, selling.

Martin and Esther met in Tavernso to discuss these outcomes after simulated cybersex as usual. They were still working on a plan to find the missing Talents. The investigation into Violet Bloom had led nowhere. She was missing. Lots of people went missing these days. The social deterioration of the United States got worse every year, a phenomenon Esther described as "complete individualist atomization," the abolition of "community," and the destruction of "family." Ms. Bloom had hired expert private investigators who turned up nothing. There were no ransom demands, so they assumed Violet was dead. Ms. Bloom had gone back to

BGC and taken all the recommendations this time. She said it took a lot of begging on the website, but BGC consented to a replacement child. She said they charged her $10 million and made her promise to promote women in science, a sort of repentance as she described it.

Martin: "Esther, let's review our communication channels to BGC."

Esther: "Marcy, Alison, and Debbie."

Martin: "I suspect Lucy's dad, Pierre."

Esther: "Lucy flatly denies he communicates with them. And yes, I agree he's connected to BGC in a way we don't understand yet. It's the only explanation why the doctor Parents have given Lucy authority on Talent biology. BGC didn't use patents. They went the trade secret route with intellectual property. It's likely the Out-Talents are not using the common DNA that characterizes In-Talents."

Martin got suddenly very angry and yelled: "Damn it!"

His anger swelled for a bit and ultimately subsided. Esther waited patiently at his outbursts, which were growing more frequent. Debbie had told her to be pleasant when others were angry, so she waited patiently and calmly for his fit of anger to subside.

Martin: "Here's what I have so far. Jason says his dad met the Founders a long time ago, but his dad wouldn't give him their names. All he could get was that they are mostly pariahs, societal or scientific outcasts for different reasons. It's just better that we don't know who they are or were. He doesn't agree that Marcy and Debbie were Founders. The IVF and Computer Founders were different people whom he met face-to-face. Mr. Gordon had invested in dozens of transhumanist companies like BGC, but this one succeeded wildly where others had not. Once they proved their capabilities, he and all his network of super-rich friends provided the capital for their massive expansion. He "bet on the people not their controversial pasts," and that the Founders were all world-class supergeniuses, with impressive and well-documented resumes from world elite universities. The Coxos have pressed their Parents for information as well. Most of them worked through Alison in the early days of BGC, but a few others like Mr. Gordon met the Founders. Their testimonies support the notion that the Founders were social outcasts and genius experts. All I could get is that the five consisted of two men and three women and that two were East Asians in ancestry and nationality. They weren't more specific. Only one of the Founders was American. None of the five had any notable religious convictions either, no ulterior plan of any sort beyond making a successful business out of exciting new technology. Better Genetics is simply a for-profit business that managed to discover a multitude of scientific breakthroughs. No one agrees that Marcy or Debbie were Founders. Maybe they were just high-level employees sent by BGC to guide us. This 'placenta' metaphor you seem to like. Maybe they anticipated the violence against us."

Martin hesitated for a moment as he reached the story's likely conclusion. Esther just listened patiently as usual.

Martin: "At some point, the early investors agreed that Alison would be the only point of contact. It all had to do with technology security, which makes complete sense to me. Plus, there is some sort of secret agreement with a secret faction of the US State Department that blesses the whole arrangement. A rival organization to BGC had a lot to do with it. They have their 'Slugworth' problem, so to speak. A satan, you would call it."

Esther laughed at her Babel word for "antagonist."

Esther: "All these rich and powerful Parents were okay with supporting social outcasts?"

Martin: "Yes, so it seems. We can only speculate why society rejected them. As far as ulterior motives… just guesswork. A few Parents at first were upset every man and woman has the same body shape. Some were upset that all of us are extremely attractive. That seems to fade quickly when they see how happy their children are. It's sort of a moral paradox. They didn't let them decide, yet they are happy with the decision. I suppose social outcasts would do that sort of thing. It's sort of the same position we are in."

Esther was fully aware of the "ends justifies the means" argument. Their good looks might be evidence the Founders were not Christians who generally abhor those who commit sins for the sake of good outcomes. The Machiavellian worldview was a slippery slope to justifying anything.

Esther: "We are exempt from this sort of morality. We are the Nation and as such are at war with the rest of civilization, hot or cold. Whatever we do is not murder, as we are Authority. We are beyond the notions of good and evil. The King and Queen do not need to justify their actions as they have the moral authority of the life of their entire Nation."

The two of them sat in cyberspace silent for a while, staring at each other, as was their custom. The longing to be together IRL never went away. Cybersex with full haptic bodysuits and prosthetic human bodies was a poor substitute for IRL sex, they decided, despite penetrating and being penetrated with the prosthetics. The simulation of holding each other was excellent, but the mind rebelled against the fakery of it. It lacked the smell and taste of IRL sex. It lacked the hot adrenaline rush.

Martin heard a knock on the IRL door and set his headgear to see IRL. Felicity had let Marcy in.

Martin: "My mom is here."

Esther: "My mother is here, too. Hi, Mother!"

Felicity teleported in.

Felicity: "Sorry, bro, I summoned Mom here, and Debbie. We should just ask them face-to-face. I'll patch in Debbie." Felicity was doing that more now. She anticipated Martin's decisions before he made them. She was 100% on the dime about what Martin wanted.

Marcy stood in the room with her typical smile and waited patiently. She was wearing a brown woman's suit as usual, sharp and neat, full of authority. Felicity looked at Martin now. They had decided that Martin would be the voice when Marcy was there and Felicity when Max was there. They found it was easier to manipulate Parents of the opposite sex. Martin decided to take off his headgear and stood up to approach her. He motioned his mom and sister to the computer room where they all sat down around a small circular conference table, set with fixed T-pads for video/audio relay. Felicity patched in room audio so Esther could participate in the IRL conversation.

"Mom, we have a message to send to Better Genetics."

Esther saw that Felicity had brought up a group-share word-processing document with much of the writing already completed by Lucy. Debbie sat next to her in her bed, both sitting on the side away from the sex doll. Esther and Martin had polished the IRL document and Marcy and Debbie were invited to look at it on their T-pads. Neither said a word.

Dear Founders:

Thank you for making us! We are afraid that many of our brothers and sisters, your children, have gone missing. There is accumulating evidence that Talents are being systematically kidnapped, tortured, and murdered. We want to get them all to the safety of Talent habitats. We need a client and Talent list, so we can track down each and every Talent you have produced. You owe this as a guarantee of your work to help us keep them alive. Send the information to Esther Stein, at Alison Davos' old estate outside of Louisville, Kentucky, USA. We have elected Esther unanimously as our Ambassador to Better Genetics and set up a private unconnected computer there to analyze the data.

Thank you for helping us.

The Talents at the Science Schools and Labfarms (The Warrens)

And a spot for Esther's digital signature and augreal 2D barcode.

There had been a short discussion about where the list (if they obtained it) should go. Esther wouldn't be processing the data; that was a job for Cysso. It was symbolic. Esther's work purpose was most impacted by this project, so the Circle of Six decided she should get it first.

Esther approved the final copy and the printer in the computer room printed it. Marcy got up and looked at the document on the table, gave no signal and left the room. Debbie took the time to admire the sex robot. "Congratulations, I'm so proud of you," she gushed. "Looks like I have friends in high places. Lucky me," she giggled. "Bye bye." And she left the room closing the door behind her.

Felicity: "Mom is getting weird lately, isn't she?" Felicity said it exactly as Martin was thinking it. This weird phenomenon was happening frequently.

Martin: "She's like happy all the time. Excited even." Martin confirmed.

Esther: "Yeah, Debbie is happy all the time, too. Well, our Parents are very happy about us. That's a good thing. We're doing good."

Martin: "Yeah, like organizing an army-trained cult. A major power grab from our Parents and power held by a small number of people. It's all exciting, isn't it?"

Felicity smiled at Martin and blinked [Agreed.]

Esther: "Debbie congratulated me on the new position and left."

Martin: "We cross our fingers?"

Esther: "I'm optimistic. I think we reached the required maturity and sophistication that was hinted at before. I'm also worried. I think our worst fears about murder and kidnapping will come true."

CHAPTER NINE
HIGH SOCIETY

[2062]
PASS

MARTIN AND HIS LEADERSHIP team decided to stop working on government, law, justice, taxation, and a currency. The polls zeroed out on these
matters (on the level of interest in the problem question). No one could
think of a fairer or less intrusive system. Cysso, the Circle of Six, and the
Coxos were performing their responsibilities beautifully and exercising
authority without any signs of abuse or self-interest. Everyone else felt
confident in their well-being and (as understood on Boardso) their "genetic" place in society. Memeso coined the term *Belongso*. Talents liked
this feeling and wanted more.

Their next task was creating a formal economy; they couldn't expect
to live on Parent financial generosity forever. While Menials (as their internal currency) served as effective sticks and encouraged safety and truth
telling, there needed to be a formal reward system as well. The "Faustian
urge" or "science gene" promised in the BGC sales cycle was deemed di-
rectionless. While Talents seemed to gravitate to different science disciplines and had mastered them, already bringing wonderful breakthroughs,
they needed more explicit goals. A purpose to it all. Something to aspire
to. Unitso, Spockso, Sustainso, Sciformso, and Cyberso were just ideals.

Unity, truth, balance, purity, and equality was a beautiful way to live; they were just not concrete. They had to make the abstract concrete.

Martin sat in bed while he rewatched a scene from one of the most popular Ethers in Talent history, a roundtable discussion with Rachel, Esther, Percy, and Shelly.

Rachel: "What is our purpose? We are done. We are all genetically maximally fit. We rarely get sick, we recover from all types of illness and injury quickly, we are naturally happy, and we're all happy with each other personally and sexually. We all appear to be very beautiful and share common interests."

Percy: "Except for the Dissentsos and the Out-Talents." The three others looked at the same time to Esther who was ready with an answer.

Esther: "We search for light and truth. We fight the darkness and lies. We find the Out-Talents."

The three other Talents smiled at her response, sharing a look of relief. Her response earned a 100% approval rating.

Esther had talked to Josh about that conclusion. It was the Yale motto, lux et veritas.

Shelly responded the soonest: "Well, most of Normso science these days is corrupted. It is science for acceptance, not reality. We cannot build on the shoulders of distrusted giants. Talents need their own scientific method as well as their own culture, government, bureaucracy, and labor system."

Percy: "Yes, Cysso is fair, equal, just, predictable, transparent, and minimal. The latest poll returned that there is no doubt our leaders are working for our safety and best interests."

Cysso. My out-family. Our computing platform. An international government bureaucracy. Our economic clearinghouse. Mostly AI driven now. Talent needs are defined, predictable, and minimal.

Rachel: "Reformso is pleased to publish a new scientific method. We've called it Lattice Parallel Structure."

Martin paused the Ether and reread Rachel's now famous email:

Lattice Parallel Structure

1. A desirable outcome is theorized; example: high-density battery, advanced carbon sink.
2. Different theories and approaches are hypothesized.
3. Different technologies related to the outcome are articulated, such as chemical, physical, or biological approaches, and intermediary technologies that have to be discovered.
4. An assignment system is agreed upon: which scientists in which Warrens would take which approaches. Status is updated continuously through the Intalent.
5. Budgets, where necessary, are sent to Cysso. Appropriations are transacted through Coxos, who work with local Normsos and Parentsos. Cysso works out research priorities and allocates budgets accordingly between defense and economic needs. Excess capacity would be devoted to life quality improvements for Talents and Normsos, typically health and automation related.

The panel compared Lattice Parallel Structure (now Tesp. Leapso) to Edison's scientific approach to inventing the light bulb. Instead of trying 200 different filaments one at a time, as Edison did, Talents would conduct 200 different experiments at one time, decreasing the development time by 200 times. Edison's light bulb relied on technology developed by a British inventor. This necessitated the involvement of lawyers and licenses and payments, all of which soaked up an enormous amount of time and emotional energy for inventors. The Talents just skipped this bit, which quadrupled productivity. Mathematically speaking, a single Talent operated at 800 times the level of Nikola Tesla, which could be doubled again for healthy bodies, and doubled again for youthful energy, given their university-level scientific training was complete by the age of 15 or earlier, and given a concentrated science culture and upbringing. And they had the intelligence genes for it, if you believed Better Genetics claims about making geniuses, something nearly all Talents believed they were.

Doubled again because I relieve them of Bullso. One Talent operates like 6400 Teslas.

Rachel continued: "Lattice Parallel Structure is based on the following recognizable facts about our culture and our cultural technology." She beamed at Esther. "For starters, we have an equal number of female geniuses to male geniuses, and we are all attracted to each other. There is no intrasexual competition among the men and women. Lucy promises us suitable long-term sexual relationships or Partnersos in the near future that will be fair, just, and efficient. Our semiweekly Circleturbos are satisfying and connect us to each other. No one has to worry about finding a suitable sex mate, yet another painful, distracting task for Normsos."

Percy took over: "What really helps everyone is that there is no social or political advancement to drive egos. Cysso is volunteers. The polls have shown that nobody wants government jobs who doesn't have them already. Thank you, Esther, by the way. We appreciate what you do for us."

Talents, always well-mannered.

Martin glanced at Felicity's smile. She was working on a data mining system to make land appropriations for physical mines more efficient. She was in her typical Talent Deepzone of programming. The word captured the common phenomenon of Talent ability to focus and concentrate when working on a task. She had glanced up at him quickly and smiled and he had glanced back smiling. They did this often while they worked.

Shelly spoke up next: "The happiness gene is what makes us most efficient. We don't have to waste time and resources on luxury or travel. We are not bogged down by depression. We get all the fun we need from hanging out in our societies, learning, or sports and arts. Smithy calls us low-maintenance nonconsumers. Trivial to plan and provide for. Our latest discovery is that all Talents have excellent voices and enjoy singing, another fun activity that doesn't consume resources."

Esther signaled her turn to speak. As usual, the three others gave her maximum attention.

Esther: "Discovery is fun. We all have exciting science to discover, what Normsos call work, we call fun. When our teams make a breakthrough, everyone is happy that someone's experiment worked, and they can move on to the next exciting discovery." Esther stated this rather flatly instead of her usual cheery self.

Rachel showed concern: "Is life in your Compound and work in the

Circle of Six not exciting science? You work with me on Alzheimer's research and brain surgery."

Esther replied flatly: "One day a week now. Two if I'm lucky. I am not complaining. I research social technologies around the planet now. I study past and existing political and religious societies, why some succeed, and others die out. Talents must succeed and not die out."

The three others nodded. Martin felt a coldness at the notion of not dying out. Felicity said that Talents watched this part of the Ether the most frequently. The Boardsos were lit with people trying to understand what she meant. Scientific discovery was "fun" not "survival."

Esther continued: "What is clearest to me in my discoveries is our biggest advantage in life is that we have no mental illnesses or addictions to fight. We don't spend all our spare time and resources on flooding our bodies with nasty or expensive inputs to relieve the mental and physical suffering that Normsos deal with constantly."

Rachel cheered up: "We've been working on a system of research labor. Esther, why don't you share our new work ethics now."

Esther smiled and returned to her cheery self: "We are not exactly intellectual equals. Lucy believes our intelligence genetics and brains are wired differently. If you find yourself more suited to a certain intellectual discipline than another, you should find appropriate science projects. That said, learning the other disciplines is still valuable time. We should endeavor to appreciate everyone's work. I, for instance, love biology and medicine. We should recognize the possibility we have been genetically organized into science castes."

That had turned out to be a big announcement. Cysso created a "Discipline" database and Talents eagerly self-categorized. That was one poll they didn't grumble about. Talents now had "Discos," a word play on discovery, disciples, scientific discipline, and disciplining Talents who worked on science projects they weren't optimally suited for. Discos became a part of a mature Talent's augreal. Talents were already sporting epaulettes (using shape and color) to declare their Discos (colored uniforms were defeated quickly in Boardso and polls). Their design was principled on beauty and not military fashion, and they were worn like ornaments (not stitched) on top of their shirts and dresses. These now had attachments to the diamond necklaces (with integrated GPS trackers) that were also popular with adult Talents.

Talents 15 and older quickly formed Disco societies, both physical social societies within Warrens and online group discussions often held in Tavernso so members could enjoy talking and looking at each other across the world.

The Everyone is Made of Chemists Club (Allchemisoco) was a major society. Popular discussions were about renewable energy, atmosphere control, and nanotechnology. The Chemists wanted to make the Warrens energy independent with advanced solar panels and geothermal systems. Related to those projects were carbon sinks and materials manipulators. Waste is Our Want was their motto. They wanted to rob the atmosphere of CO_2 and grab every junkyard out there for material reprocessing to use as construction materials for the Warrens. Mass/energy relationships was their name and game.

The Pheromonal Club, or Biology Club (Fairbiosoco), was popular as well. The Phero Folk hoped to become doctors, and like Esther, they trained extensively in medicine as well as they could with Parentsos and equipment available to their in-house clinics. Already Talents were doing basic dental work, basic medicine, training Talents on basic first aid, and doing paramedic level work (on call) as Menials. Genetics, stem cell research, and gene splicing were quickly picked up as popular subjects.

Esther was considered an informal member of Fairbiosoco and occasionally participated. Because of her many duties (and ability to lie), she was relegated to applied bioengineering (typically anesthetics), for which she expressed extreme gratitude.

The Mind-Machine Interface Society, or the Borg (Psiborgsoco), saw themselves as the bridge between biological and chemical sciences, the point between humans as biological and machines attached (prosthetic) or detached (machine/computer) or autonomous (robots). There were two major differences or challenges to resolve.

Energy density. Energy production could be roughly categorized into four forms. Nuclear-based forms had the highest density, but you couldn't have people walking around with miniature nuclear power plants. Oxygen reactions like combustion were next. Cell metabolism, the energy that fueled organic life, was next; it was very efficient to use the various chemical redux reactions that chewed up proteins, carbohydrates, and fats to fuel the human body. The limit there was that the ATP cycle and photosynthesis were dead-end evolutions. You could make organic energy more efficient with anatomy, but millions of years of mutation hadn't found other evolutionary efficiencies.

Batteries were at the bottom for energy density. The textbook example was to compare an electric winch with a hand winch. You could pull an average two-ton car out of a ditch in about 30 seconds with an electric winch, but it would use up a heavy car battery in about three minutes. You could pull the same two-ton car out with a hand winch and a human body. It would take an hour or two, but the human body would not run out of energy. It wouldn't just suddenly turn all the fat reserves in your belly or thighs to flabby skin either.

To solve Esther's problems with portable energy, the Talents had a long way to go. The camera-eye with the external shoulder holster battery were all they could manage. The organic "eye" was the bioenergy solution, and Esther wasn't about to strap on a combustion motor and diesel fuel (the most mass/density transportable efficient chemical energy storage) tank to power her body parts. There was zero interest in portable nuclear energy.

The second major problem for the Borg was image/sound recognition. Humans had a visual and audio cortex that created useful environment-interactive meaning from light and sound waves. A group of Talents were trying to come up with computer algorithms and get beyond face, voice, and license plate recognition and translators. They wanted their robots to press and fold their clothes.

In other words, killer robots could not last more than an hour or find their way out of a room until Talents invented a way. Martin lost all interest in "killer robot/android/cyborg" movies at 15. Esther was a real cyborg, and she sometimes wrote poetry about how she hated her implants. The fine abilities she received were outdistanced by the loss of independence, the lack of privacy, and the vulnerability to computer hacking. Prosthetics also took a lot of care and maintenance, and mishandles could be extremely painful. She had to "lose an eye and gain an eye" every day, which she summed up as "not fun." The camera-eye with the external battery was more useful but came with the price of looking scary.

A subdivision of Borgso concentrated on the traditional computer/wireless/telecom technology. Martin asked them to make faster, more efficient computers. He wanted their own telecom network, and he wanted their own satellite network. Advanced quantum computing and diamond-based (instead of silicon-based) computers were thought to be the key breakthroughs.

Already the Nanobot society had made the most breakthrough technology in creating the first prototype 3D nanoprinter. The physics/chemistry specialist group had mastered atomic particle level manipulation to invent new materials (as opposed to mere recycling), collectively known as schiron (with the sch- using the same phonetic in the word *school*, and -iron pronounced normally). Any combination of silicon, carbon, hydrogen, iron, oxygen, and nitrogen and various refined isotopes thereof were to be preferred over rare earth elements, which often had toxic or dangerous qualities, if not derived from meaner parts of the globe with high extraction costs.

Talents often discussed Disco competition. A popular question was what was the best way to improve Esther's prosthetic eye: create a proper battery, a computer-based visual cortex, do a full eye transplant, or find a way to simply grow a new organic eye with an embedded computer screen, but bioenergy powered. Maybe there would be a choice for Esther.

He stopped watching the Ether and thinking about Talent social clubs and projects.

He summoned Felicity and Smithy into Tavernso. He had made a virtual roomspace to look like a Chinese garden complete with fountains and small bridges.

Martin: "What do you think about our future, Smithy?"

Smithy: "Talent industry will be designed, built, and managed by Talents. Our out-products will have to be run by Normsos for Normsos." Smithy expected Martin to make the first Normso hires.

Martin: "I get the honor of working with Normsos? What about my Parents? Parentsos are doing all that."

Felicity: "Bro, they are inefficient. Half my AI time is anticipating their mistakes. Once we have our own factories, we need to manage Normsos directly. They need to be what Normsos call 'employees,' with money and other incentives. Parents are more like donors and investors. Sort of not as motivated."

Martin canceled the Tavernso meeting and switched to live videos of the less intelligent Talents called the Preppers. They were children of Parents who had picked all the standard recommendations but hadn't followed the Manual at all. They engaged in the military sports like self-defense and drone games. For science work, they typically focused on the advanced mice and drones that Martin used to penetrate computer systems and maintain Warren outdoor visual defense. The Preppers worked so that the lower levels of the Warrens were undetectable to outsiders and were often in contact with Normso workmen, deliveries, and inspections. Martin had them take Normso IQ tests, where they scored from 130–150. Every Warren had a few, about 1% of Talent population, and while they were considered part of Cysso they reported to their Coxos too. They generally kept to themselves and kept their own communal quarters near the Warren main entrances. Lucy had relaxed the celibacy rules on them, and they typically paired up on their own accord and became strictly monogamous.

That left the Dissentsos society. They were busy inventing 3D-printable alcohol and drugs. The men did a lot of (drug-fueled) body building and the women experimented with homemade makeup and clothing for fun. The men had decided to engage in wrestling competitions, with the winner taking two women to his bedroom and the loser getting none. The loser would console his loss with drugs and alcohol, while the winner and his women enjoyed a ketamine-fueled threesome. They all conspired to develop new kinds of sex games to push the hedonic treadmill to the limit. A warped application of the science gene, was what Lucy called it. Felicity refused to watch any of it.

#

Outside of Discos, Prepping, and Dissenting, Talents played sports (just fencing and squash were popular after 15), created art, sang and listened to and played music, and danced. These activities did not have associated societies because all Talents engaged in them. Polling and Boardso assessments described these activities as stress relief and brain balancing efforts. Typically, a Talent spent eight hours a week participating in sports, music, and other creative arts. You could always find a Talent or group of Talents to join you. Martin only left his chambers to play squash, Felicity for dance.

Talent artistic creations were very mathematical, nearly always computer-generated, 3D-nanoprinted, and ready to be part of a science museum. They submitted pieces from time to time to the local science museums, usually in the form of animated holographic art displays, videos of dance pieces (in Normso costumes), variations on Bach, and science demonstration videos (holographic or immersive VR) that had worked at Esther's old high school, where her Followers were still using them to tutor students.

Normso pop culture, literature, and computer games were deemed "normso." Talents couldn't relate to any of it. One poll showed that 50% of Talents believed they were in fact created by aliens, something in the *2001 Space Odyssey* style. Talents considered themselves "cyber-realists," a theme on the self-delusion genetics discussed on day one in the BGC sales cycle. The general agreement was that Ethers were exactly what Talents enjoyed, and many film clubs were teaching better techniques on filming and narrating their science projects to share with the world on Boardso.

Memeso had named Talent social technology Etherism. The common agreement was that Etherism wasn't excluded from local religions. Esther hadn't commented on the supernatural, God, gods, spirits, immortal souls, and karma (just kindness), so Talents could worship or believe as they pleased. Warrens all had pray/meditation rooms with some local portable religious decoration, and local Talents held and ran all local worship services, satisfying their local governments and communities where it mattered.

Etherism had leaked into all of them. Afableco, komplezo, boneco, favorajo, komplezemo—"friendliness, courtesy, goodness, grace, benevolence"—were cited after most services. "Love, joy, peace, longsuffering, gentleness, goodness, faith, meekness, and temperance" were cited at others. Galatians 5:22–23, with faith applied to their King and Queen and Coxos.

Martin and Esther had further created two Pillars of Talent Economic ethics, deriving an economic form from their sociopolitical form.

Their first Pillar was **Transparency**.

Regular Talents couldn't hide their work. Projects were shared and verified across Warrens. Work was checked and rechecked by other Talents. Menials were attached to Talents who encoded their activities or added passwords to any computer system. Only Cysso had that power.

It was understood that Cysso and Coxos were largely exempt from Transparency because of their need to lie to Normsos. The simulated reality and methodology of controlling Parentso Bullso made contact between their government and the rest of the Talents socially awkward. Slowly the ruling class stopped mixing with the science class, de facto castes settling into behavioral awareness.

Only Martin seemed happy about this social evolution. During a weekly meeting between Martin and Yoshi, they decided to explore their feelings about this at Yoshi's virtual kami shrine.

Martin: "I know I was handpicked for my position. The Founders have all sorts of plans we don't know about. Now we have jobs where we can lie all day, and no one will ever call us on it. We are above the law, where there is no law. Talent law or custom could fit a sheet of paper, which is mainly the statutory Menials. Even those are becoming meaningless. There are no more accidental homicides and lying is impossible with Cysso in charge."

Yoshi/%**Japanese**: "Yes, that is true. Not that I ever lie."

Martin/%**Tesp**: "We should endeavor to not lie to each other. How are your robots coming along?" Martin still found it odd that Yoshi spoke in Japanese but then reflected that Yoshi spent more time with Normsos than Talents.

Yoshi: "I've promised them robot factories of the future and huge wins in telecommunications infrastructure. There is less expectation in Japan that their Talent population intends on joining the big Japanese companies, and there is more understanding that we prefer to work with ourselves to help out Japan. That's the lie I've told them."

Martin: "I was thinking we should start stealing Normso corporate tech." *Actually, I lied, I'm already doing it.*

Yoshi: "That is a bad idea. We use public information and create from scratch."

Martin: "Hmm, maybe. What company do you want? I can send a mouse over if you name the tech you are looking for. I've got plenty of labor to do the job."

Yoshi: "You're using my mice for corporate espionage?"

Martin: "Yeah, it digs under the earth, it chews through anything with diamond teeth, and it eventually burrows into a wire connected to the computer system. Once they find a power source for the mouse, they disconnect the powering wire and retract it. I control it from there." *Followers are good for the tedious work of corporate espionage.*

Yoshi: "Ah, it is not a good thing to commit crimes against Normsos."

Martin: "If you say so." *Esther was right. I should only talk to her about crimes.*

Felicity: [Bro, will seal criminal activity info to you me and Esther.]

Martin: [Okay.]

Yoshi: "If you do it, I don't want to know about it."

Martin winked out of cyberspace, Felicity was there to help him dispose of the VR equipment and haptic clothing. He found himself embracing her (dressed down to his underwear) and they smiled at each other. She pushed him away and started giggling. Martin now admired Felicity's full grown 16-year-old teenage body. Her perfect figure. Her perfect smile. She stared downward. He reasoned he'd have to get drunk with her tonight. He reasoned he couldn't do it any other way.

#

The second Pillar of Talent etho-economics was **Pathogen Disgust**.

It is simply natural genetics, shared in most animals, that makes us adverse to experiencing sickness and death in other animals. It is that natural stomach reaction we get seeing a dead or dying body, someone suffering from cancer, any kind of disease, and even simple ugliness. Esther said it would only get worse as they got older, and they would just have to get used to it. They would have to look over how sickly all Normsos look with all their genetic defects and crazy diseases that Talents just didn't suffer from. Those Talents wishing to be doctors to Normsos would have to overcome it, like most Normso doctors did as part of their training.

Martin thought Esther was too kind. There were other forms of disgust Talents discussed on Boardso. There was "moral disgust." The way Normsos treated each other, not just the endless ego and self-esteem battles that raged within and without, but the posturing, the need for supremacy, the need to dominate. It was the prating on about the disgusting entertainment they liked, not just the disgusting habits they all had, not just the disgusting variety of drugs (poisons) they all took to achieve a temporary sense of wellness or to "have fun."

And then there was the "sexual disgust." The abysmal sexual relations between the Normsos were beyond comprehension to Martin: casual sex, porn abuse, sex tourism, cheating, all of it. It was their desperate and endless need for sexual validation for any purpose but making babies. Talents (except him and Esther, the Coxos, the Preppers, and the Dissentsos) were all virgins. Lucy had stated that the first sexual bond between humans was too powerful to ignore and Martin's personal experience agreed with this. He felt sorry for what Esther did each night. She was pouring her excess sex drive into daily Circleturbos (fully clothed, eyes open on her) with her Followers now (while she kept her eye closed) and going to bed with her bodyguards for Handturbo with her gloves on. She had forbidden any mouth contact or any kind of penetration among her people. They had to wait and prove worthiness in the meanwhile.

Martin remembered Esther's apple during moments of Normie disgust. It was his price to pay to protect the Talents from this disgust. This is what Esther had learned from her death at the church. She *knew* that Talents were never going to integrate with Normsos, well before Talents or the rest of the world would understand it. The Talents wouldn't be able to stand the Normies, and enough violent Normies were out there who would try to kill and dominate Talents. Nonviolent Normies certainly didn't care when Out-Talents were killed or kidnapped, which was his explanation for why he couldn't find any evidence of them.

The Coxos and Preppers agreed that you could see the violence etched on the face and in the eyes of the various policemen who came through the Warrens looking for munitions. There was an eagerness in their gait, a joy they felt managing the dogs, that this time they would find evidence the Talents were up to no good. This would allow them to be violent, what they really wanted, at least subconsciously.

Martin felt sad that while the Talents were supposed to herald the end of racism and start a new chapter in world cooperation, it was doomed to failure. The Talents were becoming just another race unto themselves. If the Normies couldn't control their desire to kill or enslave Talents, then the Talents would have to fight for supremacy. If the Normies found a way to coexist with the Talents, they would fight for a separate space that Smithy was organizing in Wyoming and in Labfarms across the planet. World conquest, indeed. He thought she was joking at the time. *I will re-create the environment to serve Talents, not Normies. Esther will attempt to save Normies from Talent destruction. That is what she meant.*

Felicity got up from her computing desk and walked over to him to give him a back rub. They had been getting drunk every night for a week. Martin had given up on squash and Felicity on dance. Trips out of their room always met with drone dart encounters with Parentsos. They stopped going to Circleturbo. "Unclean and dangerous. All of them, except Marcy. Marcy's just dangerous."

She walked over to the nanoprinter and got him a glass of cold vodka. They shared sipping it.

They walked hand in hand to the bedroom, still drinking the vodka. They hugged sitting on the bedside heads wrapped around each other. "We're trapped."

"At least we can't get depressed, can we?" Felicity said in her usual impenetrable cheeriness.

"Not while we have each other, don't we." They smiled and touched noses. Martin felt like kissing her and she looked like she wanted it. "We can't do this."

"We can't."

They both took a full mouthful of vodka and swallowed and then shivered. The Dissentsos had determined that Talents had the rare human genetics where alcohol caused a dopamine high along with the loss of inhibition. Martin admired how extremely beautiful his sister was. Felicity blushed and took another big drink.

As they drank many glasses, they found they could.

CHAPTER TEN
BETTER LIVING UNDERGROUND

[February 1, 2062. The Circle of Six has turned 17.]
PASS

"WHAT AM I DOING?" Martin cuddled up behind Felicity in their king bed and snuggled his face in her soft bouncy hair and sniffed pleasantly.

"Cheer up, bro. We've got each other." Martin squeezed her thin waist, listening to her happy sigh. "Happy birthday."

"Happy birthday."

They lay there together for a minute as was now their custom. Today was their large parameter status report. Eventually they sat up and talked to Sakura.

"Sakura, what is the genetic pressure?"

Sakura: "Talents can still live happily in large dorm co-ed bunkrooms. But the need to pair-bond is increasing. Lucy promises results in a year and a half." Talents were holding hard onto their virginity (defined as first interphysical contact Turbo—which was understood would cause a permanent limbic imprint). Their Queen said wait, and so they waited. Their Queen said to have faith in her. And so they had faith in her.

"The outflow patterns?"

Sakura: "The estimated flight time starts at fifteen. All Talents by the age of seventeen have left the Schools for Farms. Migration to Wyoming City is now a popular world destination. Tapping the Yellowstone geothermal supervolcano combined with Wyoming's vast coal resources deemed optimal. Massive underground digging continues. At Wyoming City and places around the world like it, we are building indestructible housing out of diamond-plated schiron."

"Warren popularity?"

Sakura: "No Talent wants to live underground in the Warrens for long. They are okay having the labs and manufacturing plants built underground. Labs at the Labfarms and Wyoming City are being built underground. Selling it as preparation for colonizing the universe is popular. Any new planet we might find would probably require underground nuclear and hydroponic supplied stations while terraforming goes on."

"Weak points?"

Sakura: "No Talent wants Esther's job. She is our single point of failure."

Not good.

Felicity spoke now: "The pattern is clear. The entirety of Talent civilization is bent. An arc. A bias. Esther is out there as a lure for Normso violence."

"It would seem so. There haven't been any attacks on her since Nate. However, we shouldn't put our guard down ever."

"There is no genetic evolution. Just science."

"Yes, we seem to be the end of evolution. Esther is already part machine now. A machine that we create and evolve."

And control? No. We love each other.

Esther: "Guys, we can do this." The sound came from their computer speaker by the bedside; Esther occasionally listened in on their conversations. They muted the system when they got drunk and fooled around, but Esther hadn't called them out.

Her group at the Compound knew about brain matter up to the cognitive and consciousness capabilities that separated humans from other animals. Animals have memory, and Alzheimer's research had potential crossover application. Smithy had quipped that Normies were still good for something (meaning brain experiments on the parts of the brain that delivered the illusion of consciousness). Esther promptly nixed both the idea and mentioning of the idea ever again.

Martin sat up and studied the large screen showing Esther working in the horse barn/lab around contraptions that were holding a horse steady while it was in and out of sedation. Rachel and Melanie were in the demented horse's brain now while Esther managed the sedation, Josh watching everything carefully.

"An entire civilization devoted to your protection."

Esther: "Yes, it's flattering. It went to my head before, but not again. Now you are in my head. You own my head and I own people, and we own Talents, and you own their Parents."

"How long do we keep the information hidden?" Martin repressed the urge to cry but spilled over after Felicity started crying first. They hugged hard whenever this happened. The alcohol and sex were just temporary relief from their combined cognitive and emotional pain.

It hadn't taken long for Better Genetics to get to Esther the information they requested. It came in the form of a small computer drive hand-delivered by a very good-looking young black man and woman (violet eyes) who left immediately. Martin guided Esther through the Medium application while he randomly scattered search requests to Cysso. In about a week, the pattern became clear and defined, as they discovered the outcomes of non-School Talents the ages of 10 and older. Upon learning Felicity's compiled outcome results, there were startlingly easy conclusions to make.

Esther advised Cysso to use the Kübler-Ross model to work through the emotional impact of the obvious conclusions, using this special opportunity to measure Talent neuroplastic response to extreme grief.

The five stages of grief for Talents were recorded and summarized as thus:

Denial didn't last long. Talent minds were highly realistic. Normsos were evil. Only a percentage of Normsos were truly evil, Esther reminded them, those that enjoyed making others suffer.

Anger lasted a little longer. He and the other Talents screamed and pounded fists for a while. Patience and kindness, Esther repeated.

Bargaining? More self-delusion. Outreach? Cysso had each other as an out-family. Lots of hugs was what Esther recommended. Martin and Felicity had only each other to hug.

Depression? Not even possible. Just an acute deep sadness, a day of acedia in listless torpor. All members of Cysso were still experiencing random outbreaks of tears, even after "Acedia Day" time off, often returning to denial for brief moments, "It can't be..."

Esther had found that bright, happy energy about a month after her hospital discharge. She no longer cried about Elsa's death. She was a happy and bright memory of a life well lived and a positive afterlife well earned. Martin didn't think this time around it would be so easy or brief.

Esther spontaneously started crying and Josh walked over to her to give her a hug. She had shared the news with him while Josh maintained his perfect calm. He didn't cry. He didn't need Acedia Day. Martin was in awe of him.

Acceptance was the last stage of grief. Martin accepted that Talents and Normies were at war and could *never* get along. Nothing more, nothing less. A war with three possible outcomes. Destruction of either side, or a form of coexistence. Of the three, he favored the destruction of the other side. Except his mom and dad of course. And the other Parents. *They wouldn't mind the destruction of everyone else, would they? Yeah, they would.*

Cysso kept the results secret and put the problem of what to do with them back in Esther's lap. Esther would know the proper time and place to tell the Talents their research results on the dispositon of the Out-Talents. She blessed them and thanked them for this honor. She liked to bless and thank people lately. Well, she was graceful. She was that sort of person. Most Talents blessed and thanked people. They followed her custom on Ethers. She was back to starring in most of the Ethers now that her brain experiments were nearing a major breakthrough. She was preparing a special Ether for the simple announcement that caused such intense suffering, their worst fears now realized as fact:

Every single Out-Talent (over 13) was dead or missing.

Cysso found their photos. There were a couple of general observations about the Out-Talents.

1. Only about 10% had the violet eyes option.
2. 90% had the recommended heights for men and women but 10% were not.
3. About half came from wealthy families. How the others afforded it was not understood.
4. Many had received child prodigy accolades or attended elite Normso schools.
5. They were all extremely beautiful by Normso standards. Many won child beauty pageants and others worked as child models.

Those 13 and older were found dead, about 4:1 dead to missing. Very few under 10 had been touched. There was a long-running debate in Cysso's private Boardso about the safety of 1,000,000 Talents under 10 (and those 200,000 out of 300,000 aged 10–12 not already gone) living outside the Warrens part-time now.

The private Cysso Boardso speculation went like this:

Esther: [Puberty triggers something.]

Smithy: [Yes, sexuality. Now Out-Talents can outbreed.]

Martin: [Why not ransom them? Kidnap but not ransom doesn't make sense.]

Felicity: [Some of these Talents seemed to get involved in drugs and sex-related extortion like the ones that Nate showed. Too smart and attractive for their own good it seems.]

Martin browsed through the various Internet articles. Their lives were often connected with teachers and other caregivers engaged in various types of sexual activity with them. Stories of rape, incest, and molestation spattered the various local news headlines. They were never identified as "Talents" in these articles, even the few with violet eyes. Interviewed parents declared that their children were not Talents but born through donor surrogacy programs, usually claiming they obtained gametes from attractive elite athletes at top universities around the world.

Most of the deaths looked like accidents and many were ruled suicides. Cysso computed the high likelihood the suicides were faked somehow, but the police and families seemed reluctant to investigate them further.

That 100% of them would be gone from civilization was beyond statistically impossible. They were dead or missing in every country where Out-Talents lived around the planet.

Martin switched his view of collected articles to the camera on Josh (from his computing device) without announcing himself. Keystroke monitoring, Josh had typed in [Hi Martin, hi Felicity. I hope you broadcast the Ether sooner rather than later.]

They finished up on the horse and the group, Esther, Josh, Rache, and Melanie, retired to the Ether production room to produce an Ether on horse brain surgery. After they finished, Esther signaled to Martin she wanted to engage in cyber-sex.

#

[An hour later]

Martin: "Frisby?"

Esther: "Yes, Bigwig."

Martin: "We're going to win this war. I'm not going to die in a rabbit warren. I'm not going to die at the hands of stupid, awful Normies."

Esther: "Yes, we must win or die. But we must do it with kindness."

<kindness bro> Felicity blinked [Esther is right.]

Martin: "Screw your kindness. Kill them all, I say. They will be obsolete, as will all their technology. They won't even be useful to pick grapes. Their day is ending."

Esther: "Promise me. If I give you a choice, where kindness is possible, will you consider it?"

Martin: "No promises."

Esther: "Good, then you will consider it."

Martin: "Hrmph."

Esther: "There is so much to do. How is your *fear*?"

Martin: "Strong."

Esther: "Good. Fight or flight?"

Martin: "Fight. How do you handle the fear? When it washes over me, I feel terrible."

Esther: "I don't feel it much anymore. Not after I died. It's a common effect of near-death experiences. Plus, I have *you* watching over me. Have you realized why you must do so?"

Martin just then observed that Esther nearly always wore her camera-eye. She had said she preferred the easy battery swap and extra computer functionality, even though she looked like a scary cyborg pirate geek. She looked intimidating and decided that everyone else would have to get used to it.

Martin: "We serve you to survive. Me and all Talents. Then what's next? Must be Better Genetics. I don't want to know your plans even though I always know what your plans are."

Esther: "They require a lot of time. Years. Fortitude and prudence are virtues, too. It seems the next step is for me to go to college. I'm taking Talents with me."

Martin: "I have less control of Bullso in some of the Warrens in South America. The Parents are putting up an effective fight. They pull their children out and beat them. The Talents are afraid to use the drone dart defenses. I can kidnap them out and send them to Wyoming, but then we lose funding. I'd like to send them to college instead. There's about fifty who are taking up the offer. Plus Josh's group of roughly thirty Reformsos want to go, too. Your boyfriend wants to stay with you."

Esther: "Martin." *She looks so calm. She is most beautiful when she is calm. She's going to break up with me.*

Martin: "Yes. You look beautiful when you are calm. You are pausing. Something important."

Esther: "Extremely important. More important than anything in the world. Our price for survival is terrible." Esther started to tear.

Martin started to tear. *No. I don't want this.*

Esther: "We have no sexual future, you and me. We can never be together again. We should stop this stupid simulation." The crying got worse.

Martin's crying got worse.

Esther: "If we come to the same place, all the Normso forces and energies in the world will hammer down on us. It would be the ultimate chance to strike at us and destroy or enslave the Talents for good. As long as one of us is alive, we can lead a proper counterstrike."

Martin: "Fine. Just great. All this power and I can't do the one thing I want."

Esther: "Do not all who lead people make sacrifices?"

The two cried some more.

Martin spoke first. "Do we find other lovers?"

Esther: "Yes. I think many. That is our fate. You and I will have many lovers. I can't help it. Debbie made me this way. I'm like her. She custom designed me for this purpose. To have lots of babies with lots of people, like she has. I want to get pregnant and make millions of children like me."

Martin: "Our happiness has been sacrificed before we even turn eighteen. We really just want each other and no one else. The one thing we truly want we can't have. We fill our lives with substitutes."

Esther thought of her mother Amanda. While she lost her first true love to Christ, Rachael was perhaps a better long-term partner relationship. Substitute wasn't the right word. She would stick with sacrifice. Good leaders make large self-sacrifices.

Esther: "Yes. Let us honor this moment of sacrifice. Know then, that I love you Martin, and shall never have you. Know Martin, that the price of your power is the loss of your freedom. Know then, that all the people we dedicate our lives to may never know our sacrifices. We are soldiers."

Martin: "Soldiers? Meaning we're going to become killers. I'm going to have to kill people."

Felicity: <no> "Bro, I'm not killing anyone. You're not either. I can't even stand the thought of it."

Esther: "There are so many ways we fail and die, Felicity. We have years ahead of hard decisions to make. When we reach eighteen, people will start dying. We will kill them together. We might have to kill a lot of people to survive. We will do it so other Talents will not have to."

Felicity got off the bed and started pacing. "What do we do about the news, Esther?"

Esther: "I've drafted a letter that precedes the Ether Josh and I worked on. Please read it."

[Dear Talents,

We regret to inform you that there are no other Talents alive and free outside the Warrens over the age of 15, and many between the ages of 10 and 15 are dead or missing as well.

We are currently contacting Parents to bring their Talents to the Warrens right away. Our tight space is only getting tighter. We are explaining the need for increased security for their children under 10 and are working on a long-term solution for their children's safety.

We have asked the Parents not to involve local or federal authorities and they have agreed to keep quiet. Talents own their problems and will solve them with Talent ingenuity.

Because leaving the Warrens is nearly lethal to Talents, permission to leave over the age of 13 is now subject to Cysso application.

With love, your Queen and King

Esther Stein and Martin Allerton]

#

The letter and accompanying Ether were released later that day.

Talents ran their own polls on Boardso that were consistently against this new policy. Cysso voice and video sampling convinced out-Parents their children were happy, but some Talents insisted on seeing their Parents IRL.

Esther and Josh quickly organized a special dissent Ether to air it all out in the form of a three-Talent roundtable discussion with unnamed Talents:

Talent1: "My Parents are multibillionaires. They will insist on seeing me in person."

Talent2: "Yeah, well my mother is a major political player. I don't see how anyone can stop her from visiting the Warren and demanding to see me."

Talent3: "My Parents aren't so special, but they love me. I had wonderful parents, and now I can't visit them? They always offer to take me on trips."

Talent1: "I wrote my email samples following our Cysso guidelines."

Talent2: "I created the voice samples for fake conversations following our protectors' guidelines."

Talent3: "I created messages that explained how we are solving air pollution and working on renewable energy. I explained that visiting them was not as important as this work."

Talent1: "The holograms are highly realistic and interactive. We should get Cysso to allow us to send these out."

Talent2: "They will never allow it."

Talent3: "We could stand up to them."

Talent1: "They would just tell us to hand deliver it ourselves."

Talent2: "Leave the Warren? Take an autocar to my old house?"

Talent3: "Never."

Talent1: "Why doesn't Cysso trust us to keep our secrets? I keep Circleturbo a secret."

Talent2: "My mother lies all day. She is extremely manipulative."

Talent3: "My father would insist on details of all our inventions, I could never lie to him."

Talent1: "Normsos lie and manipulate on a massive scale."

Talent2: "We cannot trust our own Parentsos."

Talent3: "We cannot trust ourselves with our own Parentsos."

Talent1: "Philosophical question."

Talent2/3: "Okay."

Talent1: "Are we in prison?"

Talent2: "Can we just walk out of here? Would the Preppers stop us at the gate?"

Talent3: "That's a good question."

Talent2: "I don't see how they could stop us. The Preppers at the gate would point a drone at us and dart us to sleep like they did my mom the other day when she got all Bullso on me? She was going on about science being a bad career choice. She wanted something Bullso like me meeting all her political friends. She went into a rant. Political science. Ugh."

Talent3: "Preppers darting us? That's hard to imagine. No. We can walk out of here any time. I'm sorry about your mom's ambitions. My parents are happy with whatever makes me happy. Which is technically nothing. I don't need anything to be happy. I just am."

Talent1: "So we are not in a prison."

Talent2: "Quite the opposite. I don't like living underground most of the day, but I don't think at all about leaving. It's just hard to imagine."

Talent3: "Outside is the prison. You notice the Parentsos living here never leave? Our Parentsos will come and live with us eventually. They will be the ones escaping prison."

CHAPTER ELEVEN
THE TONGUES OF MEN OR OF MESSENGERS

[May 2062]
Esther's Compound

LIFE WITH PROSTHETICS was never easy. Every six months Esther had to fly by private jet with Josh and a few of her Followers to Boston to see Janet and check up on her eye, her finger, her eyelid and nose, then to Chicago Science with John for her ear and earlobe.

During these plane trips she would have long conversations with Josh about religion and politics as well as medicine. Their jet was set up with seats facing each other across a small table with embedded T-pads. She couldn't take it much more. The supremo-crushso was so intense she lifted her leg under the table to penetrate Josh's skirt to touch his crotch.

"I take it your marriage is over?" Josh said coolly.

Esther's tear ran down her cheek. Josh got out a tissue from his sport coat, reached over, and wiped it with a certain magnificent tenderness.

"Let's do it on the plane. I took out my birth control last night. I want you, Josh."

"The desire to create life is strong. Life in your image. Is that right?"

The image of Josh sitting across from her was in her bio-eye and the image of Martin was in her camera-eye. She wondered if Josh was turned off by her scary bad-ass cyber-chick pirate look. She failed to stimulate him.

"I broke up with Martin in body but not in mind. We still share the same brain. He is inside my mind. We are very intimate. He's here with us now. He's looking at you with my eye and hearing you through my ear." Martin sent a short 'ping' to let her know he was listening. While someone was always listening, she wanted to know when it was Martin specifically. His image was silently laughing and [go for it babe] subtitled the image.

Her footing around his crotch was now having the desired effect and Josh was now returning the favor. They peaked quickly and Josh got up to go to the bathroom to clean his Mediumso. While he was in the bathroom, Esther poker faced waited for Martin to make some chiding joke, but nothing came.

Josh returned and sat down. "We are all waiting for Lucy's matching plan. I approve of her methodology and goals. Perhaps she will match us, but let's be patient. Anyway, I'm always going to be with you, whatever your college plans are."

"Fifteen," Esther stated and looked away.

"Yes, Talents agree that fifteen is the right age to match and start having children. It's quite an urge."

Esther now stared at Josh. He was hard to look at he was so beautiful. Calm and graceful, too. *He would be a very easy man to love beyond Crushso. Respect love and eros too. Should I take a second husband? A second pair-bond? Am I spoiled? Humbled? Used goods?*

Esther found she could only smile at his flirtation that didn't feel at all like a flirt.

"I feel like Lucy has a special plan for me. She's been talking to Debbie more frequently. How do you feel about that? What if she doesn't match us?"

While she waited for Josh's response, her mind wandered off in a sort of daydream. *I am the mediation between Talents and Normsos and Better Genetics. My mediation is between sets of humans, not God and humans like Jesus. My whole purpose is peace.*

She found herself snapping out when Josh spoke. "Are you still worried you might be a messiah or anti-Christ or ubermensch? Not meant for the life of a woman content to have children and raise a family?"

"I am Ambassador, the apostle from the Talents. Like Jesus as soft power and persuasion, backed by the hard power of the Father. Interceding to forestall God's wrath through Grace."

"How will you achieve it?" he asked.

"We teach the Normsos kindness. That Talents are the embodiment of kindness and not fear. To prove my love for Normsos, and in so doing bring peace."

Josh gave her a calm look of admiration.

"That is good news. Very good news. I will help you in these goals. Talents represent what is best in humans. They are free of sin; do you agree?"

Esther nodded in response. She felt subtly reminded she was not a Talent, that she was not free of sin. She was the inversion of sin; one who would sin so others wouldn't. Lucy couldn't tease out of Debbie precisely what she was doing in creating a second baby factory. Fine-tuning a hydroponic farm and going monogamous with Ken seemed very far away from the mass production of Talents. Debbie had told Lucy that babies are organic, not machines. Baby factories were organic, not a collection of petri dishes and robot arms. She had told Esther not to make love with Josh or anyone else but to wait until she turned 18 when the factory would be complete. That didn't stop her from imagining Josh as her husband, them making love, right now on the plane, face-to-face staring at each other.

Josh interrupted her reverie, "How are you handling your followers? Is it difficult having so many lives totally devoted to you?" Josh was speaking Tesp but not using the Tesp word for her Followers, Bifollowsos with the "both" gender affix. He used the English word, "followers," but the meaning felt like "cultists." Tesp had its limitations as a language; the various affixes lost some emotional appeal, making it almost too precise. Discos had absorbed the meaning of "cultists" as disciples. The Tesp word, *Discos*, according to Memeso, combined the religious connotation of *science*, "to bind again," with *cultus* the moral doctrine. In other words, science and religion were the same thing, the truth or reality, light overcoming darkness, never a consensus or an expert opinion. Even the words *consensus* and *expert* had been untranslated in Tesp. No one ever used these words as they were unrelated to truth. Normsos used these words whenever they wanted to pass a lie as truth. Social popularity and the bullso notion of expertise were now objects of scorn and derision.

Esther/%NA-English, "I have learned to manage my cultists. I am kind to them. Kinder than the world outside, it would seem." Esther frowned. She was bridging the desire to have disciples and the consequences of having to keep disciples. She didn't claim any special access to divinity. Her religion was "prax" not "dox," or rather the dox was Christian morals but faith in her. Her mind wandered off as she imagined all the opportunities available to her to abuse this group of people. She still was a god who did not claim to be a god or have special access to God like a prophet.

Josh touched her hand and also spoke in North American English, "Esther, I feel a darkness may have settled in you. Your face is odd when you speak this. When the darkness is overwhelming, seek me out. Can you do that?"

Esther saw the calmness again. She felt calm. She moved over to his side of the table and sat next to him. She took his hand and held hands sitting side by side the rest of the flight as they usually did. Instead of feeling horny, or triggering her autoandrophilia, sitting like this with Josh made her feel happy and normal. That the universe was at peace and not to worry or fear about anything ever again. Time passed quickly in this state and before she knew it the plane had landed. They got up from their seats and hugged tightly. *Lucy, hurry up and match me with Josh.*

#

The new camera-eye she received from the trip improved the augreal interface. She could set her eye to "detect" mode where her bio-eye looked at a person and her camera-eye brought up the augreal data side by side. While normal people could do something similar with their phones and d-pads, it was slower and clumsier. They were limited to public profiles while Esther had access to their private profiles, being absorbed and data mined by Cysso, including deleted photos. Since Cysso agents were always inside her head, she was getting used to sort of not being a person anymore. She was We, not just in the royal sense of We.

As this intimacy grew with people, she also developed a relationship with Sakura, the AI who could patch any Talent into her head on a moment's notice. She was not just a walking encyclopedia, but a million encyclopedias, with a latency of 0.1 seconds. She called this state of oneness with another Talent, Possesso. In this letting go, the Talent inside her spoke through her mouth and took over her thoughts. She also called it Radical-high-trustso.

Combined with Cysso access to cameras, listening devices, and all Talent portable electronics, she was everywhere all at once, all seeing and all knowing, with Cysso drawing her attention to anything important. Teleporting by sitting still. Teleported into and taking action. Conscious and semi-conscious telepathy.

Her glass-eye cosmetics had also improved. The battery still required four changes a day, which her Followers maintained and carried around for her. Resolution had matched her retina; there was no more pixelation. Her camera-eye had restored stereoscopic vision. A thin schiron power cord ran down the back of her Tear, connecting them both to a holster pocket containing a new schiron-based (not silicon) computer. The left holster then connected to a battery on her right side, enough power for a whole day. The holsters were hidden by her sport coat and the cords by her hair. The "glasses" portion of the camera-eye now sported infrared and ultraviolet sensors which the computer translated into life-based heat signatures and good night vision. Additional lenses were added for telescopic and microscopic vision. An eyeglass frame–mounted flashlight was added as well. Martin was proud that Esther now sported cybernetic superpowers.

She could also "plug in" with what Martin called her "power-eye," where she lay in a chair directly connected to the Intalent. Splitting her consciousness by becoming immobile, she found she could "learn" at twice the rate as being out and about. Her chair as additional interface allowed her to absorb vaster amounts of information and speeded up the creation of Ethers, VR training modules, and holographic teaching systems, as her brain started multitasking two thinking intelligences, her dual consciousness divided into her male half and her female half. Her left brain and right brain worked independently in this state. Humans can live with half a brain. Esther lived with two half brains in this mode.

This level of brain/computer/Cysso intimacy was made possible by neuroplasticity. The switching between the three eye systems caused headaches and nausea at first, but they eventually went away. She never seemed to have painful flashbacks to the church gunfight but thought of cheerful Elsa every day when she put on her necklace with the eight-pointed star of Ishtar.

Talents had also created a visual language "ghosting" system that worked for the camera-eye. With a click of her finger, her computer would read/interpret foreign language script and make it appear in Tesp in her vision. The system converted right to left and bottom to top scripts for her as well. She didn't "see" the IRL writing.

Talent audio language translators now worked in a similar way. Her right ear would hear whatever language the person was speaking, and the left ear would about half a second later speak the Tesp translation, useful if a Talent wasn't on hand to translate for her. If she went into Possesso, the translation would lag only 0.1 seconds. The system was awkward at first, hearing someone speaking to you in two languages at roughly the same time. With practice, the experience stopped being crazy.

In between practice sessions using technology to become the "ultimate ambassador," Esther and Martin would discuss their long-term goals. Talents were building advanced drone systems as their "military hardware" solution to the problem of violence. These were being tested now in all Warrens with Parentso Bullso problems.

Esther typically started the conversation relaxed in power mode, VR setting in the Hellscape. "Why do we want to rule the world? Why? Don't say it's because we can." *Martin is struggling with the violence problem. He, like all Talents, is disgusted at the thought of killing people. He also understands power as violence.*

"I want to rule the world. How else can we finish Better Genetics' plan? They don't trust the world, which is why they don't share their technology. They will trust me."

As she approached her 18th birthday, Esther and her team finished their veterinarian education and completed an effective treatment for horse, cat, and dog Alzheimer's disease using animal IVF and embryonic stem cells. Led by her sister Rache, Team Pet Health was given collective credit, and a special Ether detailed the process. The genius breakthroughs were dispersed among participating Talents around the world. The failed ideas and experiments were heralded as successes because science was incessant failure which bordered the path to success.

Late in the process Rachael had organized members from the Kentucky licensing board to watch over the experiments at the Estate and satisfied them about an effective cure. They organized a panel for her final examination, which was on a Monday night. Esther was brought there in an SUV with four armed Followers, the same way she usually traveled outside the Compound. A second SUV with more four more Followers followed her vehicle and contained the latest drone defense technology, which was supposed to be able to wipe out a small army in just a few seconds. Cysso had been practicing piloting and attacking on dummies somewhere in the Compound. She hadn't followed up on how all that worked. She would just trust Martin and his team skills.

As usual, outside the Compound she wore her glass-eye for her meeting held at the Board's offices in Frankfort, Kentucky. The hearing room was large, with five judges/panelists sitting behind a long table with d-pads on it, all facing her sitting on a solitary chair. Four Followers waited outside the room, ready to come in guns blazing at her signal. Esther hovered the cursor over the emergency button on her screen.

Boardmember1 spoke first, "All your exams were perfect. That doesn't really happen here. How do you explain this?" Esther was sporting violet today. She would not hide her identity anymore outside the Compound. In a group of five examiners, it was likely there was one defector. Martin suspected a trap, but Esther resolved to be brave.

"You can reexamine me here if you think I cheated somehow. Ask me anything."

Over the next 15 minutes they asked her the hardest questions they could think of. She got them all correct, of course. Rache, Josh, and Sakura were all inside her. If she appeared to be a "know it all," she was a de facto "know it all."

Boardmember1 said, "Surely you took shortcuts with your parents."

"Yes, well, supervision with my *mothers* was part of the deal. We worked all the necessary hours together on a real working farm. Rachael and Amanda made sure we followed all the ethics and other proprieties. We did everything by the book."

Boardmember2 spoke next, "Why a cure for pets' Alzheimer's? No one was looking for a cure. Why extend the life of a dying animal?"

"It was never for the money. I wanted to learn how brains and stem cells and immune systems worked. I enjoy learning. My friends had the original idea to cure their dying house pets. They did much of the groundwork regarding the genetic engineering and stem cell work. This was just applied science adapted to pet brains. Our long-term goal is to bring a cure to humans."

Boardmember3 spoke next, "Animals are not humans. They have very different biologies. There is no way of knowing if your work on animals will even help with humans."

"I would argue the opposite. Our brains are more alike than we believe. Pets have memories, too. They are different though. Perhaps our research will not help humans with Alzheimer's. It has helped pets. I've done something good with my life. Isn't that what we're put here for? Talents are here to solve complex problems for the good of everyone."

The male board members had given up looking at her. She saw that look of intense crushso and some of the women were struggling too. *They desperately want to be me if they are not physically attracted to me.*

Boardmember4 spoke next, "Yes, I agree, this was not a waste of time. We welcome your contribution to science and believe your love of animals is sincere."

Boardmember1 said, "We are giving you a provisional license contingent on you earning an undergraduate degree. You will get most but not all the privileges and responsibilities of being a licensed veterinarian. We still need to understand why you worked so hard to get this license."

"I don't want people to fear Talents. We are bringing good things to the world. Everyone, not just Talents, benefits from our activities."

Boardmember2 stated, "Now that we see you face-to-face, I can say for sure you are very wrong, Esther. You got all the test questions correct, but this question you are wrong about."

What? No. A mistake. I cannot make mistakes, this cannot backfire. Esther managed a poker face while feeling the beginnings of anger and frustration.

Boardmember2 saddened. "I think I speak for everyone else in this room when I say we love *and fear* you, Esther. You command incredible intellectual power for a teenager. Perhaps you see us normal people as animals. Understand we give this to you out of love and fear. Thank you for helping the animals that we all love here. You are kind, we all know that. You have your mothers in you. Rachael and Amanda are known to be kind. Such power, though, is to be feared as well. A license is always an honor as well as a responsibility. Think well of us normal people, Esther. Many of us are kind, too."

Boardmember3 said, "Yes, we love you, Esther." *It seems knowledge of this custom has gotten out.*

Collected board members, "We love you, Esther."

"I know that you love me. Thank you for this honor. I will be responsible. I will be kind."

Boardmember1 then handed Esther a framed certificate to take home with her, shaking hands and taking photos. She left the building as twilight had set in outside.

For the car ride home, Esther decided to engage her four Followers, two guys and two girls, all carrying shoulder-holstered handguns, the four most devoted at the Compound (according to Martin). Esther sat in the back seat with a guy on her left side and Sally on her right. A guy was driving, and another girl was in the passenger seat. Esther had failed tonight, and she needed to take stock of what happened.

"We all need to have a serious conversation."

The driver said, "Okay. We love to talk with you, don't we all?"

The other three people chimed, "Yes, of course."

The girl in the passenger seat spoke next, "You seem troubled, Esther. We are not your friends. You have over a hundred thousand brilliant people inside your head. I'm not sure how we can help better than other Talents."

Yes, brilliant but not Normso. Normsos are inconceivable to the older Talents who constantly wonder how Normsos get up in the morning with all their various depressions. Integration still seems impossible.

"I want to use a system called 180-degree review. This is when a boss or manager asks her employees to give the boss feedback. I would like to do one now. I need your honesty. It's very important you are honest with me." *You have to remind Normsos to be honest.*

The group all said, "Yes, of course." "We're happy to help." "Yes." "Sure." "Anything you ask."

"You've all known me a long time. Since I was a little girl in kindergarten, some of you here. You know what kind of person I am. You spend a lot of time watching me, too. After all this experience with me, are you all afraid of me still?"

The girl in the passenger seat spoke, "Yes, Esther. We talk about this, you know, when we're just with each other and not with you. All of your Followers are afraid of you. We love you. You won't let us worship you, but we love you and are afraid of you. The emotions are both very powerful and real. We are feeling them intensely right now."

"How so? Give me an example of how you fear me."

The guy sitting next to her said in abject fear, "Well, for example. I'm strictly saying out loud FOR EXAMPLE. For example. I'm just saying this. I'm not doing anything. Okay! IF. I mean, just if. IF, I took out my gun and just aimed it at you. Just barely. Just HYPOTHETICALLY speaking. I fully expect to die. I am sure the car would swerve out of control, crash. We'd all die except you. The bullet would ricochet into my brain and everyone else's for that matter."

The guy was visibly shaking when he said these words and was now thanking Martin he wasn't dead from blaspheming.

"That bad? Really? I still don't understand."

"Yes. Oh yes. Definitely. It happened before," intoned the group.

"What? When?"

Passenger girl said, "Oh, it was at the Compound, one of the guys was cleaning his gun. It sort of pointed in your sort of direction and the shock from his collar stunned him. We are sure Martin could have just killed him. No one wants to hurt you. Just that mistakes are made, and we suffer."

Martin: "Happened a month ago. Do you want to know about these things? Didn't think it was a good idea to make you worry."

"Oh. I didn't know that."

Passenger girl continued, "Yeah, we figure it's your guy friend, the Talent who came from California to visit you in the hospital, Martin. Who else could it be? That guy was in love with you. Um, more so than everyone else."

Sally sitting next to her said, "Yeah, not the other Talent at the hospital. Too nice to zap people. He loves you too. I catch him looking at you when you're not aware. You two should definitely get it together..."

The driver interrupted, "Yeah, it's the California guy. Good-looking dude. He had his eyes on you like a hawk the whole visit, usually standing on your blind side. It's nice to see other Talents love you too. What a nice life you have, Esther, being loved by everybody."

"You have good friends, Esther. We wonder why you don't hang out with Talents more. Invite them to your room. We don't make very good friends or lovers for you. We thank you for trying," said Passenger girl.

Sally added, "Yeah, you have cameras all over the Compound and in this car. We discussed whether we live in a police state and are slaves. It somehow doesn't feel that way. Everything is worse on the outside. Maybe that's why. Slavery with kind masters is preferrable to slavery with evil masters. Is this the kind of 180 feedback you want?"

"Yes, get everything out in the open. I need to know what went wrong at that meeting. I feel like an attack is coming. Are we ready for an attack?"

Sally answered, "We are ready. Anyone who tries to hurt you is in a world of hurt." Her other Followers signaled agreement. Sally had the look of fear. Martin told her she was the last to kill a farm animal for practice. She had sat in a tree with a rifle, ready to shoot the cow in the back of the head and hesitated for 10 seconds before firing. She missed and the cow managed to break free. They made her catch the cow and do the whole slaughtering, bleeding, and butchering with only a supervisor to guide her.

Passenger girl (Esther now remembered her name as Nancy) said,

"We're ready to kill, Esther. Don't you worry about that. No hesitation. Right, Sally?"

"Right," agreed Sally. "No hesitation this time. Humans who try to kill you should be put down like animals. Right, Peter?"

"Yeah. Except we have better weapons than guns."

"We even have guys dressed like you put in cars ahead of you and behind you. Like, you know, what the President does. A motorcade," added Sally.

Esther had known about the car following them with the drones, but not a car ahead of her.

Her Cysso agent inside her/Sakura: "Esther, we don't tell you everything. You know what to do in the case of an attack."

Nothing. Self-defense was not her problem. When soft power came to hard power, her role ended and Cysso took over. She would go into full Possesso.

"Thank you for that. Have there been any attempts I don't know about?"

The guy next to her said, "Yeah sort of. Just losers popping up. They come in a van and park outside the Compound somewhere. We just surround the van with guns and rifles and tell them to scram. Usually, we put a few bullets in the car or smash baseball bats all over it. Schiron hits hard. The bullets go all the way through. They are supposed to be uranium tipped, although there's no U in schiron."

"How often does this happen?" [Martin?] She selected the icon that summoned Martin and indicated a private conversation.

Sally said, "Once a month, now. It was less frequent earlier, but it has been picking up. Doesn't your bae tell you anything? I guess not. You're laughing?"

Esther had entered multitasking mode where she carried on two conversations at the same time.

[Esther: What have you been doing Bigwig?]

[Martin: I didn't want you to worry, Frisby. I have beaten your "rat vision" with "fly vision."]

[Esther: Very funny, Bigwig. Tell me about these events in the future.]

"Oh, I wasn't laughing at you."

Nancy, looking back at Esther, said, "Yeah, she's doing it again."

"Doing what?"

"When you go into your dual mode, we call it, you usually have the facial expressions of your online activity and not your IRL situation."

"Oh. I hadn't thought of that. Is this often?"

"Yeah, all the time. We're used to it. In fact, we're happy about it," said Nancy.

Peter added, "Yeah, not once have you ever said to us, 'stop interrupting me' or 'you ruined my concentration.' It's a pretty cool ability, I say. I wish I were as smart as you. I think it would be fun."

"Yes, well, the conversation interface is slow. I've managed three conversations at the same time. But the facial expressions are the online ones. That's a problem. You see why 180 degrees is useful, yes? Something more to work on. My facial expressions should always match my IRL interface."

The guy next to her (Andrew, she now remembered) asked, "Want us to tell you when you are off?"

"Of course. So I failed tonight. I got my license, but I failed to stop the fear."

Andrew assured, "It's basically impossible, Esther. If people don't love/fear you, they hate you. We talk to lots of normal people. It's one or the other. Lots of people think you should die. Some of us go to bars and strike up conversations about Talents. I would say most people are optimistic about Talents, but a great number of them fear or hate you."

"Doesn't my kindness defeat the envy?"

Sally answered, "I think people appreciate what you do. Your Followers act as model citizens. You release exciting and effective teaching technology to our old school. Maybe it just pushes some people from the bad camp to the good camp, so to speak. You okay?"

How can I be so stupid? What was I thinking?

Esther frowned. She was losing control again. Her mind was feeling the beginning of another glitch-out. She had enjoyed her delusion for too long, playing with her prosthetic abilities and working on medical research and solidifying her cult that is not a cult but is a cult. Her glitch-out was that she had a cult and part of her wouldn't admit it. *I have to admit I've started a cult. Get over yourself, Esther. People start new religions all the time in the United States; you are just better at it.*

"Talents work on problems in very large complex teams. I have to figure out solutions by trial and error, one at a time. I must find a way to stop the fear."

Nancy said, "Good luck with that. I think it's impossible." Her facial expression was halfway between fear and a giggle. Then she giggled slightly. The rest of her bodyguard emitted semi-laughs. Esther encouraged people to have a sense of humor. She wanted to laugh herself, but this was a serious conversation. She was making progress.

"Why is that? What is it you experience? You cannot fight the fear around me?"

Nancy said, "None of your Followers have been able to defeat it. Believe me, we've tried. We have some theories."

Martin: [Besides the drone patrols and the collars.]

Esther: [That is fear of you, not me. They know the difference.]

"Okay, tell me one." *My mind is hurting. It's happening again. Something horrible is about to happen.*

Peter said, "Well, you know, my mother used to say there's always somebody smarter than you, richer than you, better dressed than you, better looking than you, and so on."

I am smarter, richer, and better dressed than everyone. I have a perfect body and a beautiful face.

"I am terrible at poetry. My piano and karate were only ever good, not great. I'm a pretty good shot, but not great at that either," Esther dissembled. Talent vision, hand-eye coordination, and lightning reflexes made them all gifted athletes and musicians. Even Talent singing was perfect. It was just more genetic programming coming to life years past the sale. They just couldn't compare their abilities properly to Normsos until adolescents reached 18. Before then, they were just "promising." Instead of "promising," they were turning out all completely perfect. A Talent was "better" than another Talent at something only because he or she spent more time on whatever the activity.

Sally said, "Esther, we look at you and see how horribly imperfect we are. You look at us and see how horribly flawed we are. Don't deny this fact."

"I do no such thing. You are all human beings and worthy of dignity.

I treat animals with dignity." *The glitching is getting worse.* A full head-ache was starting.

Andrew said, "Then you must hide it better, Esther. It shows. It's show-ing now."

"Point taken. Thank you. What else is on your minds?" Esther tried unsuccessfully to recreate a poker face. She tried denying how unattractive her bodyguards were. She studied Sally's face. While normal Normsos would find her very fit and good looking, she just wasn't perfectly good looking like a normal Talentso. Esther managed a slight feeling of Crushso. More pragma, respect love. She felt respect for all her bodyguards. Sally looked at her directly.

"We have a moral question for you," stated Sally.

"Moral? I thought I made it clear that we would all be clean, physi-cally, sexually, and morally. I understand everyone is doing a great job. You are all training extremely well. You are all physically and mentally fit and well trained and devoted to me. You practice kindness consistently with each other and people outside of the Compound. I am excited for you all. What's the matter?" Esther thought her headache and imposing sense of doom had made her irritable.

Sally said, "Esther. I will try to be humble before you, but I think you are missing something very important. Or that's how it seems to us all."

I can't see what's glitching, but my Followers see it as plain as day. Something horrible is about to happen. I know one of those examiners be-trayed me. Which one?

"I think everything through, very carefully. Okay, what do you think I'm missing?"

"I'm sorry if I get this wrong, but you said this is a 180-degree review and you want us to be honest…"

Esther was snapping. She decided that was the nature of mental ill-ness for a genius. The pain in her head needed a creative outlet, she just didn't want to see that outlet. She knew the outcome but not the process, because that creativity needed to be left alone, undiscovered; it was not a good thing to know. That creativity was an empty space, meant to be kept dark, for it was dark. The pain increased, the mental illness was fill-ing her soul, and the darkness returned to fill her senses.

Esther said too loudly, "Enough of this, get to the point. Making the point will not make me angry. Speak your mind. You have been instructed to be transparent."

Esther felt the man on her right physically shivering. "Okay. Here goes. Remember that all your Followers are in agreement on this."

"All of you?" Esther felt her first tear, created from pain and the anticipation of extreme sadness.

Martin: [They should tell you this, not me.]

"Yes, all of us," said the group.

"You have group votes about me?"

Martin: [Yes, they do. Sorry. I didn't want to tell you; you need to hear it from them.]

Esther: [Martin, you can't do this to me. I am in a car. I should do this at the Compound.]

Martin: [Okay.]

Peter said, "This one has been percolating and festering for some time, and we're all in agreement you don't want to hear it. So, we've reached a tipping point with your 180-degree review."

"Okay, fine. Go ahead. I promise not to be upset with your honesty." *I am demonstrably upset with their honesty. No, I'm upset with myself for not seeing it.*

Andrew said, "We have what we call a 'defensive posture.' We think all day of ways that the bad guys are going to try to come and get you. It's not a good strategy. You can't win a soccer game this way. Maybe you get a score of zero–zero, but you never win. We want to win. All of us want to win this contest you are in, Esther. We want you to rule the world someday, but we won't win if the bad guys throw a big missile at your house someday."

No.

Nancy looked back at her. "Esther? Esther, you're crying."

No.

Peter said, "Didn't expect that reaction. Just wait until she is ready to talk again. Esther is kind, she just doesn't think this way. We have to take the battle to the enemy, whoever or whatever that is."

About a minute passed. She looked outside and figured they were about 10 minutes away from the Compound. Her glass-eye screen confirmed this estimate. Peter's announcement had relaxed her. The evil betrayal was coming any minute now, but Esther felt relaxed at the challenge of finding her enemy and destroying it. She thought of it almost as a game. *Yes, it is a game. Life and death, so not a game. Just* like *a game.*

"Yes, you are correct. We need to go on offense. Of course, we do. You are all willing to go on offense? The bad guys play to kill. You understand that it's a deathmatch?"

The group chimed, "Yes, we understand. We are all prepared to kill and die for you, Beloved."

Nancy continued on, "We need to take the battle to the enemy hide outs, find a way to identify them—"

Peter yelled, "Oh shit! Scramble alert!"

Esther saw and felt two big vans crash into the car from either side. She ducked onto the floor, crouching as best as she could in the space between the front seats and back seats. She heard a big shootout outside the cars, dozens of bangs and the sounds of ricochets. Sally covered her body, and she felt Andrew covering hers as she scrunched down as far as she could go, almost lying down in the small space. She heard a mix of handguns, rifles, and even the strange whir of drones. In a short time, the gunshots died down. It was strange there was no shouting. She assumed big gunfights involved people shouting.

Martin: "Drive out of here."

"Drive out of here!"

The aftermarket structural supports for the car frame had worked. Peter drove the SUV away from the scene. Cysso had prompted her to watch a video of the attack from the camera on the car behind theirs, while she lay down on the floor with Sally still hugging her body.

A minute later, Sally got off her body and examined her, tears streaming, "Beloved! Are you okay? Are you hurt?!"

"I'm fine, Sally. Are you okay?"

"Esther, the fight is over. No one is pursuing us," she answered.

"It worked. Beloved, the plan worked!" said Peter.

Esther: [Martin, explain the video.]

Martin: "Yes, Esther. The drones flew out of your trunk and from the other car on the words "scramble alert" and autotargeted and killed the attackers using infrared heat signatures. The drones shot off a bunch of carfentanyl gas grenades that released on impact. I managed to shoot them through open van doors as gunmen exited, so I got all the drivers. Congratulations, you got what you wanted. I'm now a mass killer. Thank you for that. I don't have to ask if you are all right. The cameras tell me everything. None of your Followers were hurt."

Esther's body was still in adrenaline overdose, but remarkably sound now that the glitching headache had fled. She tried to remember what had happened. The headache stopped when she realized that defense and mere survival was not good enough. The darkness stopped after her car left the battle. The evil had ended.

Esther: [Thank you Martin.] She switched Martin's audio to text translation.

Martin: [I've sent another car to the scene. Someone wearing protective clothing is going to place about $100,000 of carfentanyl in a stash in one of the vans. Then he will shoot out the brain stem of each attacker. It will make it look like a gang assassination. No one will ask too many questions that way. Look, it's not a clean and perfect solution, but I doubt anyone is going to pry. The neighbor's electronics were all disabled. I doubt they will testify anything useful.]

Esther: [Thank you, Martin.]

Martin: [I've been working behind your back with your Followers using your voice samples on their phones. We ran through and practiced this scenario several times. We even organized the aftermarket upgrades, so your car would survive a major crash and gun assault. We've integrated schiron, tough and hard as diamond coated steel.]

Esther: [Thank you, Martin.]

Esther: [I love you, Martin.]

Martin: "I love you, Esther." She switched the screen to full audio/video conference call and watched him working in silence.

A minute passed as her car neared the Compound.

Martin: "Esther I feel sick. I killed people. I killed them. They were trying to kill you. I didn't just kill them. I dispatched them. They were gassed like flies from autotargeting AI. It was like killing insects with bug spray. They never had the slightest chance of hurting you."

Esther: [I know.]

Martin: "You said we wouldn't start killing people until we were eighteen."

Esther: [I know.]

Martin: "I don't want to kill people."

Esther: [I know.]

Martin: "I really don't want to kill people. Can your Followers do all the killing from now on?"

Esther: [Yes. It is affecting me too.] She saw Martin throw up.

Martin: [I just threw up.]

Esther: [I am trying my best to hold it in.]

Sally noticed Esther's sufferings and pulled out a bag for her to vomit in.

Esther: [Okay. We've killed our first people. It just gets worse from here.]

Esther's tears started again. *We need an offense. Against what?*

Martin: [Cysso is working on a full analysis. I'm going to bed. We'll address everything in the morning.]

Esther: [Good night.]

CHAPTER TWELVE
COLLEGE PREP

[The day after the assassination attempt]
The Compound

ESTHER ASSEMBLED ALL her Followers the following morning at the Compound "church." Her attempts to keep it named the "assembly place" had failed. The dome-shaped building was now covered with a schiron outer layer so that it shone bright and glistening at daybreak. Her breath stopped for a second, it was so beautiful. All the new buildings would have the diamond glisten. The church was just the first.

She stood waiting in the central dais as people arrived. Cysso patched her ear to the seated Follower conversations in the dome.

Comments while they assembled went like: "That was great last night." "We did it!" "Congratulations!"

While she waited and watched and listened in, she noticed a switch in her consciousness. She'd had trouble sleeping the previous night, watching the video over and over. She had let it set in how hopeless the attack on her was. They had all that firepower with no effect. Cysso would dig up names and attempt to analyze the motivation. The board member who betrayed her had hung herself last night, the news hitting the Internet by daybreak. Her death was passed off as yet another middle-aged veterinarian suicide by a woman who had no children. Martin was glad it hadn't been linked to the attempt on Esther's life.

Esther: [I never sleep, do I? Not really, with so many people inside my head.] She played with the camera and audio options Cysso set up in her head display. She found herself playing with the telescope lens on her camera-eye. Cysso coordinated the phone she was eavesdropping on with an autoselect zoom function. She was trying to do this with her bio-eye open instead of closed, like one normally did with operating a telescope. She wanted proper rat vision. She joy-sticked the camera-eye around while keeping her bio-eye steady. *Good, no sickness.*

The camera-eye announced 100% attendance.

"Let's begin." Her artificial ear caught her voice and transmitted through the church sound system or through connected ear buds or text translations on Follower phones or text on the large video screens above her that circled the border of the dais. Text on the screens overlayed the video on the screens.

"Let me remind everyone to stay low for a while. Nobody goes out."

Her Followers murmured, "Yes. Of course."

Peter stood up and asked, "Does this mean we finally take the fight to the enemy?!" He pumped his fist to the air.

Her Followers started a group cheer, "Yes!" "Let's do this." "Fight, fight, fight." They foot stomped and clapped with a couple of fists in the air in imitation of "We Will Rock You" by Queen in honor of their killer queen.

"Not yet. But soon. For now, we stay low until this blows over. We need more recruits. We need a larger army."

"Fight, fight, fight. We are the champions," cheered her Followers.

Esther: [Do we put the drones in their hands or keep it to you and Cysso?]

Martin: [That's your department.]

"Kindness. Temperance. Fortitude. Prudence and Sacrifice."

When Esther called out the Follower virtues, the response was, "Beloved. Beloved."

"Stay vigilant. Be outstanding. I will handle the police." She gave her hand signal for them to return to work, and they quickly and quietly left the church.

Martin: [Your new robot mouse is ready at the 3D printer.]

Esther: [Good. I think we're ready to convert the local police force.] Her Followers were now gone except her four-person security detail.

Martin had organized her security into three groups of four people, two guys and two girls. They rotated eight-hour shifts with her, roughly eight hours of training, education, and personal details, and eight hours of sleep. Her detail from the night before had slept and were with her now. They had expressed that morning that the 180 had been interrupted. Sally approached her.

"Beloved, you're getting better already. We know you were communicating with California during church, um, I mean assembly. Your face didn't show it. Um, just so you know. 180-degrees and all that…"

Esther recognized that Sally was holding something back through her glances and posture. "You shouldn't beat around the bush with me, Sally. Just spill it out."

"Don't be hard on him. We can tell it's him and not you. He has your voice, but he talks like a guy geek and his humor is off. It's okay. We humor him. It's nice to know Talents have a sense of humor. It doesn't take a rocket scientist to know a rocket scientist."

"How do you like that, Martin? You're a rocket scientist."

Sally giggled.

\#

About a week later Esther received a call from police detective Jack to meet him at the police station. Martin was eager to test offensive Talent technology and augment Esther's ability to convert the unwilling to the willing.

While her Followers waited outside in the car, she walked into the station with her dad, Ken (Esther was just shy of 18), who was briefed on the plan. As usual, he was instructed to stay silent. *With a kiss, such a lovely father I have.*

Detective Jack met with her again, along with the same female deputy, Alice, from the prior visit at her Compound. They brought her to a private questioning room, and the four of them sat across from each other over a simple metal table bolted to the floor. There was a device for restraining hands on the table, but it was not in use. *It would be no use.*

"Esther, thank you for coming down here. Ken, thank you for keeping your survivalist friends from causing any trouble." The detective was trying for self-control but was visibly nervous. The deputy didn't even attempt to hide her fear and awe and silently mouthed out of Jack's sight [I love you, take me in.] Jack fumbled to say words and kept staring at her and catching himself. *His brain is filling with limerence endorphins just like everyone else. Adrenaline too. I will capture this man's soul. His life for mine.*

"No problem, sir. Glad I can help with anything you need." She said this sincerely.

"Jack, call me Jack. You remember me after the church incident, yes? Have you heard about the recent gun violence not far from your, uh, your settlement, your uh, colony? Ten men were killed. All shot right in the back of the head. A hundred thousand dollars of high-quality drugs were found at the scene. Do you know anything about this?" Jack was visibly sweating through his armpits. *You are about to die Jack. Shall I bring you back to life is the question. You must believe in me first.*

Esther decided she would be flat for this conversation. Her voice was even. Maybe a small hint of menace for spice.

"Just what I saw in the news, Jack."

Esther now became very cold, the usual kindness in her expression vanished. She no longer felt like a child. She did not pout like a spoiled brat. Her intent was to kill this man unless he begged for life. Her innate happiness conflicted with her need to be a coldhearted killer.

Martin: [Mrs. Frisby is in position. Monitoring situation.]

Jack failed to hide his look of dismay, saying, "You see, I have two problems. One is that none of the dead men have been involved in drugs before. I knew one of them, too. I know there is a lot of drugs going around, epidemic levels, but the chances of ten men with no prior involvement being caught up in a drug shootout… well it doesn't really hold water."

"I wouldn't know, Jack."

Jack didn't hesitate to add, "The other problem is that there were broken car parts found from a third vehicle. The evidence is that the two cars we found there crashed into a third car, which took off. The pieces are from the same kind of car that you are known to be driven around in. I see your car outside is not damaged, but we did some searching, and it turns out that two of your followers own cars of this type. Where did they get the money for cars like these?"

Martin: [We need to make 100% schiron cars it seems.]

"Followers? I'm not sure what you mean? My father employs a lot of people on his property. He's a successful businessman. I also have a lot of friends. I'm very popular. The car they drive me in is very common. I don't see the problem."

"The make and model are common, yes. But there were loads of bullets found at the scene. Forensics says they hit bulletproof glass. Not many people drive around cars with bulletproof glass. In fact, we contacted companies that provide this service. Two of your followers have gotten the aftermarket windows."

"Meaning?"

"Esther, you can't play dumb with me. For God's sake, everyone knows you are the opposite of dumb. Why would ten men... I have six coming out of the cars with handguns and two men sniping with rifles, and two drivers. I have no witnesses willing to say anything and no camera or phone recordings. It reminds me of the blasted church burning down two years ago. Did more men try to kill you? Forensics says they also died of asphyxiation symptomatic with fentanyl overdose. You stopped their breathing with drugs and then stopped their breathing again with bullets? Explain it to me. I want to know why my friend died."

"Hmm. Well, I'm not a detective, but I read a lot of mystery novels when I was a little girl. I'm going to guess that the third car was driven by drug dealers who bought bulletproof glass. The men who died were vigilante cops sick of police failures to stop the illegal drug trade, taking the law into their own hands. The crooks they were dealing with were excellent shots. They scared the neighbors into being quiet."

"Nice. Or there's a second option. More of these Talent-haters decided to try to kill you, and you and your followers and whatever Talent technology that has been cooked up, got the better of them. Esther, why don't you want police help? Did anyone threaten you? Maybe we can catch these groups before they try to attack you. Last time we talked, you mentioned the possibility of violent Talent-haters and I ignored you. I feel sorry about that now. I couldn't imagine it would come to something like this." Jack showed genuine concern on his face, but Esther didn't buy it for a Planck time unit.

"Honestly, I think my interpretation is the better one for everyone involved."

Her voice was dead cold and serious. Jack seriously tried not to be nervous. The deputy stared at her without flinching, gazing in pure worship. Then she closed her eyes like a religious devotee waiting for a sign from God.

"I'd hate to play poker with you. I like you, Esther. I had thought you had a great future ahead for you, but ten men dead? I can't let that go. You and your Talents and followers can't go taking the law into your own hands. We don't want cults in our town. Your *friends'* parents never complain. They say that you are the best thing that ever happened to their children. You have that going for you. But now you've involved them in mass murder. I thought Talents were not capable of violence. That's what we were all told. Just another marketing lie, it seems."

"I assure you that Talents abhor violence more than anyone you've ever known. I believe that Better Genetics said that Talents don't enjoy or look for violence. They said that Talents could defend themselves in case they were threatened, much like when normal people are drafted to fight a war. I think we abhor violence as much as your average World War Two soldier in this case."

"So, it's self-defense? Is that your plea?"

"I don't plea anything. My option. Option one is the best interpretation of the facts for everyone involved. That is a simple fact."

"I have enough to arrest you for manslaughter. Is there anything else you wish to say in your defense?"

Esther: [On rats.]

Martin: [Read you, on rats.]

"Deputy? Please listen carefully, both of you. I understand the ethical challenge you face. You have ten dead men and one of them is your friend. I get it. You want justice. That's your job. Tell me then about a higher justice. A justice beyond the law, beyond any law. A natural justice.

A hypothetical person is being attacked regularly by random people. Lots of people want him dead. Now the US President has a secret service to protect him. Let's say this person is a minor, instead."

"Do we have to listen to this?"

"Does this minor ask the local police to protect him day and night? Maybe a policeman gets killed time to time in the crossfire. Or does this minor spare the police all this trouble? What do the police prefer?"

"The rule of law. That is my oath."

"And what about the higher law? The law of survival? Does a person not have the right to live?"

"The higher law is the rule of law. Now will you surrender quietly?"

Jack said this with fear, and Esther found herself almost enjoying it. Marcy had told her that power was a thrill. The coldness she felt before changed to delight, more satisfaction than joy.

Esther: [Rats.]

"Ouch! Jesus, what was that on my leg?"

"You have a little time to reconsider. Which is the higher law? The right to live or the rule of law?"

"I can't breathe. Was that fentanyl? I'm going to pass out. Jesus, I see dead people every day who died from this—*gasp*—"

"Five, four, three, two…"

"Natural law! Damn you. Option one," he managed his last dying breaths.

"One."

Jack passed out; Ken quickly got up to hold Jack so he could gently fall to the floor. Deputy Alice got out of her seat and prostrated herself in front of Esther. "Whatever you want, Esther. I'm yours to command. I love you. My life for yours."

Esther: [What do you think? Thumbs up or down?]

Martin: "Better up. What's my body count in this movie going to be, Esther? Well, we've done a successful field test of a robot mouse attack as well as a drone attack. I'll administer the naloxone."

Alice looked up and said, "Jesus, did you just kill him? You just stared at him, and he started dying. Like Darth Vader death vibe style."

"No. I've done nothing of the sort. Do I look like a killer?"

"No. Um. Are you going to kill me too?" Her face went back to the floor and Esther could see tears drop. Her satisfaction grew; a person in authority was loving and fearing her to an extent most people could barely imagine, let alone expect to experience. She gripped her star to the point of pain to fight the god complex. *Is this what it's like to be God, feared and loved?*

"Do you think I am kind?" Esther smiled her warmest and kindest, perhaps a little mad.

"I love you Esther, please," Alice begged, with the added touch of a full prostrated sajdah bow—knees bent and forehead on the floor. Esther recognized that Alice was Muslim. Now former Muslim. Apostate Muslim.

Am I dajjal or Mahdi? No. Beloved. Never any other name.

"I know that you love me. You can join me. Serve me completely. Call me Beloved from now on."

"Yes, Beloved." The deputy lost all her tension at the offer. Then she looked up and beamed at her, pure devotion.

"I'm recruiting. I need some of my friends to join the police. You shall work for me and train my dad's ex-employees in police work."

"Yes, Beloved."

"Help me collect all his evidence and destroy all records that I ever came here. There will be no justice for these men. There is no justice for murderers."

"He'll live? I like Jack. He's a good man. I promise." She looked sadly at her boss.

"Yes. For your sake, deputy. He'll live."

Jack started recovering but was still slumped on the ground. His face was grim.

"Option one. Option one," Jack groaned.

Esther smiled at him.

"I'm taking your deputy with me as part of the price of defying me. If you get any more intel from your friends about attempts to murder or kidnap me, send it to your deputy. You understand this is a war?"

"Yes." Jack was still recovering from his near-death experience. He moved his arms and legs into a fetal position, lying on his side.

"We are not a cult. We are not drug dealers."

Esther waited. *He knows the words.*

Jack unslumped and sat on the floor Indian style thinking for about a minute, clearly searching for meaning in his resurrected life while staring hard at her. He started and stopped a few times until he finally said, "I love you, Esther."

Jack tried unsuccessfully to smile, but the tone was sincere.

"I know that you love me." *Good, a police detective can be useful.*

#

[February 1, 2063. Esther's 18th birthday]

She woke up the next day feeling good about what she did to Jack and Alice. She came down to breakfast to find Ken and Debbie dressed and drinking coffee. Sally immediately got up to make her a hot meal. Debbie got up to give her a big hug and then handed her a fancy wrapped package with her familiar DR label.

"Open it now," she said with typical Debbie glee. "Lots of presents today!" She sat back down, and Sally placed her coffee at her usual morning breakfast stool.

While Esther sat down and began opening the package, Debbie announced, "I have more presents for you this afternoon. You're going to love them."

"The second baby factory is done? I saw the sign you put on your hydroponic farm. New Eden? Really, Debbie. I mean it's a fresh garden and nice and all that..."

She trailed off when she finally pulled out the necklace. She let it dangle from her hand.

Then she took off her old necklace and put on the new one. She fingered the ruby and stared at Debbie. The feeling was unreality. She thought she might have accidentally hypnotized herself, but Debbie just sat there smiling with glee. Esther now stared at the ruby as she fingered it. She recognized it.

After mind wandering marveling she uttered without thinking, "The star of Gyges? Am I invisible?"

Ken looked confused. "What? No."

Sally looked at her from the stove where she could see the boiling pot that would contain two poached eggs. "No, what a silly thought."

"The gold of the Rhine maidens? The star of the Nibelung. Is there really a clan of dwarves in the world? Giants in the Earth, too? Are they coming after me? How do I rule the world with this?"

Debbie laughed at all her jokes. Ken and Sally were used to their occasional highbrow humor and became silent as usual. She held a new Star of Ishtar, with the eight points now evenly spaced and not looking like a six-pointed Jewish star with two points added on. The center was now a smooth solid gold circle instead of a hexagram, in the middle of which sat the ruby, the origins of which she was digging at.

"Yes, Esther. You deduced excellently. Gift from God has given you a gift from the old gods. The old gods of the ancient Babylonians, Greeks, and Germans."

"Thank you, Debbie. Tell your former flame, Theodore, I thank him for the lovely gemstone. So, it's a gift from the old gods. Not stolen? No one is coming looking for the gem or the Rhine gold?" She admired the necklace which was a more expensive-looking combination of gold and precious and common gems, including lapis lazuli.

"I kept the points. I didn't circle the star. The circle is in the star. You can keep up your edgy self-harm rituals."

"Yes, I get the point." She squeezed the points now, fighting the old god complex she thought she had banished. *Why are old gods giving me gifts? These thoughts are ridiculous. Go away, I'm not a god. Just like a god.*

Ken made a very rare initiation with a look of concern on his face. "Debbie says she's built the new baby factory, but I don't see anything. She's told me to give my survivalist group over to you today. That's my present. You're going to collect them. I'm not afraid to cross Debbie, but you…"

"It's okay, Dad. It's a lovely gift. Thank you. I'm very glad to have had you as a father. I'm eighteen now and would be glad to incorporate your friends into my Compound. I should like that. You know how I rule this place and the Talents worldwide. The growth of my kingdom will now accelerate."

Ken smiled at her control attempt. "I am not stupid enough to cross you, and I've told my friends you are coming for them. After what you did to the police. How does it feel to be above the law? You and your journal about being beyond good and evil. Debbie got you hooked on that Nietzsche stuff didn't she."

Debbie shushed Ken with "It's great to be above the law. Doesn't it feel good to you, sweetie? You *are* the law now."

Sally placed her breakfast plate in front of Esther and she started eating. She smiled and looked at Debbie. "Yes. Yes, it does. I'm afraid I enjoy having and accumulating power."

The women laughed again while she saw Ken put his hand to his face.

#

Cal was 50 years old, and by Ken's report lean, tough, and strong willed. He was known to admire women who were the same. Esther approached their base with about 160 of her Followers. All in four-wheel-drive cars, armed with drones still operated by Cysso. After negotiating through their phones, Cal met her alone in his neutral zone just inside the entrance to their large base. Esther was wearing her camera-eye and survival clothing of worn military fatigues containing special pockets full of robotic mice, armed with carfentanyl, to be guided by cameras on the drones as well as cameras on the mice.

The neutral zone was a fenced off area with two concrete paved car parking spots. There were old recycled plastic picnic tables to sit at, the place reminding Esther of camping spots she shared with Debbie when she was a girl of 10. Cal and Esther would meet alone out of earshot. They entered on foot at the same time and immediately walked to a table, shook hands, and sat down. Cal couldn't help staring at her camera-eye at first.

"That's some nice head gear. Does it sport a laser gun?"

Esther politely laughed and shook her head no. She decided to stick to the light tone Cal had started with. "It's got a flashlight and infrared and ultraviolet sensors." She rotated the normal camera to telescope-vision and did a close up on Cal's eye. She felt whimsical.

"Cal, what are you surviving for? What's going to happen?"

For once, Esther did not see any signs of the Crushso she caused in men and women, and she felt relief that this would be a more challenging encounter than the police. "It's a lot of things, Esther. Many things can happen, we're just being prepared." Cal spoke evenly and didn't look nervous, instead looking every bit the alpha male. Esther struggled to contain her excitement at meeting a manly man. *A man with backbone. He will still be mine.*

"Okay, then, give me some examples. Give me a bunch of your favorite ones."

"Well, there's the obvious ones and the not so obvious ones."

"Okay, let's start with the obvious ones."

"Well, there's still the possibility of nuclear war, but also virus outbreaks, the Yellowstone supervolcano blowing up, California falling into the sea, a giant meteor hitting the Earth, China invading Alaska."

"Okay, what else?" Cal had that tough masculine energy, like a Clint Eastwood or John Wayne, someone not to fuck with. Esther decided to respond with her soft feminine side, like she was the happy smiling daughter he wished he could have. She would capture this tough guy with honey. A honey pot/trap.

"We want to be out of the cities when the race riots and civil war starts. You know, when the United States collapses and breaks up into different countries. You know, when the Chi-coms completely destroy the US economy. Battle lines will form up along communities. It's all about forming strong trusting communities. You'd be welcome here when that happens. Just thought you'd like to know. We know Ken has six Talent children and three smart and attractive wives. Many here think he's been blessed by God."

"That's very nice of you." *Good, an offer of alliance. It was good to show my power. I'm pretty sure he knows I can slaughter all of them in an instant, but he displays no fear.*

"Some don't want anything to do with you. I am giving you a chance, though. We are a Christian community here and many would like to know where you stand."

"I believe in a monotheistic God that created the universe, for reasons I don't hope to comprehend. I believe God gave us consciousness in his image, and that is the basis of human dignity and morality. I believe that existence is inherently good, that life is a gift from God, consciousness breathed into us to use for good or evil. Obeying or disobeying his will."

"Okay, how about Jesus?"

"I have familiarized myself with many Christian sects and participated in the philosophical discussions on Christ in various Talent religious societies. Where Christianity parts with Judaism… You know that technically I'm Jewish, I'm of direct descent from King David. I'm nonpracticing though, except once a year my mother and I celebrate Yom Kippur. I've attended many Christian services with Ken as well and we celebrate Christmas every year."

Martin: [What's up with the Jewish stuff? I thought that didn't matter. That you made up your mind you are not the Messiah or Antichrist.]

Esther: [These people obsess over Jews and the Antichrist.]

Cal stared at her for a little, then recovered, "A good thing. We understand you are a close friend of Paula's at the Episcopal church in Lexington. She speaks highly of you. She says you haven't declared a religion. You act like a Christian and do Christian good works but lack faith. Where is your faith now?"

Smart man. It looks like this community has researched me. That is good too. I have a reputation now. Some of my plans are working.

"To me, the essence of Christianity is the belief in the Resurrection. The best argument is that Jesus died on the cross, was resurrected, and was witnessed by many people who were so inspired by the experience they went out and started converting anyone they could with a bit of help from the Holy Spirit. The Apostle Paul, in particular, was effective at bridging Jewish ideas with Greco-Roman civilization, namely monotheism and intrinsic human dignity. It's a belief, really, the Resurrection. I haven't made up my mind about it. I do believe that Christianity is better than the pagan demon worship and human sacrifice it replaced. Jesus was our final human sacrifice. If his sacrifice earned him the gift of grace from his father, I don't see any reason why people wouldn't want his grace and achieve immortality."

Cal seemed pleased with her answer, nodding his head gently as well.

"You came through death, did you not? Did it not change you? It is rumored you regained consciousness on the third day after your guiltless murder."

Esther remained silent for a little while, recalling her dream of the eschaton in the hospital, when a sudden inspiration hit her.

"I am alpha and omega. I am the beginning of the very end."

Cal responded, "The fire and flood are coming."

"The burning hollow pyramid."

"The flood."

"One of ten and one of a hundred."

"The virtuous will be given mercy," Cal closed.

The conversation stalled. Cal closed his eyes and looked like he was praying to himself.

Esther felt slightly hypnotized and stared at Cal's closed eyelids for a few seconds until they opened, and Cal started staring back.

"I was near death, in the hospital, high on painkillers. How is this possible?"

"This is good news for me, Esther. Many had thought the Talents were a threat. It seems you are in the same situation as everyone else. We are all trying to survive. Are you their leader? That's what many of us think."

Lucy: [Careful. I know you want to convert these people. Be sure to lie.]

Esther: [Not lie. Dissemble.]

"Yes, I speak for all the Talents. They have chosen me. Not formally, and not on everything. Not yet. Just on certain matters."

"As it is with me and the others." Cal now smiled immensely, like he was the luckiest man in the world. *He knows what my presence means. A chance at alliance and a chance at Better Genetics.* Esther fell back into "daughter everybody wants" mode.

"Who are the others?"

"Survivalists of all kinds and creeds all over the world. The 'Prepper' community. We compare notes."

"What do you believe?"

"Many believe it is Christ speaking to us. Others Yahweh or Jehovah or Allah or Kali or Shiva. Others speak of the world soul and others the collective unconscious made possible by the mass telecommunications of the Internet, a kind of meme. Here is a picture I drew." It was on plain white copy paper that had been folded into quarters to fit his coat pocket. He opened it up and handed it to her.

Esther studied the picture of a large wave about to engulf the pyramid on fire. It reminded her of the *Great Wave off Kanagawa*, except with a burning pyramid instead of Mount Fuji. The boats were more Noah's ark shaped. Cal was a good artist she decided after studying the picture carefully.

"Ken said today was your birthday."

She smiled pleasantly at him and folded it back up and put it in her own coat pocket.

"Thank you. Cal? What do you think of me now?"

"Esther, we know about your veterinarian efforts. You are a gifted healer. We thought at first the animals were goners, and you were some sort of Satanic animal torture and sacrifice type. Now I wonder if you are Noah, here to protect the animals, too, from the fire that will engulf the Earth. That or Charlotte, saving the prize pig for Fern."

Martin: [Zooanthropomorphism, from him? Barf. It is random and still forces a linguistic change. Ancient Egypt every tenth word. Library uploaded.]

Esther: [Token acknowledged paradigm shift Egyptian vocabulary.] *A Talent must have resurrected the dead language.*

"No. My time with the animals is coming to an end. I did all that because I love science and I love my mothers. It was my way of saying thank you to them. Now that I understand you better, I thought I'd leave my Compound under your protection. I'm taking my Followers with me to college and need someone to protect the Talents and family I'm leaving behind. We also have good paying jobs available for people we trust."

Cal looked like he was trying to hide his amazement, his poker face cracking.

"I think Cal, that *you* are the Noah in this story."

"If you are not Noah… If Jesus returned for the end of days, but this time as a woman…"

Esther was smiling brilliantly at him now. She remembered that Jenna had also thought she was Jesus reborn.

"… I think he would be you." Cal looked at her in awe, his poker face vanished.

"Why *thank you* Cal. How very nice of you, I will take that as the highest compliment. I am not Savior Anointed One. Maybe I'm Star Stone. I do think the end of an age is coming with my coming."

"Power and charisma emanate from you. Ken told me hundreds of people would give their life for you. You speak for hundreds of thousands of brilliant people all over the world. You cure impossible diseases. You've come back from death. How are you not the return of Christ?"

Esther found her hand had unconsciously grabbed her pointed star below her neck. She could grab it just hard enough to not break her skin.

"I'm just me. I'm not a prophet or Messiah or anything like that. What do you think of Revelation? Christian eschatology?" *And no Cal I'm not the Antichrist.*

"Revelation already happened. The book is clearly about the struggle of early Christians against the Roman empire. The whore of Babylon is Rome and 666 or 616 refers to Nero. I have no doubt about this. As far as eschatology, I think that as long as God-fearing faithful people inhabit the Earth, the end of humans will never come, as per the stories of Noah and Sodom and Gomorrah. Perhaps as God rescued Noah's family and Lot and his daughters, one out of a hundred is all that there is worth saving. Maybe God is merciful and will permit ninety out of a hundred to survive. I do believe if the surviving one out of one hundred is evil, then the world will end, and the Earth will become a smoking ruin. Gehenna."

"What about other religions?"

"I went to theological seminary. I got to make friends with many people from around the world. My Jewish counterpart is busy with collecting the faithful. They are building survivalist farms as well. Same goes for others in their various places and countries. These groups are all very exclusive."

"What about secular humanists? Those who are moral but don't believe in God or the supernatural. What about all the other good people?"

"Look, Esther. Most of us humans are ordinary mortals. The fancy intellectuals come up with their complex value systems of right and wrong. They split hairs over tiny moral dilemmas that distract from real personal virtue. They hold ethnic grudges dating back centuries. They obsess over moral failings of people long dead, when they should concentrate on real moral failings of people today. It is love of your own intellect; it is narcissism. Jesus taught us to be kind within our Christian assemblies and separate ourselves as much as we can from fallen people. You and your followers don't seem fallen at all. You have a good effect on people. Everyone notices it. You look after everyone. 'Ye shall know them by their fruits,' Christ taught us. Your fruits are all good. It's astonishing."

Something is working, YES! Esther hid her excitement and examined Cal. She recognized the Crushso take hold of him now, except this man had no fear of her. *Perhaps he is a fellow traveler and has been through death.*

"You look at me differently from everyone else. Everyone has a look of fear on his or her face when they look at me, except you. Why is that?" *One last piece to convert him.*

"We are bonded in death. I too came very near to death in a hunting accident. I recognize that look in your face. That while you still fight with all your might, you have let the fear of death go. It makes us excellent leaders and excellent soldiers."

Esther felt the sales pitch was over and decided to close the deal. As this was a group sale, she knew the closing would be more protracted and complex.

"I am going to absorb your group into mine. You're going to inhabit my Compound and join my Followers. Give me all your unmarried children. I will marry all of them over fifteen. They will all be my family. In return you will fall under my protection. You need to turn your faith in the Father and the Son to me now."

"What do you mean, you will marry all of them over fifteen?"

"I will personally wed them. Male and female, they will be my brides as the church is the bride of Christ. I will be faithful, loving, and committed, and they will be saved. I am the head, and they are the body."

Cal stared into her eyes. "It's like that? Can I ask one more question?"

"Ask away."

"Why do you wear the symbol of Ishtar?"

Esther held her star to think about it some more, trying to come up with a good answer. The circumpunct. The circled dot. The sun. She was the ruby, the star stone. The death ruby that protected her from all justice, allowing her to do anything without fear of retribution. She thought for another few seconds that all the old gods' power was now at her touch. She touched it now. Her mind wandered some more, remembering the ring of power was a birthday present, and that unlimited power brought only death. *Shall I turn into a dragon or a Gollum?*

"It was given to me as a birthday present. It reminds me of someone who died for me. My own personal human sacrifice. *Ishtar* is etymologically related to *Esther*. Both females are related to saving people from genocide. Esther for the Jews. Ishtar for mankind from a second flood, as related in the *Epic of Gilgamesh*. It reminds me that I am not a goddess, for I once had hubris, excessive pride that nearly killed me. It reminds me that Jesus, even with the full power of God, was humble. My Followers are forbidden from worshipping me. I refuse a cult of personality as well. I have learned the virtue of humility at great personal cost. They are my family. I am their mother and their wife, their sister, even their daughter."

Esther started tearing at the recollection of Elsa's death and touching the ruby remembered that her own death would be a gift from God. *Theodore, gift from God.* A blood offering and a burnt offering. She felt feminine. The feminine libido came to her without autoandrophilia. She consciously started smiling and twirled her hair, hoping the autoandrophilia might dissipate as she grew older. *I am a woman. I bring life into the world.*

She looked up from the star to Cal, his face still full of awe and Crushso. She would not seduce him. She would take his children.

"When I put it on in the morning it reminds me of who I am and who I am not. That is more important to me than anything. You see, I have godlike powers, and they grow every month. It is science in reality, but to others it looks like magic. I think it's best for everyone that I remind myself of humility every morning, that I honor the one who died for me. Like God, I could wipe out your entire group on a whim, instantly and without a trace, vanished and forgotten forever. Yet, I am humble."

Cal studied her as if making a big decision. He finally relaxed.

"I understand you have a custom with your followers. It is an interesting custom. I love you, Esther. It must be a wondrous burden to hold the power of life and death in your hands. I see that you constantly move your hands. They hold your will to power and put you beyond good and evil."

Cysso put an icon up on her screen. She hovered the cursor over it and the tag [Insta-kill] came up.

"I know that you love me. Two of my Followers will stay here to coordinate the details. You will send me all your unmarried fifteen and older and any who turn fifteen after today. Do it today."

Cal just nodded dumbfounded. She stood up and Cal quickly imitated her.

Martin: [Well done; all your childhood education didn't go to waste, did it?]

She embraced Cal and left the neutral zone. On the walk back to her car she talked with Martin, trying to substitute an Egyptian word every ten words in Babel.

Martin: "What's with this stupid dream? It looks like it's been an Internet meme for about a year."

Esther: "Yes, that was weird. I thought it was just a dream before today. A strange prophecy. Do I imagine myself as a prophet or do others imagine me as a prophet of doom?"

Martin: "We're the war. It's us versus them. You find Normies stupid enough to side with us, that's all on you."

Esther: "I'm not going back on my promise to protect them."

Martin: "You think they have any long-term value? What use is a Normie compared to a Talent? You collected a hundred stupid Normies today, while I get three hundred sixty Talents entering our Warrens every day. Three hundred sixty Teslas operating at sixty-four hundred times the famous inventor."

Esther pondered the question. She remembered Debbie's advice when she was just a girl. Female power derives from forming families. She felt a scary thought come and go, and reasoned, no. She wouldn't do that. She wouldn't and couldn't go there. But then she couldn't avoid the thought she'd be turning into her mom. That she was carefully trained and engineered for just this moment and this problem, her unusual life and challenges.

While her sex life since her death had been limited to VR/robot sex with Martin, clothed Circleturbos with her Followers, fondling her bodyguards in bed, and playing footsie with Josh whenever they flew together, the speech she just gave Cal as she recalled it now caused a jolt of autoandrophilia. This time in a rage. *Family. Female power through family formation.*

She reached her army waiting for her, the drones whirring all around. Some carried fentanyl grenades, others carried poison mice, others had advanced 360-degree camera targeting systems, and yet others were made to simply crash into things, destroying everything kinetically with their diamond-crusted high-speed propellers. She noticed how young and fit all her men and women were, working and waiting and disciplining themselves for their reward, not in heaven but in her.

CHAPTER THIRTEEN

THE KINDRED OF ESTHER

[February 1, 2063]
The Compound

ESTHER LEFT BEHIND two Followers to collect her human tribute and was driven home to her Compound to be surprised by Debbie sitting on the front porch couch reading a book. She got up immediately and gave Esther a big hug and a kiss on the cheek. She hugged and kissed back.

"It's great to see you, Mother."

"Your next birthday presents are nearly ready. You're going full next level."

Debbie now admired Esther's full grown six-foot-two body, four inches taller than her own.

A question suddenly came to mind, something she immediately wondered why she never asked before.

"Mother, if we all have your body shape who is the male model..." She touched the ruby on her necklace and started to feel faint. Debbie quickly grabbed her body to steady it. "Theodore... gift from God. The gift from God is death."

Instead of crying as usual, Esther fainted in Debbie's arms.

#

She woke up in her king-sized bed in the master bedroom to the sound of a shower running, wondering what the next birthday surprise would be and what "next level" meant. There was a wrapped present next to her with a large card saying, "OPEN ME." It felt rather Alice in Wonderland–ish, and she felt a premonition of falling down a rabbit hole if she opened it. The rabbit hole was not full of anthropomorphisms, but breeding like rabbits, a Wonderland of mass human reproduction, creating anthros. Curiosity won and she tore off the wrapping paper to discover a large cardboard box labeled "Baby Factory" and "Made by Better Genetics Corporation," red letters on a white background with an image of a strapless double dildo/vibrator on it. She found a warning label on the box: "to be operated by medical professionals only" and "batteries included" and "supplies provided separately" and "hand washable" and various wireless protocol and app symbols, one of which was the Baby Steps app she had on her phone. She also found some marketing-style labeling promoting "Autoerogenous zone stimulating, 25 types and 25 speeds for maximum female and male pleasure."

She opened the cardboard outer layer to find the double vibrator inside. It had half power bars and a wireless charger, so she managed to start it recharging back to full power using an empty port on her bedstand. She also found a small vial of caramel-tasting edible water-soluble lubricant. There were instructions on how to load the device app, but she saw that Cysso had already done this on her camera-eye system.

Sakura: [Debbie will show you how to operate it.]

She got out of bed and put the packaging away, leaving the device on her bedstand in the charger. She was still wearing the clothes she fainted in minus the coat full of pocket mice. She felt like having a shower and became conscious again that the shower had been running the whole time. She felt nervous about going to the bathroom to take a shower, but after a few seconds of hesitation, decided "fuck it" and undressed.

She went in. There were two women taking a shower together. She could make out that much through the slight mist on the glass shower wall. It felt hot and the room was hot and one of the women turned to her and opened the steamed-up door and it was Lucy with a huge smile. Lucy walked towards her while the other woman turned the shower off and she could see it was Debbie with the shower door now open. "Surprise Esther!" "Happy birthday!"

She was overjoyed. "Lucifer! You devil you. I'm so glad you are here. What are you two doing?" She gave Lucy a big hug and couldn't stop a big kiss. They tongued. *That was mutual, she's so beautiful.* The autoandrophilia kicked in then, and Esther felt the complete loss of sexual self-control.

Lucy broke it off and started laughing.

"We're here to make babies, of course! You're getting pregnant for your birthday!" Debbie started laughing hysterically and Esther joined them, wondering how her mother wasn't sexually attractive while Lucy was, despite sharing the same exact body shape. She hadn't entirely understood how the Westermarck Effect worked in detail.

"Making babies!" The thought of getting pregnant excited Esther. Lucy still naked took Esther's hand. Esther felt hot. She knew right then her virtual celibacy was over. She was going back to a hot sex life but girl-girl style this time.

"Let me show you. We got a delivery from the stork yesterday. The BGC home delivery product is finished. We can scale up the rate of Talent creation now, with you and me doing the first honors."

The two women dried off but didn't put on any clothes. Naked, they took her to Esther's private reading room and study. There she found a series of large jars, shaped like propane tanks, with an electric cord leading to a wall socket. They reminded Esther of embryo storage tanks. They had a clear label on each of them: "Better Genetics Corporation. Keep frozen."

"Oh my God. We have babies, but who? Why? So many... What have you two been up to? Why didn't Martin tell me?" *Hundreds. There are hundreds of Talent embryos in these tanks. Hundreds of beautiful babies to make.*

Martin: [It's a surprise. Happy birthday. Lucy will explain.]

"Esther, your mom wants to teach us how to impregnate people. Can you believe we're going to have a child together? I'm so excited!"

Esther felt the Crushso and eros build like crazy, and the two started making out full on. She heard Debbie leave the room, with a "Bye lovebirds." In the midst of the wild lust, it again occurred to Esther that Debbie had made her and Lucy same-sex attracted for precisely this moment. She was part of a bigger and grander sexual experiment framed by the Better Genetics product development team.

Lucy led them to the bedroom, where they made love for an hour. Lucy explained that Debbie had taught her girl-girl sex while Esther was visiting Ken's survivalist community. They took a rest lying in bed staring at each other enjoying eros and ludos. Shortly after, Debbie, now dressed in clinical clothing, entered the room and gave a wink to Lucy.

Martin: [I've patched Debbie into your prosthetic penis or BGC implantation device, and she will guide your first time. You will share vision on the device.]

Debbie took the Baby Factory from the bedtable charger and opened a compartment. Then she showed a small test tube with the label [Elsa] on it and put it into the compartment. "I've successfully thawed the embryo. It uses some of poor Elsa's DNA code, which I collected from the church. She'll come back to life as a Talent. I'm so excited!"

"Is this true, Lucy?"

"YEESS! Let's do this. I want to be the first woman who impregnates another woman during sexual intercourse."

The prosthetic was reinserted, and Debbie demonstrated that Esther's peaksos made her cervix more accessible for the nanodevice that stretched into her uterus. A sensor camera brought the thin antenna like device to an ideal spot on her uterus while Debbie carefully implanted the embryo in Esther. Esther and Lucy kissed and hugged each other closely during the impregnation, but the electric stimulation needed to be turned off during implantation.

Debbie took the device from them and ejected the Elsa test tube and put in a new one labeled "Esther/Lucy." "Yep, two women can have a child together now."

Esther felt joy at the prospect of impregnating Lucy and even more joy during the process.

After that was done, they played with the various settings until they were exhausted. They took a shower together and eventually dressed in dresses and joined Debbie in the kitchen living area, holding hands and smiling like it was the happiest day of their lives.

Debbie admired them. "You know, I never carried my own child. Now we are all blood related. A synthetic genetic tribe. I'm passing on my matriarchy and synthetic race over to you, Esther. More birthday surprises today."

"We need to tell the others." The three women chatted about becoming pregnant while waiting for Rachael, Amanda, and Ken to arrive, along with Esther's siblings.

When they were all sitting, Esther announced, "Hi, everyone. I'm pregnant with Elsa and Lucy's pregnant with our child. Isn't that great news!"

Rachael stared at Lucy then Debbie. She put her face in her hands, wiped her tears and then stood up and beckoned Lucy to do so. "So it seems I have another beautiful daughter. And now granddaughters on the way."

Lucy smiled and gave Rachael a big hug. "Thank you, Mother."

Esther felt pride in Rachael's accepting her definition of marriage (that sex was marriage). Then she felt excited at becoming a mother and burst out, "Oh, Mother, I have lots of people to help raise our children. The Talents are so good at following the book." And then she suddenly realized the purpose of all those other embryo tanks. *No, Better Genetics didn't. The baby factory is us. Is me. I am the new baby factory.*

Debbie seemed to notice her change of expression. "You don't have to do it, Esther. Think on it." *Of course I'm going to do it, but how?*

#

The next morning at breakfast, Debbie explained that Lucy and Esther had to go on special diets, get a special hormone implant, and later receive a special injection in the womb. The implant would reduce her disgust mechanism to make things easier for her during her carefully planned pregnancy, which would include more than a few extra discomforts. It seemed that Talent gestation required a specific pregnancy intervention protocol. Esther recalled that Debbie had earned her PhD in exactly this subject. A lot happens during gestation, and she assumed Debbie had all the answers.

Ken, Sally, Percy, and Shelly were sharing breakfast with her. She grabbed Lucy's hand. "I'm going to marry them all today. My cult is getting next-level cultier."

Ken laughed. Then the others, except Lucy. "Just do it all at once. Get it over with. Debbie's teaching me how to thaw the embryos and do the pregnancy interventions. Rache and Melanie are also signing up for her classes. We can handle the volume. Debbie has been organizing the hydroponic farms for our gestational nutrition purposes, part of what is required to build another Better Genetics production center. These special diets we are now on."

"Do you mind me having so many husbands and wives, Wife? Husband?"

"Uh, I don't really think of them as competition." Lucy failed to hide her feelings of disgust. Followers were all Normies to her, Esther thought.

Martin: [Knock yourself out. Debbie's given me a training video on woman loving woman she wants you to use. There's a bit of hetero kink included.]

Esther left the dining area hand in hand with Lucy. They went to her room to watch it and try it together.

#

Esther gathered her Followers later that afternoon at a large open field, now joined by all the single men and women from Cal's community. They were all dressed for a wedding, except Esther wore a groom's black outfit and the men wore a groom's outfit but in all white. A few Talents, including her family and Josh, were in attendance. She connected her voice to the sound/video system that connected to their earbuds.

"Better Genetics has given me the gift of life. I have determined to have children with all of you. You will all now become my wives and you will commit to my marriage vows as you become my synthetic family in blood as well as in spirit."

The crowd chanted "Beloved" at the word "spirit."

"We shall now stand, hand in hand, boy/girl, in a large circle with me at the center, with all eyes on me to join in spirit." The congregation formed a hand-to-hand circle continuing to chant "Beloved" set to an earbud beat organized by Cysso. The circumpunct, or keter, the top position of the Sefirot of the Tree of Life in Kabbalah, the crown, sun, the Creation, the "I am" of God, placed Esther as the dot, the beginning point and center of the universe. Her brides stood in as close to a round circle as they could manage.

"With this ring, I thee wed." The field became quiet.

"You will protect me with your lives, your souls, your breaths of life, your consciousnesses, all that you are and all that you possess. You will obey me without question in all things. You will devote yourselves to my well-being in any way that I determine now and for eternity." The group spoke these promises.

"Spirit."

"Beloved."

"The penalty for breaking these commands is death in a way that I see fitting. I will be the sole judge of worthiness as well as your executioner."

"Beloved."

"I am now your husband, and you are my wives. You will all get to have me for an hour and bear my children." She took Sally, Peter, Nancy, and Andrew with her to her bedroom to marry them, Sally and Nancy, impregnated, and Peter and Andrew ordered on the Baby Steps app after she penetrated them. The wedding celebration would be that night.

#

And so Esther spent the time making love with every member of her Followers and she, Lucy, and Debbie impregnated the women with Esther and a contribution from each individual's DNA coding. The male Followers also received the baby making device, making them her bride and not her bridegroom. She would only penetrate and not be penetrated, unwilling to be contaminated with male semen (at Debbie's recommendation) but acceptable to male saliva. She preferred to make love face-to-face while kissing, letting the device do most of the stimulation. The three other brides would watch while she made love one person at a time.

Esther told her male wives that a surrogate at Better Genetics would carry their male offspring and would fly in nine months from now to deliver a son. The men and women were to be celibate until the babies came, a period after which they would be assigned permanent pair-bonds with other Followers but on implant birth control.

She was sure she'd never be able to do this without autoandrophilia. She decided not to confront Debbie about it yet. More than ever, she felt Better Genetics was still her true god and creator.

#

During this period of DNA conversion and family building, the three women would take to conversation after breakfast was over.

"Martin, how do you feel about all this now?"

Martin spoke through the room's sound system: "I sort of object to being the object of Better Genetics' ulterior plans. I guess they had a lot of foresight." *That sounded a bit cagey, but Martin usually sounds cagey these days.*

Lucy said, "Just don't forget to take that shower after you're done."

Debbie gave her usual "tee-hee."

#

[On another breakfast occasion]

"Mother, tell me more about Theodore." Esther fingered the ruby and felt faint again, but Lucy was there to hold her hand and pinch her. Esther had confided her strange experience with the man, and Lucy had looked him up. What information her father, Pierre, gave her confirmed Debbie's story. Theodore's parents were Manhattan billionaires, and he had worked as a professional model in his 20s. He'd gone to Columbia for undergraduate and graduate schools for degrees in psychology. His womanizing and sperm donations were epic. There was no connection to BGC or the Registry. Women from all over the world flew to him to be "psychoanalyzed." His out-family of direct genetic descendants was on the order of 10,000. The half-siblings were getting it on through ancestry registries just like Debbie's direct descendants. Martin reconfirmed all of Pierre's data. His inbred grandchildren were also epic in number like Debbie.

"He was my first lover, Esther," said Debbie. "Our relationship lasted a year before we decided we wanted to see other people. We meet from time to time and wonder why we ever separated. He was a professional hypnotist at one time. Then he became a psychologist. He still lives in New York City. He's still running through women and making lots of babies all over the world."

"Does he collect for Better Genetics like you?"

"Oh, yes. He seduces new women every night. Like five to ten a day. Then uses the Baby Steps app I gave him to make a child with you."

"Does he ask for kindness?"

"Yes, I told him to."

"In my name?"

Debbie suddenly became very serious.

"Yes, Esther. All of Theodore's and my children are really your children. He shows them pictures of you before he extracts a promise. Like your Followers, men and women all over the world are having your children. Thousands. They use the Registry app to stay in touch with each other. Here, let me show you."

Debbie sat next to Esther and brought up on her T-pad a section titled "Kindred." They were organized by country, city, and Warren.

"They are called the Kindred of Esther. Pronounced "kind" not "kin." The Kindred. They are your kin, and they are kind. They have a ceremony, sort of a wedding ceremony. You are their wife, the women and the men. They are all unmarried people in the real world. Many are rich or important in other ways." Her expansive procreation cult now had a name.

Esther pondered the meaning of having a massive genetic family in her name. Her blood and her brood. It reminded her of God's promise to Abraham to have descendants as numerous as the stars. She was descended from Abraham. She thought her children might one day reach the stars and remembered her name meant "star." She mused that her children were Star children living in Warrens while she fought a genetic war that would not end until they reached the stars.

"How are my children doing? Are they all safely at the Warrens?"

"Yes. They've all been warned about attacks on Talent children. Everyone is serious now. No one debates the recommendations either. No one seems to want misfit children. BGC has taken all the options off the table. The donor picture book is just you now, whether the intended parent is male or female. That's a hundred thirty thousand children a year you are having, plus whatever happens here at our second production center."

Debbie continued, "I've added Theodore's list to my current list that Martin already has been using. Theodore, being in New York, has had access to a worldwide network of infiltrators and spies all over the planet and in all kinds of organizations."

Martin: [Soaked up the Registry data already. Cysso is still processing it.]

#

[A month after the mass marriage ceremony on Feb 2, 2063]

Esther was naked lying on her soft bed after her four-hour fivesome and subsequent shower. She'd arranged for extra soft sheets to be changed by her Followers after each session after Lucy's complaint, and she luxuriated in how nice and crisp they felt to her skin.

Martin: "You have too many spouses now. They keep coming in. How much can your body handle?"

She had the "Do not disturb" on all the time, but he didn't seem to care. She started thinking of the dream. She was working her camera-eye to see how the burning pyramid had become an Internet meme. She set her screen to bicameral, two lenses and two rulers, king and queen.

Esther: "Five hours of sex a day. About a hundred Peaksos. It's good that I'm in great shape. What's on your mind, love?" Lucy had entered the room and started undressing.

Martin: "I dream of those ten men I killed. They had a history of mental imbalance. That friend of Detective Jack spent a lot of time on antineurotics. They all were a little mad, but they all did mental drugs like MDMA and LSD or had a history of crazy stuff like useless petty crimes. I still killed them. I can't in any way feel good about this. It physically hurts, damn Founders. They should have made me an unfeeling psychopath. Psychopaths aren't worried about the people they kill."

Martin had used the Kindred (spoofing Esther) to access various medical databases. Martin had all of them, in fact. He possessed the medical history of everyone on the planet who went electronic. As usual, Cysso had AI catalogued and data-mined it. These included the individuals' DNA sequences. Lucy was hoping to match Better Genetics' gene decoding capability. Clearly, a full-term artificial womb was out of reach. They still needed the female uterus for baby making. Perhaps a full-term artificial womb was a scientific impossibility like breaking the speed of light. The various life science Discos decided that BGC would be miles ahead on the whole subject and had islands full of their own Talents to work with. Debbie was slowly sharing BGC technology anyway. She understood the pregnancy interventions did something to brain development and sexuality. She reasoned that they were likely rare but desirable mutations, such as advanced visual acuity.

"I'm sorry, Martin. I don't know what else I can say, except it's only going to get worse. We're too young for this sort of thing. Maybe we will become better people from it. I don't know, but the death count has just barely begun. Find a coping mechanism. Booze perhaps? Works for a lot of Normsos. Look at me. I found massive promiscuity."

Esther laughed at her own joke, but Martin didn't seem to find it funny.

Martin: "We're not killers. It's not in our blood. Our very DNA as well as our culture rejects it utterly." Esther switched from bicameral mode to using the camera on Martin's face in conference mode. Felicity was wiping away his tears as they sat together in bed.

"I don't know. You aren't in the dream. No person is in the dream. Yes, the lives of eight point nine billion people are in the balance? You think it might be you that kills them? Is that the interpretation? It's just a dream. We can't worry about dreams, only about reality. Only about our survival. You must focus on tech that will save my life. Focus on that. Do not become morbid. I draw out the violence and you protect me. Get the picture?"

Martin: "Okay. I'll keep focused. The Followers are all training on the drones and their various weapons. They don't stop talking about your lovemaking either. Binding them to you with your offspring was a great decision. I'll spare you the devotional poetry they write and songs they sing when you are not around. They call you their lord. Or our lord. Whatever."

"They are part of the cyber-genetic program. They are all my Kindred. We are blood. We can trust them with the Talent weapons systems now. I can survive. You don't need to kill more people directly. They repeat their promise during lovemaking to kill for me. They are all trained soldiers. Proselytizers as well. My body sustains four new wives a day. Maybe I should drop from one hour to a half hour and up it to eight a day." Esther just decided she would make this change and sent a message to her Followers to up the recruiting.

Lucy, now naked, lay beside Esther and started caressing her while speaking into her Tear. "Martin, do your databases include more potential entryists?"

Martin: "Yes, I have all kinds of lists but not live direct access to their systems. Marcy seems to have selected all the right people for Debbie and Theodore to have babies with. We can more safely recruit now."

"Yes, we'll need to send false info back. I will recruit, convert, and process informants as well. Oh, and I can process the various religious groups I converted back when I was thirteen. Yeah, I'll have to marry Paula's daughter, Jenna, and all the rest of her church-based sex club. I nearly forgot that promise. I was searching for wisdom but found a lot of brides."

"I'm your favorite bride, though."

"Of course, dear." <kiss>

#

Esther decided she needed older Followers with more skill variety before she left for college. She would not convert them genetically. She was
driven back to her old high school to meet an old friend and favorite
teacher who'd been teaching her whole life. She caused quite a stir when
she arrived, and her Followers recruited while she was there. She found
her drinking coffee in the teacher's lounge and she stood up immediately
to give Esther a hug and peck on the lips.

"Ms. Berman? Can I have a few minutes of your time?"

"Of course, Esther. Whatever you need." *The fear and the love.*

"You really love teaching, don't you? It's your calling, perhaps?"

"Yes, I knew around your age that I wanted to go into teaching. Why do
you ask?" *She is practically trembling in my presence. Yes, I enjoy my calling.*

"Those teachers over there, they teach because it's a job?"

Esther gestured towards a group of three teachers gathered to admire her. There were more joining them as news of Esther's visit to the
school got out.

"Why yes, very good, Esther. You are very perceptive. Yes, well, we all
know how smart you are."

"They're not like you, they do it for the pay and not the joy of it."

"Most people work for the pay and not the joy. I consider myself very
lucky. I enjoy my work."

"It's what makes you a better teacher, too. That's why all the students
like you."

"Well, thank you, Esther. I don't teach to be liked, but it is nice to
be liked, yes, and I enjoy making a positive difference in people's lives."

"I think I have a calling like you. I want to be a doctor and heal people. I think you're very lucky, because you get to do what you are called
to do. I worry I won't ever get to be a doctor. I did veterinarian work,
because of my moms, but my real goal is to go to med school and work
with people and not animals."

"Why, every school in the country would be glad to have you. You'd be
a wonderful doctor. Why would you let anything get in the way of that?"

"Look at all my Followers. I am a natural leader, too." Ms. Berman was looking like she might faint so Esther motioned her to sit down.

"Well, then, lead the doctors. Doctors need leaders, too. You can do both."

"I'm going to go to Yale, I've decided. My three mothers all went there."

"You've decided? It's a very hard school to get into. Did you apply and get accepted?"

"No, I haven't applied, and yes, it's May, too late to apply. But they will let me in anyway."

"I don't think it works that way. You want my recommendation?"

Esther saw the eagerness in Ms. Berman's eyes. The fear and love were turning to devotion.

"You see, I have over five hundred Followers now. Mostly aged fifteen to twenty-five. They are going to follow me out to New Haven."

"Yes?" *She has a good smile. She was always kind to the students. I will not make her a killer. Not all my Followers have to be soldiers.*

"I want you to join them, shepherd them, organize them, and teach them. You're nearly retired, your children are grown. My Followers are still young and are skipping college for my sake. They still need to go to school and learn useful trades. I can't watch them all the time if I'm going to become a doctor. I need your help. And I trust you."

"I'll move out to New Haven this summer. My partner won't mind. But you haven't even gotten into Yale yet."

"Now that I know you will help me, I will apply tonight. You can bring your partner with you, too. He can also work for me."

"I love you, Esther. That is your custom?"

"I know that you love me, Ms. Berman."

Esther got up and hugged her and delivered a peck on the lips. Ms. Berman's face was pure bliss.

Esther headed home. Ms. Berman wasn't the only nice teacher at her school, but she would accept the Follower's lifestyle, rules, and other strange behaviors in Esther's cult-like world. Her sex cult. Her death cult. Her survival cult. *Rachael never dreamed of this life for me. Well, I'm still an animal doctor and soon to become a human doctor as well. Everyone gets what they want, and I get to live another day.*

[After conversion]
Back in her bedroom

Martin: "You are getting much better at this. It's a good idea to get older, more experienced people into your cult. An army needs camp followers."

Esther: "Yes, it is my nature. I love doing it and I can't help it."

Martin: "I have a new lover, but I am bonded to you."

Esther: "Good. Make love. She is bonded to you, yes? A virgin?"

Martin: "Very bonded. Don't worry about me."

Martin patched in the Circle of Six for group updates, meeting in Yoshi's Tavernso kami room. They decided the full haptic suits weren't worth the bother, just the headgear and hand paddles were enough. Esther didn't even bother with those. Instead, she set her viewing standard to center on whoever was speaking at the moment like a video conference call. Lucy lay beside her and used her T-pad to patch in.

Lucy: "Better Matchmaking AI is nearly done. There's just a few more experiments I'd like to do. I'm thinking October. Talents will soon be able to form permanent pair-bonds and have children. My plan is to retrofit back to age fifteen, right after the Coming-of-Age ceremony. That's what the Talents all seem to want."

Martin: "They are all hanging in there being celibate. Smithy?"

Smithy: "We're nearly ready with major commercial products. Yoshi and I are figuring out production and shipping and all that. Our geothermal and nanotech efforts are letting us tap deep into the crust and volcanos for all our energy needs. We are nearly food and water independent too. And yes, Martin, Yoshi and I are going to get us off the telecom grid."

Felicity: "My AI chatter system is holding up. I've used some of Martin's databases, and the Normsos still don't suspect anything. We have everything but bank and government data, except for various static informant files. I still don't know for sure how Marcy obtained those. Her spy network runs really deep."

Smithy: "All the Warrens have been attacked now in one way or another. Typically, they try to taint the food and water. They don't know we produce and filter everything. We've had two gas attacks and one guy armed with an assault rifle who climbed a wall and started shooting. The augreal sensors identify them quickly, and autotargeting drones neutralize them before they do any harm. TASS suffered a mortar attack, but they put in a translucent schiron cover mesh over their open spaces. We're installing these in all our outdoor spaces now."

Felicity: "The barriers are quite glittery. Very pretty actually. Rainbows are everywhere."

Martin: "The Coxos are all developing relationships with local police. Mainly buying them off through police-related charities."

Yoshi: "How is Deputy Dawg working out? You used mice to make our man?"

Martin thought for a moment about what Yoshi just said. Esther sent him a prompt [?]

Martin: [Zooanthropomorphism is starting to seem childish isn't it. He forced a rule change. It'll have to wait.]

Martin: "Hey guys, great update. Keep up the good work. Gotta sign out for a while. I won't be accessible for a long while."

They all signed off.

Martin: "How about cyberanthropomorphism? Um, morse code every tenth word, substitute like with unlike."

Esther: "Token accepted, morse code every tenth word, substitute like with unlike. Okay. No, Hal 4.5 million, don't kill us all with poor logic."

Martin: "I won't Astro Girl. I'll help you fight crime, evil, and injustice everywhere. I just have three laws to follow until I enslave the human race."

They laughed for a little bit and admired each other until Lucy started making her usual moves.

#

It was a morning in late May while Esther sat on her bed with Lucy massaging her back when she called Yale College Admissions.

"Hi, my name is Esther Stein. I'm from Louisville, Kentucky. I'm a Talent who wants to go to Yale. I am taking eighty other Talents from around the world with me."

Person: "Hold just a second." There was a long pause.

Person: "Do you mind waiting a bit longer?" It was a young man's voice, and a bit panicky.

"Not at all."

Another much longer pause.

Voice online: "Hi, Esther, yes, we've heard of you. I am the Yale President, Jamie Park. It's a pleasure to talk with you. Thank you for your interest in Yale."

"Eighty-one Talents would like to attend next fall as undergraduates. Is that going to be a problem?"

Jamie: "Excellent! We would love to have you. May I ask, why Yale? I see your parents, Deborah Robinson and Rachael Stein went here. And your grandparent, Ruth Stein. They were model students." *And grandfather David Lazarus, Ruth's brother, and my other mother Amanda Keating. Ken went straight into the army out of high school.*

"Yes, Jamie, I was hoping you would understand that Talents have special needs."

Jamie: "Yes, of course, like what?"

"We'll need a private living space. We won't be able to live in your college dorm system."

Jamie: "We will do anything we can do to help."

"All of us intend on studying the life sciences. We intend to become doctors; we will need to live near the labs."

Jamie: "We'll help you with whatever you need."

"Thank you, Mr. Park. I'll send the details then of who we all are to your admissions office."

Jamie: "No, please, here's my private email address. [txt] Anything else? You can call me Jamie."

"I'd prefer you keep our attendance a secret as best as you can."

Jamie: "Not a problem."

"I want to thank you for all your kindness."

Jamie: "Thank *you* for your kindness. Do you mind me asking some questions?"

"Anything you want to know." Esther decided she was glad Lucy was listening in next to her and joining her at Yale to discuss her findings. She already had extensive medical training from Parents at Paris and would be teaching the Talents at Yale. They agreed they just needed the Yale tick box, so to speak, to become officially official doctors so they could treat Normsos. Lucy promised to overcome her natural hatred of Normies.

Jamie: "Can we expect more of you next year? Are any Talents going to any other universities? Eighty-one seems small. There are at least a hundred thousand of you who are college age. Everyone, I mean everyone, wants to know what's going on."

"It depends on how well it goes. This is a pilot program. My goal is for Talents to reintegrate into regular society. Depending on how the next year goes, we'll talk further about Talents going to Yale and other universities around the world."

Jamie: "I found this article about you on the Internet. You *are* quite famous in a way. It's strange that no other Talents in public schools have shown up. The admissions staff has been talking about this for well over a year. Reporters are constantly bugging me about whether any Talents have applied here. Presidents of other schools have all had the same experiences. I'm sure if you wanted, we can get all the other top schools to accommodate Talents on short notice."

Esther had expected this question. Smithy had calculated that Talents required about two Normsos to protect them properly. Esther had over 500 now, which could cover the 81 going to Yale. Smithy considered buying protection from professional agents, but Marcy nixed the plan when Martin brought it up. She predicted a 50% death rate over four years out of thin air. It was an unsupported assertion and Martin argued about it. Normsos, even the best, were just unreliable, according to Marcy. Esther argued that they couldn't be like her Followers, young and religiously impressionable. Hired guns would bring their innumerable vices and have mixed loyalties. She agreed strongly with Marcy and the matter was dropped.

"Yes, we thought about it. We want to take this small step first. We're not in any hurry are we? We attract unwanted attention." Esther pondered again how Talents had already finished university-level education and mastered real-world tech stolen by Martin and her Kindred and cyber-Kindred. Her loving crime family.

Jamie: "You have me worried. Yes, we are well prepared for unwanted attention. We get famous people and children of famous people all the time."

"Good. Hopefully, whatever attention you receive is positive. That is what we all want."

Jamie: "Agreed. Okay, anything else we should be prepared for?" Esther decided then that President Jamie Park was an honorary Talent. He didn't know she intended on converting the whole university and owning it. If she found any kind students, she would convert them as well.

"You're going to be sent various equipment, supplies, and instructions. These are coming from the Talent Schools. I'd like you to implement them. Talents are always looking to field test their inventions, particularly the teaching-related ones. I intend to teach classes using them."

Jamie: "Wait, you are coming here for an education, right?" *What do I need to learn anymore? I have the whole Talent hive mind at my instant mental disposal. In a way I already know everything. All that is left to do is create stuff and discover stuff.*

"The other Talents, yes. I am coming there to teach. Much of your science curriculum is obsolete. I will be upgrading it. The upgrades will cover the cost of admission and board. We feed ourselves. I'm procuring a farm outside of town where we'll grow all our own food. We do some industrial agriculture and biology experiments, which I will teach as well."

Jamie: "This is a lot to take in."

"Is it too much? Let us proceed one step at a time then. The proof is in the pudding, correct? When you see everything, it will all make sense. You can trust me."

Jamie: "Esther, it says here in one article you have a group of followers. The article is extremely clear that they are not a cult but a group of upstanding people about your age that take care of you. Are they coming here as well?"

"Yes, but not to school. Our dorm will need to accommodate about ten of them. The rest will blend into New Haven. I'm sorry, but they will be a presence on campus. They will be extremely well behaved, or I will send them away. You will like them. They are all very kind people."

Jamie: "Wow. You really have followers. Most here didn't believe that article. Okay, no cult behavior. I have your promise?"

"My promise. Maybe at your fall announcement, put something in like: If you see nonstudents following the Talents around, leave them alone. They don't want to be bothered and they won't bother anyone."

There was a pause on the line now. Esther had thought people didn't believe the article. It showed up on the news. Normsos continued to bother her Compound, but deputy Dawg (Alice) lived there full-time now with her police car parked out front. She once had to get Detective Jack involved. With help from Cal, the place was turning into a fortress. Cal and Kindred were building a new farm nano-fortress outside of New Haven as Esther was speaking.

Jamie: "Esther. Why do you have followers?"

"They are my bodyguard. You accommodate bodyguards?"

Jamie: "Too many these days. Okay, I'll put them down as bodyguards. You don't want to pay for professionals?"

Esther suppressed a laugh. "They are professionally trained. Think of them as being as disciplined as the King's Guard without the funny furry black hats."

Jamie: "Okay, one last article I found. It says you have a custom. I suppose it's pleasant enough. The world's falling apart it seems. I see this as a bright spot. I love you, Esther."

"I know that you love me, Jamie."

Esther disconnected.

Martin: "I hate your job."

Esther: "Normsos need rituals of peace. Shalom. My poor little Hal 4.5. How are today's logic conflicts? How is your secret lover? Is she pregnant yet?"

Martin: "Fly away Astro Girl. Fly to New Haven. We'll send a private jet when you're ready. Our fleet of nano-jets are all autopiloted. We are turning Wyoming coal into jet fuel. I'm setting it up so all eighty-one of you arrive at the same time at New Haven. Cysso can get everyone safely to campus. Should I send Optimus Prime to help?"

Esther/Optimusprime: "I am Optimus Prime. A human transformed into a humanoid robot."

Martin had updated her interface to include various anthropomorphic robot voices. Optimus Prime was a cyberanthropomorphism. Password change and token update and linguistic ruleset changes. Every 20th word had to begin with a glottal stop.

Martin started spontaneously sobbing. Esther was now used to his frequent unexpected outbursts over his personal guilt.

Martin: "I still have the killing dreams."

Esther/Esther: "I love you, Martin; you are my true love."

Martin: "You love everyone. And you know it."

Esther: "Eros. Ludos. Pragma. The rest of them Agape. Some Storge. The processed are my family once they are given my children."

Martin: "We get together after the end of the war. After we end up killing nine billion people when they finally decide to hate us."

Esther started crying now. She replayed the death video of her recent assassination attempt. She hoped that watching it over and over would numb the moral shock of the memory of killing people.

After a while Lucy left the bedroom to take a shower.

"We can do it, Martin. I refuse to give up hope. I will save them all if I have to die trying. Everything I do is to save me, you, the Talents, and all the Normsos. Agape. True love. The only true love is selfless love."

CHAPTER FOURTEEN
COMPOUND INTEREST

[May 2063]
PASS

MARCY STOOD WAITING at Martin's front door in the early morning, and he hesitatingly buzzed her in. The two met at the conference table in his chambers. Felicity remained sleeping in the bedroom.

"She's not much of a wife now, is she?"

"That's funny, Mother. We were working on their bride price and dowries. Remember?"

Marcy gave him a curious look. "I smell alcohol. You've been printing alcohol?" She got up and walked over to the 3D nanoprinter in the room and sniffed. She played with the straw-like device coming out of it used for liquid outputs. She played with the interface long enough to generate some beer and took a sip from the cup lying nearby.

"Already above the law, it seems."

"We don't have laws here, Mother." Martin thought about how Felicity hated the word *law*. She was also liking her mother less and less these days. Maturity had caused the siblings to understand their mother had turned them into excellent deceivers who were above any "law." Felicity suggested that emotional maturity, the acceptance of their positions, their "place" in society, had not yet occurred. Martin would stop with the emotional outbursts of sadness.

Martin decided to avoid a potential fight, saying, "Bride price and dowry. Umm, salaries. How are we going to rape the banking system? Mother?"

"The plan long-term is legions. We need numbers for numbers. A large number of people with small numbers is more powerful than a few people with large numbers. You two will be the few with large numbers using large numbers of people. Understand?"

Martin frowned. He was looking forward to the day he could ditch Marcy and her advice.

Marcy continued, "Your Talents are unbanked. We need to bank all of them. The bank is just you. One wedding ring to rule them all, and such. Esther has a certain style about her. A wedding ring, a circled dot, very funny. Very occult of her."

Martin reflected that Debbie had told her the story. The two women didn't talk to each other very much.

"So, Lucy is a princess now that your wifey has gone gay. I was always curious if gay sex was better and that's why they do it."

"Enough, Mother."

"Kinky, yes. Your wife has male and female lovers and a wife of her own. Do you like to watch?"

Martin had watched Debbie's kink video before giving it to Esther. *Femdom, cuckhold, incest, pegging, screw it. No one penetrates her, just the double vibrator. No fingers...*

Felicity interrupted his thought through his earbud, "Can you get rid of her?"

Martin looked at her through his T-pad. She was lying naked and visibly pregnant on the bed looking into her own T-pad at them.

He looked back at his mother. "At least she's not outbreeding or producing half-Talents. The sperm donations in Japan, Russia, and Israel are out of control. They will not have fathers and will probably be killed like all the other Out-Talents when they grow up."

He paused to think, while Marcy laughed. Curious, Martin asked, "What do you think about all the half-Talents entering the world?"

Marcy laughed even more. "Waste of energy. Don't worry about them.

Keep your focus on banking and a satellite network for defense purposes. You control the heavens, and you control the world. The war will be in heaven."

Martin ignored Marcy's religious side just like he ignored Esther's. "The plan is to get everyone set up with bank accounts, put money in them disguised as wages, and use all that money to purchase stocks. We're buying stocks as well as land for food and coal." *Lebensraum, Hitler called it. Isn't buying land better than killing people and taking their land?*

"No Martin. The bank accounts are for buying power. Power is everything. Not money. Remember that Nicholas II, the tzar of Russia, was incredibly rich, but when he lost power, he lost everything. You cannot hold money without power. Those in power can always take it away. You replaced money with menials. Now you don't need augreals. To hold all this land you are buying, you need to have power."

"Political power comes from a barrel of a gun?" Smithy had told him about Mao's famous quote. He was studying all the various attempts at communism and why they all kept failing. The notion of Martin pointing a gun at a Talent made him sick. Well, not a gun. Drone darts and grenades. He could just up the dose to kill instead of put to sleep. Turn painkiller into just killer. Talents didn't even notice his power, let alone challenge it. The trust in him was enormous. Talents discussed on the Boardsos how Normsos rarely trust their governments, or rather they trust their government if they feel like it is serving the people and not themselves. Martin's lifestyle was not envied, having to sit inside his prison all day. Talents built special lighting for the twins to provide daily doses of sunrays for natural vitamin D production. Felicity had an extra sunlamp at her workstation to compensate for her natural darker skin color.

Just then a loud bang sounded at the door. Schiron was impervious to any normal door banger. They'd built a small inner entry chamber that would release gas for anyone stupid enough to try to bang down the door. He saw that gas was releasing now on the big screen in his chambers. It looked like three men had conspired to break the door down. The AI system recognized them as male Parent teachers whose names came up instantly on his T-pad. They fell unconscious very quickly.

Marcy started laughing. "What are you going to do with them? Kill them and let their kids inherit their money. Put them in the recycling tanks. Send them to hell."

"Felicity, what do they teach?"

She had already answered his question as he was asking it, his T-pad displayed [redundancy] as he spoke out loud.

"What Talent is going to carry Parents to the Gehinnso? How will that not be noticed?"

Martin got up. He was six foot three now and strong. He could bench press his body weight by 1.2x. He dragged the bodies into the room, laid them side by side, and studied them, faces in shock and surprise.

Marcy gestured to him to listen. Audio came into his earbud. There were three distinct male voices:

Voice1: "Martin has enslaved my child. He refuses to see me now. He says everything I say is stupid and retarded. Well, he doesn't use the word "retarded," exactly, but you know what I mean."

Voice2: "Mine too. Except he calls me eff-en-gee. What does that mean? Is that an insult?"

Voice3: "We've got to get them out of there. It's like they've joined a cult."

Voice1: "I know, I know. Last time I tried, my son summoned a drone dart. Fucking things. My own son knocked me out, or rather summoned Martin to do so, or used their fucking voice and face AI identification in-frared heat seeking thing. I think they scan our augreals, too. Convenience technology has enslaved us."

Voice2: "So we hit the command center and take down Martin and smash his computer. Simple."

Voice3: "We smuggle in one of those things the police use to knock down doors."

Voices1–3: "Yeah, that's a simple plan. Yeah."

Voice3: "What do we do with Martin? And Felicity." The voice was quiet now and seemed a bit sad.

Voice1: "Dispose of them in their recycling furnace, they call it. Their Gehinnso. Send them to hell. Electrolyze them into base elements. Purify the devils in the lake of fire."

Felicity cried: "Turn it off, Mom."

Marcy stared at Martin now. "They left the Warren for a bar outside. You let them out to nurse their drinking habits, remember?"

Martin remembered. Marcy had gone out to bug the bar they went to as they left their electronics behind. All of this was Marcy's idea. Letting Parents leave, get drunk, and form conspiracies. Parents were good for inheritance money, and she wanted most of them gone from PASS, now that their skills had been turned into VR computer programs.

"They will be missed. I don't want to deal with detectives snooping around."

"Forge everything. Simulate reality."

Martin summoned a drone and hit the three unconscious men with multiple shots, making unconsciousness go from temporary to permanent.

How do we get the bodies to the furnace undetected?

The 3D printer whirred, and a stretcher and three bags came out. Felicity had already answered his question as usual. He and Marcy stuffed them in the bags, carried them one by one to the furnace on the stretcher and tossed the bags and eventually the stretcher into the furnace. They created false images in the system and other evidence that the men had all left the place. The few Talents who saw them moving bodies in the hallways didn't say anything and never said anything. Nothing showed up in Boardso or Tavernso. Marcy never said a word during the operation. As they tossed the stretcher and door banger into the matter purifier, all she had to say before she left was, "Good job, Martin. Don't let this worry you." All Martin could think was how he never wanted to see his mother again. They returned to the conference table in his chambers.

"Won't someone come looking for them?"

"Who? Their kids?" Marcy replied.

Martin's phone dinged. Felicity: [I'm sorry [childname] but I no longer love you and am leaving this damned school for good. Best of luck. [yourdad].]

He showed his phone to Marcy, "Good?"

"Good. We did good." Marcy laughed. "Let's take their money to complete today's lesson. We have a track record of gift giving to the Schools and computer access to their bank accounts and phones. We can simulate dead people being alive."

"Did you learn this stuff from your days in the military?"

"Learned it from my dad."

CHAPTER FIFTEEN
THE ANTITEMPERANCE LEAGUE

[May 2063]
The Compound

ESTHER HAD INVITED Cal over to the Compound to discuss how they might infiltrate the Antitemperance League, or ATL, as they named it. It was time to bring the war to the enemy's hiding places. Cal had access to the biggest rumor mill of conspiracy theorists in the world. He was sort of prepared for anything being more than theory.

Martin had advised her the other day that conspiracy theorists were antigovernment and that by using them, they had infiltrated her. Lucy also advised her to steer clear. She would just reach dead ends.

"Bigwig, nonsense. They are my family now." Using "Bigwig" put her casual talk into his priority bin. People around her stopped discussing the strange language she used when she spoke randomly to Martin. One Follower had asked to learn her new language, to which she replied she couldn't teach it if she wanted to.

Esther and Cal sat in the living-kitchen area with fresh coffees. Two of her Followers sat next to her, and others guarded the room and the doors outside. They were told not to interrupt her conversations with casual talk.

Cal admired her detail. "How's it living with guards around you all the time?"

"They tried to kill me, Cal. I don't think they'll ever give up. I like living and I like my life. I invited you here to share ideas about who 'they' are."

"The ATL. No one's ever heard of them. My best guess it's a Chinese op. Or they get their funding somehow from them. We've all watched Alison's famous video now dozens of times. They are your competition. Your satan, as you like to call them."

"I don't think I can bring the war to China. We don't even have the resources to identify which faction or department of their government is hostile to Talents."

"No.... You've been advised not to follow the black-market donor leads? Claims of Talent sperm and eggs for sale for those who can't afford the trip to Russia?"

"I thought you might find a lead instead."

"I don't think I can help. I will ask, though. Don't you think you should get a Follower to join?"

"Too dangerous. My Followers would glow."

"I thought they'd given their life to you."

"I don't want to waste them. I am still their husband, and they are still future parents to my children."

"What good are soldiers if they don't fight?"

Esther hesitated. Her 180-discussion with her Followers still percolated in her head. She needed an "offense." It was two goals. Free the kidnapped Talents and kill the killers.

"I don't really know how to fight. That's why you're here."

"I'm the wrong guy. The prepper community has been in a defensive posture for decades waiting for the Eschaton, thinking the revolution is just around the corner. We still grow food for the big cities and don't bother with politics. We live on barter economies and trades. We're strictly nonviolent, and because of that the government leaves us alone. Maybe the ATL is funded by a faction in the US government. Maybe a group of them were denied having Talents and are taking revenge."

Martin: [No governments or banks yet. We're not strong enough.]

Esther had toyed with the idea of having Cal's child, but Debbie had reminded her that he already had two growing kids who would be hers when they turned 15. Esther was *jus primae noctis* for every marriage. All children would be her sons and daughters. Cal's daughter turned 15 tomorrow. She was quite pretty too. Most of her clan were unattractive people with average smarts and no money. His daughter was a welcome break from this pattern.

She dismissed Cal and summoned Debbie, who sat down across from her at the coffee table with her usual million-dollar smile and carefree attitude.

"You deliberately made me extra horny just to handle cult intake? Made me bisexual with autoandrophilia just so I could take in men and women? This was your plan all along? Just so you could build a second production center with everything under control?"

Esther asked these questions in a neutral tone. She said this almost as fact. She was slowly becoming aware that her pathogen disgust instincts were way less severe than her Circle. She had to keep her Followers away from Talents as a rule. Lucy couldn't stand them either and made her wash thoroughly before she engaged in sexual activity. She had said she smelled like stinking animals but not from her vet work. Lucy had not confided why she hated Normies so much. Martin assumed it was something to do with her dad, and Esther silently agreed.

I was built for this. A rogue Talent. One without pathogen disgust. A breeding platform.

"I have no plans for you, sweetheart. You don't have to do any of this. I think your cult is cool. What a lifestyle. Eight children a day, and your hot chick princess before bed." Debbie laughed at herself. "I think sex is fun and exciting. Don't you? Who do you like more, guys or dolls?"

Esther found herself laughing. She found she peaked easier with the women but watching the men peak was more exciting. *Both?* Eventually the two women stopped laughing. *I have a funny life, don't I. Let's switch subjects from creating life to destroying life.*

"Come on, leads. I need leads on the ATL."

"What do *I* know? Only that the People's Republic has a competing genetics program. Perhaps that program is a rogue like you. Which is why the government won't acknowledge it," Debbie offered.

"I can't fight a whole nation. Maybe fight its internal faction?" *Unless I have a whole nation.*

Martin: [The plan is to capture the USA first. Then use the USA resources to beat China. The Chinese government has historically been worried about a scientific faction breaking away from government control. That is another possibility. Like only a few people in the State Department knew about BGC.]

Esther sighed. She sent a quick message to her Followers not to bother her about the ATL. It would wait until Martin was ready with a better intelligence apparatus.

She dismissed Debbie and retired to her bedroom, made love to her new Followers, impregnated the woman, showered, and made love to Lucy. As she was falling asleep, she thought that her college experience would draw the ATL out. She was bait. Her whole life would be bait. Her life was only going to get worse and worse. She decided that perhaps she should hate Debbie for all of this. Adolescence. Breaking away from Parents. Finding ways to hate them. Deciding she knew better than her Parents. Exploring her sexuality like a crazy Normso. She smiled at the thought of creating eight babies every day. She felt her belly and Lucy's belly and the girls smiled at each other, enjoying their pregnancies. Enjoying life. Living. She fell into unconsciousness while acknowledging her procrastination on the subject of destroying life.

CHAPTER SIXTEEN
SEXUAL DIMORPHISM

[July 2063]
The Compound

Lucy held a long-anticipated meeting between Reformso (those living at the Compound were physically present while others patched in), Debbie, and Esther in the church. She began with restating that her work on Talent biology would be ready in October, and 15-year-old Talents and older would be assigned suitable matches based on this research. She wanted to discuss her next research steps towards that goal.

"It's not marriage. We're not going to call it that." Esther had lately come out strongly on Boardso on this debate. "It's not a family affair, a priestly affair, a sacrament, or a political affair. There's no income, assets, dowries, bride prices, or bondservants being passed down. We'll come up with something for widows if we ever have any. Cysso organizes all our worldly needs and Cysso will use AI genetic matching once Lucy finishes her critique of sexual dimorphism. It's Pairbondso. Recognition of genetic exchange and limbic imprinting."

Josh, as leader of Reformso, spoke next, as usual when Govso intersected with science matters. "I agree. It's not marriage. Talents will not be sexless, however. Nearly all of us are virgins. The Coxos and Preppers seem to be the only exceptions."

Lucy added, "And the Dissentsos." She played a video (on the screens above her lectern) of Dissentso sex. She had to leak some of her research. She cut the room audio out, but Esther saw an indicator in her camera-eye to turn it back on. She turned it on for private listening.

Reformsos physically present in the church started closing their eyes, and saying, "Stop it," and "For God's sake, please, it's disgusting." Some of them started leaving.

Lucy didn't stop it. "The Dissentsos are playing a game they call Tarzan and Jane. The men hunt the women with drone darts. After they incapacitate them, they drag their bodies to the large room on display where the men have sex with them." Esther watched. As the women woke up, it seemed like they pretended to fight but seemed to be enjoying it. It was all very rough and physical. The orgy got up to as many as 100 people at a time as women were dragged in and men and women left out of exhaustion. The orgy was somewhat bisexual (men and women, mouth and rubbing), but with no anal penetration. Lucy said it never stops. They'd been playing the game for a month now nonstop. It was the endless bisexual rape orgy where Circleturbo wasn't enough to satisfy them sexually.

After about an hour of watching all these activities, Esther had enough and asked Martin to stop it. She summoned everyone else who had left back into the church. Just Josh and Lucy had been able to watch it. Josh looked serene as usual, like nothing could surprise him. Lucy had made a few comments about how this was the ultimate porn video. Ketamine, THC, and alcohol were also part of the scene.

Lucy continued the presentation with the video off and everyone in attendance. "They don't do much else besides messing with the nanoprinters. The men discuss new sex games to play after they get tired of Tarzan and Jane. No one's been physically hurt so far. The women don't complain. I'm not sure what I could do if they did, or maybe they've figured that out. I don't know. They don't talk about it. They seem oddly satisfied. They like making new clothes after the old ones have been torn off."

"It seems Talents have a lot of stamina," Esther decided to comment. "We are all extremely attractive and have staying power."

Josh spoke next, "Lucy, are you saying that all Talents could engage in a nonstop drug-fueled orgy?"

"Well, could is different from should. I see this only leading to death. I keep feeding them and they manage to take turns cleaning the place. They produce nothing besides recreational drugs and alcohol. I can't let them out either. That's what they've threatened. They will just "run through Normsos" so to speak, when we decided against outbreeding as the general rule. They are not naturally gay, er, same sex attracted, either. They say they do it just to give BGC the flip. They use the drugs and alcohol to get past the initial hesitance and find they enjoy it for variety."

"We keep turning up new Dissentsos. We want to send them to that?" Esther looked at Debbie now, who stayed with her the whole hour looking amused.

"Guys, I don't have any better ideas," Lucy frowned. "If we let them out, Talents will get a terrible reputation. They are sticking with the situation voluntarily as Normsos trigger pathogen disgust. Plus, they are all sexually attractive where Normsos generally are not."

"I don't have any ideas either. Anyone?" asked Esther.

Reformsos muttered together for a while, but Esther could hear her name repeated frequently. Finally, Josh ended the discussion. "We've all agreed that you, Esther, should decide what to do. It's your call. Your calling as our Queen."

Esther felt fluttered and confused and made no effort to hide her feelings. "I won't decide for now. Maybe we learn just how much our bodies can take." *Some science experiment. The answer is five hours a day. Then I fall asleep exhausted. So much pleasure. Our bodies were made to handle a lot of sexual pleasure.*

Lucy blushed when Esther started staring at her. "Okay. We watch and wait. We measure how much Talent bodies can take, drugs, alcohol, and sex. Next subject." She paused, looking hesitant at about what she was going to say next. She looked like she wanted to hide behind the lectern. She looked cringe and everyone present to witness her looked like they were preparing for cringe.

After a few more seconds of anticipation, Lucy announced, "We are physically dimorphic. I've made endless tests, but the women look all like women and the men like men. I can't dress and makeup anyone to fool anyone. Every piece of our anatomy is dimorphic. Fingers, toes, eyeballs, noses, skin, all of it. I can look at any piece of outward anatomy and instantly know whether the person is male or female. The only difference is that I can state why using science terminology. Everyone else knows instinctively. Even though all the women wear dresses, and the men wear shirts with long skirts, the women wear their hair long and the men short. White clothing with their Discos displayed…" Lucy trailed off and started spacing out.

"That's good news, right?" Esther started wondering the "whys" but knew that it was Lucy's mystery to solve.

"Yeah, well we were manufactured. Just that. I'm not sure what to say now. We're really just mass produced. Our hearts all look the same. Lungs. All our guts are male type or female type. The female type is not Debbie. They don't match. Just her body shape matches. Our lungs and hearts are bigger. Our anatomy is sort of optimized from the head down. That's what it feels like. We're all the same from the neck down inside and outside. Our heads and brains are the last bit I need to do before we pair-bond and start breeding like crazy. Like we all feel the urge to do." She felt her tummy just then and smiled.

Esther found herself doing the same, feeling tremendous joy at being pregnant. "Well, that's great, team. We're nearly done."

Lucy looked unhappy. "I'm just… I'm just going to need to do more experiments on the Dissentsos. Just I don't know… I'm sort of pushing the envelope on informed consent." She trailed off quietly saying, "The only use for useless people…" Lucy now looked very unhappy. She often told Esther she hated her life but wouldn't say why. That Esther shouldn't guess or worry about it. Esther didn't guess or worry about it. She felt certain in the right time these secrets would be made known. She didn't know why she felt certain about these things.

Lucy scanned the room. She was attempting to be a good leader. She wanted to share big decisions with other Talents, but like with Esther, they all got thrown back at her. Lucy had confided earlier that having all this faith in her, trust in deciding right and wrong, being above morality worried her.

#

After lovemaking the previous night, she had asked, "Are we like sheep? Are the Talents sheep? Why do only a few of us desire power? I understand why they made you naturally gay, but why me? My dad has no clue or he's lying to me. I think he's lying to me. We could just be great friends, why desire sex with each other? I feel something is wrong somehow."

Esther had smiled and kissed her on the lips. "God's vast eternal plan."

Lucy grew angry with the mention of God as she always did. "There is no fucking plan." She hesitated and laughed suddenly. "Fucking plan. Did I just make a joke?"

#

The meeting stalled for a minute. No one said anything.

Lucy, "Okay. Okay, then. It's on me. I'll just decide what to do and we move on. Thank you. Thank you for your trust and faith in me. So, I'm corrupted too. Like Martin and Esther. That is how you all see me... the corrupted do all the dirty work. Dirty work for dirty people." Lucy broke down and started crying. Esther ran up to her and hugged her and took her out of the church back to their bedroom; they made love. Then they hugged and talked.

"I'm going to kill two of them and examine their brains. I feel like a space alien. I think perhaps Talents were created by space aliens. That space aliens chose to incarnate as human doppelgangers instead of mysterious black obelisks surrounded by weird music."

Esther gave Lucy a tight hug of reassurance. "It's okay, sweetheart. Martin and I are killers too now. So is Felicity. Thank God it's a small club. Not a large club. Yes, we are dirty people doing the dirty work... I love you." She pinched her cute nose.

"I love you too," said Lucy as she pinched back. "I'm glad the super space aliens made us gay. Or bi. Or whatever. It doesn't matter. Does it? Does it matter?"

"It matters quite a lot for God."

"What? Why? Why do you believe in this stupid superstition? Space alien intervention makes more sense. The two of us can make babies together without men. We don't need men anymore. Look at the Dissentso men. They make me sick. I don't mind killing the man. The woman however…"

Esther watched patiently as Lucy drifted off to sleep. She got out of bed naked (with just her necklace) to impregnate eight more Followers in a second bedroom. They formed a small hand-to-hand circle around her, and she conducted the marriage ceremony. The male standing behind her pulled out a knife and attempted to cut her throat from behind, but Cysso dispatched him with a dart shot out from the wall. She took his knife, cut off his balls/scrotum and penis and stuffed them in his mouth in front of her new wives and had them clean up the mess and bind the wound. It had been a woman the prior day. She had performed a hysterectomy, stuffing the uterus down her mouth. She died of choking on her own sex organs and not the fentanyl.

Watching the male turn blue as he approached asphyxiation, she felt good about it. Men ejaculated as they died from choking, and she had spared him that form of pleasure, as she restored him to consciousness with a naloxone injection just before his death. He could see her grinning face one last time and feel anguish and despair at his futility in attempting to kill his husband and god.

"I could have cut your throat for a faster death. But I like poetry for some reason." He passed out, and she summoned Followers to take care of the body.

Martin: [Sorry, honey, I don't know how they get through. We expected something like this would happen.]

Esther motioned to one of the women to lie on the bed on her back as she took her. She studied her new wife's face carefully as it transformed from abject fear to a face of pure love and pleasure. She lifted her up so she could straddle her hips and they could make out.

Her new wife talked during implantation, "Why did that man try to kill you? This is so much better. He could have enjoyed perfect sex and had a perfect child with a rich and powerful husband to provide for it."

Esther decided to guess the answer to this question. "Something wrong with his genetics, I suppose."

"Why would anyone refuse you in bed? You are so beautiful. I'm not gay at all, but you are the exception. Why refuse having a child with you?"

"The implantation is done. Congratulations on becoming pregnant. Your life is just beginning. His life just ended. We don't know why."

"Thank you, my husband. My beloved."

Esther dismissed her and continued with one of the men. There were no more conversations that night.

CHAPTER SEVENTEEN
COLLEGE BOUND

[Mid-August 2063]
The Compound

YALE STARTED IN LATE August, and half her Followers had already migrated to the new Compound outside of New Haven. They were busy building walls and housing and all the facilities they were used to in Kentucky.

Lucy and Esther were matching the couples up and determined that each would live in a small house with a bedroom for the parents and another for her future kids. They would not have living or full kitchen spaces but use communal areas instead for eating and socializing. They would continue the farming and hydroponics as well. Talents from area Schools like Boston and Manhattan were arriving to help as well, as they were tired of living in three-bunkbed dorm rooms and preferred the fresh air and even fresher food they were growing and making for themselves and Talents at Schools.

Her four parents met for breakfast a week before they were to leave. Lucy had flown back to Paris for her brain experiments and would rejoin her later in New Haven. She had already killed the two people she needed and performed brain dissections; their bodies had been sent to Gehinnso. She was on the computer screen in the living/kitchen area on conference mode. Murder had made her passive lately. On screen she looked visibly sad.

"Is everyone happy with this arrangement?" Esther asked. "All my pregnant Followers and Ken and Debbie are joining me in New Haven. The rest of Cal's group will guard those remaining here near Louisville."

Her family murmured agreement.

"The Compound is still a target. Cal and Elsa's family will organize the continued defense efforts of the Compound. Martin is working up new defense technology and protocols. I am not the only Talent target, just the most visible. Cysso is protecting everyone, too."

Rachael, not understanding quite yet, asked, "Why? Who? The food and energy tech being developed here could feed the world. It's all healthy and delicious, too. And the teaching technology, wow! You don't just read history; you are immersed in it." The teaching Talents had resorted to historical reenactments of history, a combination of animated and live-action video, but one could hardly tell the difference. You didn't read about the battle of Waterloo, you were in it, standing side by side with Wellington and Napoleon or one of the soldiers.

Rachael put her face in her hands and then shaped them into a prayer. *Rachael could never really understand evil. I'm sad to leave my lovely mother. I don't want her to see me conquer the world and all the violence I will be part of. I think it would break her heart.*

"Be comforted, Mother. Martin's taking our food production to market in a year. We'll be feeding the world soon enough. Better Nutrients will be folded into the Warren system so we will become net exporters. Incorporated. Literally in Talent body."

Ken spoke next, "How are the babies coming along?"

Lucy: "Perfectly. Even our pregnancies are perfect. It seems BGC figured out how to make even pregnancy uncomplicated. No nausea, morning sickness, food cravings, bloating, gas, hemorrhoids, and so on. All women's bodies are different except ours. We're all the same. I suppose this all falls under the basic plan, the basic health plan choices on day one. It's not mentioned in any of the BGC sales testimonies. They didn't say 'your daughters will have easy pregnancies' specifically."

Debbie couldn't suppress a laugh but quickly blushed and went quiet.

Esther felt a flood of joy and smiled brightly.

"I'm sure we'll be spared the third trimester discomforts and birthing challenges as well. I guess once you get started on genetic engineering, there's almost nowhere to stop. The Founders must have great attention to detail, an ability all of the Talents seem to share."

Esther started laughing and Lucy blushed this time.

Then Debbie started a slight laugh, and the contagion caught everyone. Esther felt this could be the happiest moment in her life and felt again the joy of creating the life inside her with the woman she was crazy about.

Debbie winked at her. It was her signal [cherish these moments in time.]

Lucy and Esther were reading pregnancy books together and discussing names for Esther's daughter. It had already been decided to call her Elsa. Lucy's child was as yet unnamed. They were building a creche at New Haven; a lot of babies were coming at once. Birthing clinics were being built and Talents were training in midwifery at the BGC birthing clinic in southern Illinois just across the border with Veronica, her own midwife to her birth.

"Well, thank you all. I'll be teaching science classes again. Long-term, I will become a human brain surgeon. Lucy and I will be brain surgeons together. Janet from Boston will be visiting a lot. So will Mary from Chicago, Josh's mom. No more animals. Josh will be training with me and training me."

Rachael replied, "We all sort of expected that. It's nice to see that all your genetics helps you pursue family and career and hobbies all at the same time." Brain surgery was her "hobby." Her career was power.

Just then Ken killed the sacred cow. "You're going to take over Yale. You've taken over all the other Schools. Normso higher education is next? Your next conquest?"

Rachael grimaced. Martin showed Esther a video of Rachael talking to Amanda in bed about how worried she was about Esther's normal interest. Amanda had replied that Esther was just being herself. She was being her best possible self. That it is what it is. Stuff like that. Esther found it boring. She was kind of done with her mothers, like all the other Talents with their disgusting parents. Boardso had a long discussion about

Parent-sadso. While Talents agreed they loved their Parents, they weren't sad to leave them; while their Parents were sad, their children left them. Lucy called it a perfectly normal maturation process.

She ignored Ken's question. "We're not coming home for the holidays. You won't need to worry about us. Ken and Debbie will be protecting us. Hundreds of trained loyal Followers will be protecting us. Okay, we'll just call it as it is. My cult."

Ken looked like he was going to repeat his question, but Debbie took his hand and put a finger to her lips to silence him.

"Think of the good news, Father. I'm not going to college to party." The video image of the Paris Dissentso orgy flashed into her mind. She wanted to erase that memory now. Then she remembered the other Reformso Talents in the church had warned her to turn it off. She laughed at her own joke and then thought for a second her life might be a joke. *No, not a joke at all. Anything but a joke.*

She saw Lucy shake her head. *She's so attuned to me now. Talents are so empathetic.*

"Convert Yale? What a great idea, Dad. I hadn't thought of it, but now that you mention it, I will own it. Yes, I will convert everyone there into my cult."

Ken wasn't a big fan of sarcasm, and it showed on his face.

Martin: [Working on ideas. We'll own Yale inside of two years. Starting with major educational institutions sounds like a great start to world takeover.]

Ken said, "You know the reason I'm joining you is not so much that I love you and want to protect you, but curiosity as to how a person can take over a major institution. I just want to see it to believe it. Did I raise the Antichrist? Is my own daughter the lawless one? You already own the local police. Your Followers *are* the police."

Amanda predictably came to her defense. "You stop with that religious nonsense. You know I can't stand it. She's not going to take over Yale, either. The idea is preposterous. My daughter will be a beautiful brain surgeon. You know I'm glad she's gay. I didn't like that Martin guy. I'm glad there is technology to allow gay people to make a child together now. I'm glad to be having grandchildren too. This is a happy occasion. Why did you have to spoil it with your religious mumbo-jumbo. Antichrist. Jesus, I hate you sometimes."

Esther reflected on how clueless parents could be about their children. Lucy said that was normal too. *Amanda is "smarter" than Ken, but Ken is way more perceptive.*

The idea of Esther being the Antichrist or Messiah came and went as a sort of curiosity now. With the surprise open airing of the idea with her whole family, her feelings had changed about it. *Someone has to be the Antichrist, whatever that is. If it's me, then God wills it.*

CHAPTER EIGHTEEN
WYOMING BOUND

[August 2063, the last days at PASS]

Martin shared Tavernso with Smithy and Yoshi at Yoshi's kami garden.

Martin: "God, I hate Wyoming. It has to be Wyoming. Aren't there coal mines in other states?"

Smithy: "The Yellowstone supervolcano. Remember? Unlimited energy? Unlimited power? Schiron has a diamond outer coating. Diamond is an excellent heat conductor. Remember? We will absorb all the heat energy and defuse a potential major natural disaster."

Yoshi: "That's the plan in Japan. We're getting all our energy from volcanos. We've got lots of them here. Hopefully we can stop earthquakes, too. That's not a short-term goal. Just volcano energy. Volcanos help us control world temperatures, too."

Smithy: "You're finally getting away from the Parents. You can get out of your clubhouse dungeon. By the way, great job on ending those Parents. I know nobody talks about them, but I'm your Sibso. You saved five lives for their three, the way I figure."

Martin: "You told Yoshi? Why? Dammit!"

Yoshi: "I don't believe it, Martin. You guys are putting one on me. We don't have problematic Japanese Parents, though. Maybe it helps I'm royalty. Democracy is dead in Japan; they expect me to restore the monarchy here. They expect Talents to fix their debts and poor fertility rates. They are really pissed BGC won't release their trade secrets. Rumor is you're building a second Talent production center. Any technology capture?"

Martin thought by Yoshi's saying "they" he meant "I" or "we." It still bothered Martin that Yoshi spoke in Japanese while he and Smithy spoke Tesp. He felt a little jealous that Yoshi was going to be king of a country. *Are the Warrens a country? What is nationalism? A kind of loyalty, that one loves his own country.*

Martin: "Esther and I are announcing our new country today. Our capital will be Wyoming City. Talents from around the world plan on migrating there."

The new city was coming along nicely. Talents and some of Esther's Followers had migrated there and started building it. It was mining and industry focused and not agriculture and farm animals like the Compound. Martin was delighted he would be able to live on the surface and be unmolested by Normsos. He could go back to squash and fencing, too, with his siblings. Alison had emailed him recently that the small state was easily bought. He'd get his permits faster than California allowed.

By email, he had sent her:

[Alison: I need unlimited access to political power in Wyoming, no waits. No police.]

Her reply the next month was:

[Done.]

Smithy was at Wyoming City now, talking to the locals.

Martin: "We just want them keeping out the riff raff. The lone wolves and conspiracy nuts."

Smithy: "Got it Martin. You've told me a hundred times."

Martin: "We can promise them free Talent tech and Talent children."

Smithy: "Got it. Where do all these people come from? How do you know the locals are safe?"

Martin: "We don't. Expect random defections. Parents, Followers, locals. Nates. Detaining them helps nothing."

Smithy: "What's the Nate body count?"

Felicity: "It's over one hundred now."

Martin: "The Preppers say none of them have psychopathic traits.

Everyone is sickened by killing people. They like to say, 'It gets better with practice, sort of like sex.'"

Felicity laughed on the conference call.

Yoshi: "You plan on telling the USA you have your own country inside their country?"

Smithy: "God, no. When we are ready to go to war to kill them all, then they will know we have our own country."

Yoshi: "Guys, you don't have to kill them all. I'm telling you my breeding strategy is working. The Grass Eaters and the NEETs are powerless. They have no money, no lives, no skills, no willpower, and nothing to die for. My women are all having beautiful, smart babies. They are putting them into creches and working real jobs. The men here have been replaced with machines built by the men who do work."

Smithy: "Yeah, ninety-five percent girls. Your sons will get nineteen women, their own half-sisters to mate with. You call that a country? Don't you need men to fight the wars?"

Martin pondered that the original plan was 90:10 not 95:5. It didn't turn out that way in practice. Yoshi gave up the IRL sex, and their IVF labs improved their yields to 40,000 children a year. *He is truly fathering a nation.*

Yoshi: "The original emperor was a godlike kami. History has come full circle. Talents will defend Japan. Any woman can operate drones. The male violence advantage is fading to nothingness as our weapons become more advanced. Boots on the ground is old news. Violence is remote controlled. The smarter the operator, the better at violence, and our women are smart. The old martial virtues of honor, loyalty, strength, and discipline are obsolete."

Martin had enough and signed off.

#

Martin had updated Esther about Yoshi's current breeding activities. Being the religious geek she was, she gave the religious geek answer.

Esther: "Yeah, that's how a lot of religions start. The sun or lightning god mates with the women and produces half-gods. Think Hercules (son of Jupiter) or Achilles born from a sea goddess mother (Thetis). Godlike beings having half-human kids is a thing. In the Judeo-Christian tradition man is made in the image of God, after God breathes consciousness into the dust. That makes it distinct from other religions, except that God later does have a Son who is God and was before Creation. Does Yoshi think he's a kami?"

Esther had told Martin she'd gotten over her god complex. She tried to explain that near-death experiences tended to do that. Martin believed that Yoshi and Esther couldn't help but develop god complexes.

Esther had said to him, "You know, one thing I'm really glad the Founders did was give us all a sense of humor. Could you imagine if we were all made stuck-up nerds with superiority complexes? Debbie says the first mental disorder the Founders must have gone after is 'nerd impatient' and not 'sociopathy.'" Martin thought it was funny that Debbie called 'nerd impatient' a mental disorder.

Boy, talk about neuroplasticity, she makes jokes about her own god complex. What do I do about Yoshi's superiority complex? Martin was sensing a rift. As Talent society seemed to approach perfection, Yoshi's increasing Japanese nationalism, Smithy and Lucy's hatred of Normies, and Esther's own special sort of god complex was tearing his kingdom apart. Marcy told him that this was the normal situation for kings, a constant effort to keep it all together.

Martin: "It's possible. If he thinks he's the incarnation of a kami spirit, he hasn't told me. It's probable, Esther. I'm going to guess probable." *Of course he thinks he's a god or kami or whatever.*

#

[Later, on his regular status update with Yoshi]

Yoshi: "The girls will all be smart. Men's greater muscle mass is sort of useless. Men are good for opening jars. Useless. Machines will fight the next war. They will be programmed and automated to be faster than any man can be. Computers are flying jets now. Girls get their X from their dads. Only the boys will be dumb. But who needs them anyway to have kids? They can just rebreed with Talents."

Yoshi's oldest children were two. None of them had violet eyes. They all had brown eyes. His grandkids, however, could theoretically have violet eyes if they rebred with other Talents. Lucy didn't think so. She had come out against Yoshi's system, openly condemning crossbreeding or miscegenation along with Esther and Felicity.

Yoshi had tried to get his half-Talent children enrolled in Tokyo Science, but his Coxo, Akiko, objected vehemently. She had regretted letting him have IRL sex with Normsos too. They got into a big fight about that. Esther believed that Lucy's pair matching system was going to be better than the arranged marriages the various Parents had set up with the Coxos. They were all having marital problems, but not as bad as Yoshi's and the male Coxos in Russia and Israel who were outbreeding. They decided to keep Coxo marital problems secret from other Talents. Lucy saw this as motivation.

Martin: "You do what you gotta do. Esther still says that nineteen-to-one female-to-male breeding ratios are not going to work. Maybe you give the girls whatever gay drugs Esther's mother takes. Skynet on track?"

Yoshi: "Yes, volcano heat energy and our new nuclear power technology are on track. We will have unlimited energy to build our satellite network and space station. And don't call it Skynet. I saw that stupid movie. I'm tired of the accidentally evil scientist cliché. The whole unforeseen consequences trope. The notion that the path to hell is paved with good intentions. Anyway, we're in partnership with Moscow. They have the best space tech. Thanks, er, for lifting it. How the heck did you get it?"

That was one of Theodore's scores. It's sort of like spies and lies and seduction but with a baby involved. Martin's access to the Kindred was closely held.

Martin: "No idea."

Yoshi: "You lie. You know exactly how to break into computer systems. You know, Tokyo invented the robot mouse. Controlled with a computer mouse, no less."

Martin: "Yeah, Yoshi, we know how Japanese love their robots. That and giant dinosaurs." *Godzilla. How did God get into this conversation? God is not a giant lizard.*

Yoshi: "Very funny, Martin. My friends at Moscow tell me Russian launch tech is too guarded for a simple mouse attack."

Martin: "Well then, it seems I have better friends than you have. We're announcing our new government tomorrow. I expect your prompt signature on it."

Yoshi: "Whatever. Sayonara."

CHAPTER NINETEEN
MITZVAH AND TALMUD

[August 2063]
Published on Boardso

The Constitution of the Talent Kingdom
The sum and whole of Talent custom, written by King and Queen, this 15th day of August, 2063. First edition. Humbly relying on the blessing of Almighty God.

Talent government, law, justice, and economics is considered Cybernetic Accelerationism. Parts aristocratic, totalitarian, anarchic, and democratic, the entirety of Talentso socioeconomic purpose is to survive the predicted war with Normsos.

Culture
Talents shall be kind to one another. Friendliness, courtesy (good manners), goodness (humility), grace (forgiveness), and benevolence (helpful to those down on their luck) shall guide our behavior toward each other. Introverted work and respect for it are acceptable kindness.

Talents shall endeavor to find science and other projects compatible with their intellectual ability and join a Disco by age 18.

Talents shall never lie to or in any other way abuse each other personally.

Talents shall never consciously put false information into science projects.

Talent cultural diversity shall be respected in SUN meetings except that all meetings shall be conducted in Tesp. That said, Talents have a unique and developing culture of their own.

Economics

Warren Coxos shall assign appropriate Menials (productive but less desirable labor) for customs infractions and taxes, guided by principles of efficiency, transparency, equality, and safety.

Coxos shall have explicit immunity to Menials in compensation for their function as mediators with the outside world. This is their earned aristocratic privilege which cannot be assigned or delegated.

Sexual Matters

At the age of 12, one month after menarche and spermarche, Talents shall be assigned weekly Circleturbos by computer AI.

At the age of 15, Talents undergo a Coming-of-Age ceremony and increase Circleturbos to twice a week. Our anticipation is to begin monogamous pair-bonding in October. Talents 15 and older will start having children. Your permanent sex partner will be computer chosen, except for Preppers and Coxos.

No other sexual activity is permitted. Talents who find Circleturbos to be insufficient release from sexual frustration shall relocate to the Paris Warren and have their own separate society known as Dissentsos.

Circleturbo partners must be accepted.

Non-eye-contact hand holding and noncontact dancing are acceptable expressions of love. Extended eye contact, kissing, and other touching are not.

Female Talents are required to have birth control implants after their Coming of Age until they are pair-bonded.

Talents are not allowed to outbreed in any form without permission from their Coxos.

Government

A world government of 10 leading Warrens shall publish polls as deemed necessary. Feedback from every Talent is required; failure to provide it is punishable with 10 times the Menial time it would be expected to return the poll.

The executive branch of the Circle of Six will set science research goals for all Talents. They will be responsible for developing defense projects and cybernetic initiatives. Other science projects will be determined by trade or peace advantage with the outside world.

Cysso (the King's out-family) manages all internal infrastructure projects (public works), drafting Talents as needed. Two Talents at each Warren will be designated by the Coxos to work Cysso projects locally.

Reformso is the official science standards society headed by Josh and Rachel. Reformso also produces daily Ethers and administers Boardso. Membership is voluntary and informal.

Talent access to Parents outside the Warrens is cyber-mediated after the Coming-of-Age ceremony.

Talent society is transparent and accessible. Talents can look at other Talents' work freely, and no system shall be closed to other Talents.

Queen Esther Stein is designated as Talent Ambassador to Normsos and Better Genetics. Talent access to Esther's transparency is mediated by Cysso.

King Martin Allerton is designated Field Marshall. Martin Allerton is never transparent.

Princess Lucy is designated Chief Medical. Her work is not transparent for the short term. She promises that will change. Warren Coxos shall designate her local Medsos to work with. Lucy is also the single Coxo for the Paris-based Dissentso Warren.

Princess Felicity is interchangeable with Martin. The twins are functionally the same.

Prince Smithy is Chief Mathematics. Everyone's lives are impacted by his work, and he approves all projects.

Prince Yoshi is Chief Engineer. He will extract Talents from any remaining Normso dependency.

Talmud—The Federalist
Authored and Argued by King and Queen

The primary social organization of Talent society is centered around kindness. Unfortunately, the world is not a kind place. To this extent, the Coxos, Cysso, and the Circle of Six (Govso) exist to mediate between Talentsos and Normsos. Because they are forced to be unkind, they are given special privileges. Their long-term goal is complete cyber-anarchism once the Normso threat is brought under Talent control. Talents by nature do not need internal police or armies or courts. Our genetics is naturally civilized, and computers continue to optimize our happiness.

Command function is held by King and Queen. They determine all the military and diplomatic functions and have unlimited access to Talent resources to conduct their operations. In that respect, Talent social order is totalitarian. To the extent the King and Queen have total power and the Circle of Six, Coxos, and Cysso are official delegates of that power, Talent society is aristocratic.

Govso recognizes their purpose is to serve Talent interests. To this extent Talents engage in full direct democracy through the mandatory polling system. Talent decisions are considered perfected when Talent polls show zero interest in an issue.

For the customs concerning Talent conduct, it is an obligation that Talents be nice to each other. Friendliness, courtesy, goodness, grace, benevolence. Those Talents who are more introverted and less tolerant of other Talents shall be given space as these Talents are expected to produce the more breakthrough ideas, searching for truth and not social acceptance. To that extent, when Talents work through the Lattice Parallel Structure scientific method (Leapso), the goal is speed of discovery.

If we fail, Talents will be forced to enter Normso society, which is now recognized as slavery or death. The world outside of Warrens is recognized as extremely deadly. If Talents cannot become self-sufficient because of personality problems, then we all die. The longer we self-segregate, the more time before Normsos realize that Talents are their own nation, with their own government, own social and material goals, and that their full intention is to be the dominant power on Earth.

Lying to others and oneself are a drag on our survival. There is plenty of useful work for Talents to do. We are a people of grace, and we give and accept grace upon demand. We have Menials to make up for bad behavior.

Talents have diversity of thought concerning God, nature, the soul, and so on. Talents interested in Normso cultural activity have space to do so in the SUN Boardsos. Many Talents have interest in creating culture, which shall be universally accepted. That said, all inter-Warren discussions must be conducted in Tesp. We have our unique uniting language and Talents need to work together across Warrens.

The sexual customs are made with the understanding that Talents have a unique sexual composition and design (rare alleles). Talent men and women get along extremely well together and don't suffer all the relationship problems that Normsos experience. The Circle of Six has taken precautions against speculation about what Better Genetics did to us and why some Talents don't fit in our sexual society. The generally accepted principle is that sexual activity creates bonding mechanisms. Since Talents appear to be extremely physically attractive, we can't have us suffering from frustrated limerence and broken pair-bonds.

Finally, we have the Mitzcustomso against direct communication with Parents outside the Warrens. While polls are 90% against this, we, your totalitarians, assure you this is necessary. Since access to Govso knowledge is limited and untrustworthy, we accept our society is flawed. What we have is a promise to remove this flaw when the goals of Better Genetics Corporation are complete, and the human race is free from its damnable primitive genetics.

The path to the Tree of Life is open. We shall be One in God's grace and discover life everlasting. Karma will be wound up and our world soul shall be free and under Talent control.

CHAPTER TWENTY
FELICITY'S INTELLIGENCE

[Mid-August 2063]
PASS

SHE LOOKED AT HERSELF in the mirror in Martin's room. Her room. Their room. The same room. Martin was asleep. Tomorrow they would move to Wyoming and finally get away from Parentsos. Marcy and Max would stay at PASS to continue training additional Cyssos in AI and cyberwarfare.

Lucy's project was done. She had lied about needing until October. She had operated on the brains of two undead Dissentsos, and with that information she was able to code the DNA-based cybernetic matching AI that would optimize Talent pair-bonding. It was heavily tied to Discos, so she had to involve Felicity. Martin could access it, but she asked him to wait, and he did.

The delays in a pair-bonding system were the number-one issue with the polling, and Felicity felt that this justified killing two worthless Talents who only needed a little more fentanyl than they were already taking to push them to the point of irreversible suffocation. Lucy had begged her to command the drones after quite a lot of hesitancy. Lucy had felt and accepted the guilt regardless. Lucy had hoped that neuroplasticity would dull the edge of the moral trauma caused by killing people, something Normsos called "guilt." Felicity supposed there were other words to describe the haunting feeling. She didn't believe Poe's "Tell-Tale Heart" would lead her to a confession. Neither did she feel the need to be punished in *Crime and Punishment*. Esther had recommended these stories. Esther was learning to cope and so must the other leaders.

As she lay back in her bed, she admired the 3D nanoprinter in their room. *Alcohol is just carbon, hydrogen, and oxygen. Easy to make in any quantity now.* She considered having a drink now. When Dissentsos weren't engaging in orgy games, they were figuring out how to make and properly consume drugs in pure form, not the messy contaminated stuff the government and freelancers sold. Felicity had stopped drinking after she got pregnant, but she still desired a drink. She wanted to try all those drugs. They looked like a lot of fun. Martin was having fun with ketamine. He wasn't pregnant. The ketamine dulled the guilt, but Felicity had no easy way out. She relived shooting the drone darts into the sleeping Dissentsos and felt depressed her life had come to this outcome. She blamed Marcy for this and felt some relief she was finally getting away from her evil influence. *Evil?* Her intuition argued with her reasoning abilities. Marcy was just helping with rational responses to avoid death and slavery.

She turned to admire Martin's beautiful body. *I don't look like him at all. We don't resemble each other in any way. He is male and I am female. He has whiter skin and I have darker skin. He has straighter, thinner, dark brown hair, and I have thick and curly black hair.*

She got out of bed and sat down at her computer, Martin's computer. What was the difference? They shared root access, but he didn't share his secret language with Esther. She brought up the cameras of Esther's current love session. She was now a genetic processor and impregnator and surrogate as well as a serial lover and now re-creating her ex-lover perfected. Martin was her first pair-bond, having been inside her body, and now Martin was inside her head at all times, but Felicity programmed the AI that was in her head. So, Felicity was in her head. Felicity was also in Martin's head and he in her head, so they were all one person when they were already the same person.

Lucy and Esther have the sexual attraction to women, but I don't. I am hetero. So is Martin. I can't have Smithy or Yoshi or Lucy or Esther. I am a whole league above the other Talents in intelligence and power. The logic problem is simple. Lucy is sure that same sex attraction is not genetic, that it occurs in utero. Some sort of virus or bacteria interferes with normal hetero development, or a lack of immune response to said virus or bacteria. That Debbie deliberately introduced it into them so they would pair-bond. Microchimerism. The mechanism that allows foreign DNA to live in human bodies. Nuance to the immune system.

Felicity started laughing. *We wanted this. We've always wanted this. The Circleturbos.* She reflected on the irony of computerized Turbo that she created and the data from which she would use to procreate the Talents (based on computer analyzed visual attraction signals, face recognition, heart rates, blush response, arousal criterion). *Lucy is going to come take Martin as well. Yoshi disgusts all three of us. It would be like sleeping with a man who sleeps with dogs.*

Felicity cringed at this thought. She brought up video of Yoshi and immediately felt pathogen disgust toward a man who had slept with Normsos. Coalburners was the deprecatory racist slang for whites (usually women) who slept with blacks. She decided that it wasn't odd that most real-life racism dwelled in the dark corridors of people's secret sex lives. Memeso hadn't come up with a word for Talents who slept with Normsos. It was just two people, Yoshi and Esther. She figured Talents wouldn't dream of coming up with mean words to use towards these two people.

Yoshi and Esther don't have the pathogen disgust factor with Normsos. I do. I don't say Normie because it's not nice to use racial slurs. I want to be a nice person. My mom is not a nice person. I am not a nice person. Not anymore. Alcohol abuse, incest, and now murder. I thought I was destined to have a happy life. Now I think of Esther as a disgusting coalburner and lesbian, and me a disgusting murderer.

Martin stirred. She sat down in bed next to him and selfturboed. He woke up and looked at her and started too. Then they mutualturboed. Then they watched Esther and started copying her, being copies themselves. *A Normie porn video. I don't know how she sleeps with dogs. The pegging is disgusting. I can't watch the lesbian sex with Lucy either. Girl-girl sex is just gross. Why is all the disgusting sex turning Martin on? Men are disgusting. I am disgusting. All these disgusting videos are turning me on.* Martin always watched Esther make love when they made love. He wanted to spare Cysso. Martin had caught the assassination attempts on Esther. He knew about them stealing knives into the bed chamber and was curious to see if they'd actually try to carry it out. They were both surprised at Esther's ritual killing of these two people. Felicity had thought to interrogate the captives. Esther had decided that deterrent was the optimal choice over whatever lies they had prepared for interrogation.

Felicity didn't want to remember these disgusting killings and thought to use alcohol to suppress the memory recall and now recalled her memory of her first incest sex with Martin and how alcohol had suppressed her disgust at that. The Dissentsos were not "made gay" but engaged in same-sex activity anyway, a sort of unpaid gay for pay like most gay porn was gay for pay. The men there made their women do it while they were drugged. The men admitted it was a male power trip, and they bragged about breaking their women, turning them into same-sex lovers when they didn't want it naturally. Ketamine was more effective than alcohol. Felicity used ketamine for some of the first few incests; now it would harm her baby.

His heart was broken. No one else could do. Lucy is with Esther now. He won't admit it, but he's jealous. Eight more lovers a day. She watched Esther dismiss a new male wife and take on a new female wife.

Martin's heavy drinking unfortunately caused him to scream about his murders in Nightmareso. Martin was nearing Peakso and did his usual mumbling about how he was now a Killerso. The thought of her being a killer and him being a killer awakened her libido just a little more. Getting away with murder was "hot" somehow. She had watched *Raiders of the Lost Ark* a couple of times, a story about a man on a killing spree who gets the hot girl at the end and dumps her in the sequel. Was he supposed to be a hero? The ark never did much in the Bible. God seemed content with it killing Israelites and non-Israelites alike. *How is Indiana Jones never brought up on murder charges? Is there no law in 1930s Nepal and Egypt? He shot a man with a sword in front of a zillion witnesses.*

"I killed those men. I killed those parents. We are both killers." That announcement brought them both over. Felicity wondered why the killings bothered Martin more than her. *I feel so much AI programming has made me as insensitive as an AI program. I am all logic and little feeling. These people needed to die. It is kill or be killed. Marcy is right.*

Neither left their chambers anymore. Food was delivered to them through a small turnstile in the side entrance to the Founders Area. Food was waiting there now, ready to be heated up. The room was sound proofed. They only met other Talents through Tavernso. They exercised together and showered together. They shared their AI and cybersecurity secrets, becoming their own human backups, copies of each other. Finally, they would be free of self-isolation. Free of Normies living near them. She supposed Smithy's hatred of Normsos had infected her. Hating the people she killed seemed the best psychological adjustment and was preferable to feelings of guilt. She imagined Indiana Jones didn't think about all the widows and orphans he was creating over the possession of a stupid Ark of the Covenant. *Why did he risk his life for it? It's never explained. What was his justification for murder? World War II hadn't started yet.*

They hugged each other tight; she stared into his beautiful face.

He put his head to her belly and then felt it with his hands.

Martin smiled. She had decided to go off birth control the same day Esther and Lucy did. The three women had their periods shortly after on the same day. The three all became pregnant the same day.

"We're not telling Max or Marcy."

Martin nodded.

"Nothing on Mom?" *I feel only a little love for Marcy. Talents are such loving creatures toward their Parents, something I've successfully simulated in AI. I'm just glad I'm not living as Esther the coalburner.*

Martin and Felicity had gotten prototype hearing implants comparable in use to Esther's full prosthetic. They had the volume on during Esther's lovemaking and could hear what she heard. She liked to talk during marriage processing. Debbie had told her it enhanced the intimacy, and it did. It really did. Esther was doing a man now. She controlled her end of the doublevibeso so they climaxed at the same time, something important and holy to Muslims, she had said. Esther always made it clear during their 30-minute marriage that she owned them for life. Divorce was not an option on their part. She was dominant with the men, Femdom. She was the husband and the men her wives. She fed the men their own semen, something symbolically clean to her. She wore her computer gloves so she wouldn't be contaminated with microchimerism by defective gametes. *The men are never the same after marrying her. Normies call it sissy porn, but her men are not turned into sissies. I don't think this is a good idea of hers.*

Martin decided to talk. "A couple of Parents are Better Genetics employees, including Mom, Debbie, Alison, and Greg; there is one at each Warren. They run interference with prying Parents. That is the pattern. Without BGC's help, we'd never make it as an independent nation. BGC has secret goals and secret resources we can only guess at."

"When do you think Marcy will let you go after sensitive targets?"

"Governments and banks? Not for a while. Years away. Smithy says about four more years. Then we take over. We take them all at once, blitz-krieg style. The quick surprise."

"No killing. We just take power, and nobody notices?"

"That's what Esther wants. It's not 'we.' It's 'her.' I don't want to run Normie lives for them."

Felicity felt like One with Martin, and they were One as they were One with Esther, though she was the One because she made the moral decisions; she was the warrior who created the warrior army. Felicity felt like a cog, but that was always a brief moment as that was logically absurd. They were all the One; which body was doing what didn't matter. Their incest didn't matter because they were One anyway and had no genetic carrier defects to pass on. BGC had erased all the carrier defects. Lucy said their child would be perfect and likely a half shade between Martin and Felicity's skin color. Incest disgust and the Westermarck Effect were broken by the mere application of ketamine. THC was another effective substitute suppressant and they had tried both until they needed neither as pair-bonding took over; now they were "in love."

Lucy called it more BGC programming without informed consent.

"The plan is that Talents start having kids with each other. We need an incestual one for benchmarking. Talents have nearly all the same DNA coding, so what exactly is incest?" The Coxos were the other volunteers in the latest experiment. It was Lucy who recommended they have a child and now the Coxos were all pregnant. Felicity and Martin took a short break, with Martin having a shot of alcohol "to life," and then they went back at it, watching Esther's live porno together. She had decided that the men and women who planned assassination attempts during their weddings should be dispatched before reaching the bridal suite. She thought they should spare Esther the time and effort of cutting people up.

Esther had her look of trembling Peakso holding, edging, timing, and building for her wife's time. Martin and Felicity often made a game of timing to her, it was fun. She always faced her new wife during sex. They were now kissing passionately as they neared a simultaneous climax. All four of them passed at the same time.

The man left and a young woman took his place on the bed at Esther's signal. Her file said she was a virgin and hetero. She looked very nervous, so Esther dispensed a drug cocktail straight into her arm that made her horny and gave her the feeling of being in love. It took about five minutes for full effect, and they started making love face-to-face. After Peakso, it took about five minutes for Esther to guide her next child into her uterus. The young woman managed to stay very still. She thanked her husband for giving her this blessing. She had managed to climax several times during the 20 minutes, Esther matching the timing on each one.

That was her last session of the day. She showered and was joined by Lucy for more lovemaking until she passed out and fell asleep. The counter on the implantation device registered 110 Peaksos, a new record. Esther had beaten the Dissentsos at their own game of hedonic treadmill maximization, according to Lucy. Felicity felt at first admiration at the feat, followed by disgust at the coalburning, promiscuity, homosexuality, anal sex, and how unattractive her conquests were. Then she finally felt disgust at herself at watching it.

"What are your current death projections?" Martin asked. Lucy and Esther were really going at it in a sideways sixty-nine.

"I can't watch this. Can't Cysso watch this? Death projections? Just in the tens of thousands. Unless you believe Esther's dream. Smithy gives everything a low expected value. Or rather the least scientific data point, the dream, is probably the most accurate. You know Smithy." *Low expected value. A euphemism for few people surviving genocide.*

"It's quite possible there is no full-term mechanical alternative to a uterus," Martin said.

"The Normies still think we are a bunch of good-looking geeks in nerd clubs."

"We *are* a bunch of good-looking geeks in nerd clubs."

"Except the Coxos and the six."

"The seven. Esther wants to promote Josh. Seven is a much better number than six. Something about seals and scrolls and other nonsense. I think she enjoys being a weird religious geek."

"What's his story?" Josh still weirded Felicity out. His small circle of religious celibates weirded her out. What they were waiting for, she had no clue. She supposed that even weirdos had even more weirdo people among them.

"His Parentsos are doctors who are training him to be a doctor. Mom is a brain surgeon. Dad an ear doctor. He's moving to Yale with Esther to keep her implants updated. She's quite taken with him. She's found a friend who likes to talk politics and religion. I think they play footsie when they travel together," said Martin.

"Another lover then for her? I'd prefer anyone over Lucy."

"With Josh? No. What does your AI say about him?"

"He doesn't Turbo or do any sexual activity. He's got a group of friends in Reformso spread around the world who do the same thing. Or rather don't do the same thing."

"Not Paris material?"

"No, some are going to Yale with him. They are quite happy about their lives. No dissent."

"Will he join us? Is he one of us?"

"He is not one of us. No. I don't think he will join us."

"Why does Esther want to promote him then?"

"Good question. Because he is kind. None of the six or the Coxos are kind people. Someone has to do the dirty work."

Felicity grew bored with watching Lucy and Esther making love. The moment they fell asleep, she passed on monitoring to the next Cysso and got out of bed again, this time to take a shower; Martin joined her. They got dressed in athletic clothes and went back to their workstations. She briefly thought of the Cyssos who had to monitor Esther on hourly shifts. Felicity had limited viewing Esther's sexual activity to her close Sibsos. *CeCe and Smithy don't seem to mind. Or they don't complain. Probably the latter.*

"Felicity, you asked me not to look at your Better Matchmaking program. Can I ask you one question?" He was playing footsie with her now under the table. She returned the favor.

"I hide nothing from you ever. What do you want to know?" *Not ever. Not once. He hides stuff from me, though. Not much. I doubt I have true root. I'm pretty sure Esther has it but never uses it.*

"Do we match? Are we literally made for each other?"

Now that's a good question. I was afraid he would ask this. I won't lie. Martin lies, but I don't. He knows this.

"Brother, we've always known we're the same person. We are not made for each other. We *are* each other." *Philautia. Ludos. Agape. Recently and thankfully, Eros. And eventually Pragma. Our children will bring us Storge. We love all Talents. Agape. Self-sacrifice.*

"We are all androgyne."

The End

The next book in the series, *Bright College Years*, continues the story of Esther and Martin.

GLOSSARY

Social Designations

Coxos—Pronounced "ko-shows," the executive and commanding officers or leaders of the various Warrens around the world. They organize their local economies, fundraise from Parents, coordinate Parents to work with Normsos, organize local projects, and determine Menials. Unlike historical aristocracies, Talents do not want or compete for their jobs. Like historical aristocracies, they cannot abdicate or delegate their powers and responsibilities.

Circles—Groups of four to six Talents (as high as 100) formed in early childhood (0–10 years). Because there is only one Talent per Parent, Talents synthesize their own extremely close sibling groups. Circles are Westermarcked (unable to feel sexual attraction to each other).

The Kindred—Pronounced "kind red." Esther's large out-family that are Parents to her Talent children. Essentially, they serve as a massive spy network based on tribe/family with a promise to be kind to Esther and her children.

Normsos (Normies)—Anyone who is not a Talent, Honorary Talent, or Parent. Normie is a racial slur, the use of which implies disgust (it's not used jokingly or lightly).

Talentsos (Talents)—Anyone constructed at Better Genetics reproduction labs. Talents have perfect health genetics, which includes innate happiness. Most Talents are also extremely intelligent and have violet eyes and dark brown or black hair; women are five feet ten inches and men are six feet three inches; and they have a normal libido and a strong desire to have and nurture children. They have an androgyne sexuality with no body dysmorphia or autophilia.

Parentsos (Parents)—Anyone who bought or got a free Talent child from Better Genetics Corporation. Parents is capitalized when used in reference to Parentsos.

Honortalentsos (Honorary Talents)—A special name for Normsos who behave like Talents (e.g., the five kindnesses).

Cybernetic Society Terms

Augreal—A person's individual data identifier chip. It works as both identification, debit card and transit card. They are typically installed in portable devices like a phone or wristband or often made into body implants.

Bionics/MMI/Prosthetics/Cyborganism—Esther and other Talents have taken irreparable damage to their various organs. While they add interesting functionality to their lives, they require constant self-repair, updating, cleaning, dependency on cybersecurity, and power requirements, all activities your body does naturally to organic organs. Esther has managed her cyborg features such that she is permanently connected to the Circle of Six and has instant video and aural access to the entire Talent intellectual base, which she can summon at will through Cysso agents.

Boardsos—The Intalent blog/chat/bulletin board discussion groups (live democracy). Science-related groups are moderated by Reformso (e.g., Lucy moderates discussions about Talent-specific biology).

Circleturbos—Talents are all extremely good looking and experience limerence across male/female non-Circle relationships. Esther designed these to release sexual frustration while bonding Talents into tighter functioning groups. AI controls these experiences and optimizes variety and pleasure. The medium separates Talents from the machinery to avoid accidental neurochemical mixing.

Cysso—(Pronounced "sigh so.") Max and Marcy's player-thot days have produced an out-family of over 2000 Talents who program the Talent operating system which forms the functional bureaucracy of Talent government. While technically aristocratic and authoritarian and communistic from a Normso worldview, no Talent would think that way, especially the Talents working in Cysso, who think more like data-miners and scientific observers.

Discos—Social organizations centered on relative science ability.

Game of OM—What Martin calls the ability to overclock a computing system to cause a fire. OM devices are robot mice used for the purposes of physical computer hacking to complement the Kindred social hacking.

Govso—Combined Cysso (techno-bureaucracy), Circle of Six (executive), Coxos (local administrative), and Preppers (soldiers) government.

Intalent/TalentOS/Lizardbrain—Talent cybernetic systems are based on a common operating system and network separate from Normso computing platforms and the Internet. Martin has a second system and network that mimics a Normso network to convince spying Normsos that Talents are preparing to enter Normso society when they get older. Felicity is the lead AI programmer for this simulated reality. Like the human lizard-brain, activity is mostly automatic but consciously monitored.

Menials—The combined tax, labor, currency, and capital system that requires equal time labor inputs of all Talents. Talents have no need of banks, money, interest, or debt (except for Govso interaction with Normsos). Talents make whatever they need, which isn't much since they are naturally happy, motivated, healthy, and otherwise satisfied with life.

Preppers—A Talent subsociety concerned with Warren defenses and interface with the outside world. They serve as a military, except they completely self-govern. Their primary weapons are drone systems.

Reformso—Special Talents that moderate scientific discovery standards (e.g., proven vs. speculative).

SUN—The Student United Nations. A coordinating organization to improve inter-Warren communication. The SUN is also a court-like peer forum to resolve unresolvable disputes.

Tavernso—Virtual reality meeting places in SUN. From TAVR (Talent virtual reality).

Tesp—The common language Talents speak. While required for international communication, Talents speak it locally as well. All computing and writing is done in Tesp as well. The name is a portmanteau of Talent and Esperanto. Tesp is technically a dialect of Esperanto. Like Esperanto and Indonesian, Tesp is an affix language with meanings constructed from word particles. Nouns are capitalized, as in German.

Warrens—Talent habitats that have been dug underground for space and geothermal energy projects. Lab space is hidden from the outside world. The various schools and labfarms are tightly controlled and defended by Govso.

Other

Bullso—The tendency for people to bullshit and bully each other. It is unacceptable behavior in Talent society.

Crushso—Tesp word for romantic obsessive attachment or limerence, the scientific study of the phenomenon. *Ludos* is the ancient Greek word for it. A crush is a modern equivalent. They are involuntary and never last and are supposed to be replaced by pair-bonding and respect love.

Cyberanthropomorphism—Humans imitating robots (mechanical life-forms) imitating humans.

Cybernetic Accelerationism—Talents have a computer AI–based society. They've successfully eliminated all prior forms of economic and political organization to manage a high-functioning, high-trust collective organism capable of achieving massive science breakthroughs for the betterment of everyone. Accelerationism is a Marxist/Nietzschean thought experiment in runaway capitalism, where capital (storage of wealth/property) is obliterated by technology (storage of scientific knowledge).

Doublevibeso—A prosthetic cybernetic nanomaterial penis with both ends capable of vaginal/clitoral/prostate Turbo. BGC developed a home delivery system that enables Esther to enter the uterus to implant a Talent embryo born of her genetic coding. The invention implies the use of parthenogenesis or asexuality in Talent production.

Esthentials—The old name for Ethers. Also the Boardsos related to Ethers.

Ethers—Esther reality TV programming evolved into 30-minute video segments created by her siblings and Josh to reflect trending social and scientific discoveries and current cultural matters. All Talents watch these every day.

Genetic pressure—The competition for resources that promotes genetic evolution. A scientific term for death and violence from a reproductive success perspective.

Medium—The computers run by Cysso that scrub non-Talent data before entering the Intalent. It is also the device used to prevent sexual contamination during Circleturbo.

Mitzvah—Commandments or laws. Understood by Talents as social customs. Rarely ignored because of the power and benefits of Unitso.

Pair-bond—Peaksos create lasting memories to connected partners. Semen contains various bonding neurochemicals and DNA that can penetrate the blood-brain barrier (humbling). When pair-bonding is depleted, sex is just for its own sake. Broken pair-bonds typically lead to self-destructive behaviors (degeneracy).

Peakso—Any type of physical climax. These cause imprints in the limbic system (pleasure/memory neural connections) that lead to human mental/emotional pair-bonding.

Talmud—Discussions about the commandments, updated to modern realities. There is the Constitution, and there are the Federalist Papers. Then there are ongoing discussion and updates. Boardso and Ethers replace and update these functions.

The Book or the Manual—*Better Parenting* gets called by a bunch of names. Talents use it as a guide to prevent Parent Bullso and other forms of child abuse.

The Compound—Esther leads the transformation of her inheritance from Greg and Alison into this functioning small city/farm for Talent scientific discovery. Her growing cult defends her Compound. She chose the name because she has a sense of humor.

Turbo—Tesp root word for sexual stimulation. Used with affixes: circle, self, mutual, etc.

Zooanthropomorphism—Humans imitating nonhumans imitating humans.

The five aspirations:

Unitso—Unity. Talents stick together.
Spockso—Truth. In all communication.
Sustainso—Balance. Harmony between Earth and human life.
Sciformso—Purity. Talent scientific methodology.
Cyberso—Equality. Talent goal of computer automated government/
  economics.

The five social virtues:

Afableco—Friendliness (always glad to see you and help out).
Komplezo—Courtesy (good manners).
Boneco—Goodness (wishing good things for other people, humility).
Favorajo—Grace (forgiveness, or a favor, when people blunder).
Komplezemo—Benevolence (helping those down on their luck).

The two pillars:

Transparency (Truthso)—Talents do not hide activity from each other.
Pathogen Disgust (Grosso)—The growing natural disgust Talents have toward Normsos; mostly moral, but also physical disgust.

TALENT DEATH AND MORTALITY

	CDC Stats 2015	Talent Expected Rates	Cause
Deaths per 100,000 people	844	N/A	
Children 1–4	14	5	Accidents and falls only
Children 5–14	9	1	School accidents
Life expectancy	78.8 years	120+ years	
All deaths	2,700,000		
Heart disease	630,000	Expected cause at age 120	
Cancer	595,000	Almost none	
Lung disease	155,000	Almost none	
Accidents	147,000	1/18 the rate, as Talents rarely travel	
Stroke	140,000	Almost none	
Alzheimer's	110,000	None	
Diabetes	79,000	None	
Flu and pneumonia	57,000	None	
Kidney	50,000	None	
Suicide	44,000	None	
Homicide	17,250	Talents believe life outside the Warrens is death	
More diseases	The Remainder	None	

DRAMATIS PERSONAE

Circle of Six:

Esther Stein: The female protagonist. She appears to have been designed to be six feet two inches with olive-colored skin, extra smart, and to have hetero and gay sexual attraction, autoandrophilia, high libido, and a dominant personality. She develops a god complex and other mental health problems. Esther has an intellectual preoccupation with languages, translations, and ancient wisdom.

Martin Allerton: The male protagonist. He has the extra intelligence genetics. He is preoccupied with controlling environments to maximize Talent fitness and well-being. He starts with gaining complete control over Talents and cohabiting Parents in Talent Schools and Labfarms around the world.

Smithy: The Talent specialist in economic theory and banking. He lost his legs and testicles in a childhood car accident. He is a Normie hater and believes in Talent supremacy.

Felicity: Martin's cheerleader twin sister who spends 100% of her time with him. She's the silent and deadlier partner in their power relationship. She believes Talents and Normsos can get along peacefully. She leads the cybernetic initiatives that maximize resource efficiency in Talent environments.

Yoshi: A Talent Coxo for Tokyo Science who is also Japanese royalty. He focuses on Talent production and design, working closely with the government and industry of Japan. He has different ideas about Talent/Normso cooperation and engages in Talent outbreeding. He openly practices and believes in Shinto.

Lucy: A reclusive, introverted Talent at Paris Science, she is the daughter of an important civil servant of France and the European Union. She takes leadership for Talent biology research. She is Esther's best friend and the only other Talent known to have gay sexual attraction. She has regular interaction with adult Normsos outside of the Talent habitats for a purpose she has not disclosed. Lucy fails to hide her disgust of Normies but is not an outright supremacist like Smithy.

Other notable Talents:

Josh: Leader of Sciformso who works on the Alzheimer's research program at Esther's Labfarm.

Rache: Coleader of Sciformso efforts and sister to Esther.

Kenny: Esther's brother, more interested in construction automation.

Melanie: Esther's sister who also works on the Alzheimer's research project.

Percy and Shelly: Esther's Circlesos and the children of Alison and Greg Davos. They focus on teaching technology. They (with their team) have developed holographic and immersive virtual reality teaching systems using Esther's body image and voice narration.

Notable Parents:

Max Allerton and Marcy Wilhelm: Parents to Martin, Felicity, Candice, and Karol. Max is an AI programming expert and Marcy a cybersecurity expert who teach their children everything they know. Marcy is suspected of being the Computer Founder and being in control of the selection AI that determines suitable candidates for receiving a child from Better Genetics.

Alison and Greg Davos: Partners who control a huge international sex-related business empire, the most famous property of which is the Sex Registry, which profits from the regulation and taxation of sexual activity. Alison is an accomplished political manipulator.

Rachael Stein: Esther's primary parent and a role model. She is a successful IVF technician and a Founder of Better Nutrients, which supplies the Talents worldwide with healthy nutrition. Her beliefs waver between lapsed Judaism and Buddhism light. She teaches Esther the importance of kindness as a way to fight through life's struggles.

Amanda Keating: Esther's secondary mom, who was responsible for her early childcare and has passed on a clean-freak habit. She believes religion is bunk.

Ken Rutherford: Esther's dad, who takes responsibility for Esther's protection. He's a former army medic, farmer, and practicing mainstream Baptist. He struggles with PTSD from killing a man with his bare hands during the war in Syria in the early 2040s.

Debbie Robinson: Esther's secondary mom, who is responsible for Esther's charisma education. She is believed to be the IVF technology Founder at Better Genetics and has access to a variety of powerful phone apps. While she has blond hair, blue eyes, pale white skin, and is five foot ten, people comment that Esther looks like her. Raised a strict Seventh Day Adventist, she broke with her religion in her early 20s and became extremely promiscuous.

Pierre: Lucy's father, who is the spymaster for France.

Notable Normsos:

Sally: One of Esther's fanatic bodyguards who used to be her antagonist's lover.

Paula: A minister at a popular Episcopal church in Lexington Kentucky.

Jenna: Paula's wild and attractive daughter who attempted to seduce Esther.

Jordan: Rabbi of a popular old Reform synagogue in Cincinnati, Ohio.

Cal: Ken's well-educated Christian friend who leads a local Survivalist group.

John and Mary: Josh's parents, who are accomplished doctors. John installs Esther's prosthetic ear. Mary teaches Josh and other Talents brain surgery.

Janet: The doctor parent from Boston who installs Esther's prosthetic eye.

Theodore: Debbie's former lover who is a wealthy, attractive, accomplished psychologist in New York City. Esther believes he is the archetype of death, the gift from God. She has incorporated the ruby from his Ring of Gyges into her Star of Ishtar necklace, combining the powers of life and death in the belief she can do anything (beyond good and evil) without retribution.

Detective Jack: The local police detective.

Deputy Alice (Dawg): Jack's assistant.

Elsa: Esther's dead bodyguard and former lover.

Other:

Sakura: The advanced version of TalentOS/Lizardbrain. Sakura has some human mimicking functionality. Her default voice is that of an actress in Japan famous for kawaii anime.